BOOK THREE OF T

DISTORTION

R. L. BLALOCK

Cover Artwork by Deranged Doctor Designs
Editing by Lana Mowry
Proofing by Jack Appell

For all the fans of the zombie apocalypse,
May the zombies remain forever locked in our minds..

ACKNOWLEDGMENTS

When a book finally makes it to publication it is through the efforts of dozens of people. We authors can't do it on our own. I couldn't have finished this book without the support of my friends, family, and all of my wonderful readers.

There are so many people who have helped. I'll only name a few here. My author friends Rachel E. Carter, R. J. Spears, and Baileigh Higgins pushed me to get this book written. Their encouragement kept me going when I struggled to get the words down. My husband, Craig, who takes care of everything else so I could focus on my writing. My parents, who always encouraged me to follow my dreams. And finally to every reader whoever took a chance on my books, I wouldn't be doing this without you. To my editors and cover artist who helped make this book shine.

Thank you all. I couldn't have done it without you.

DAY 9

Liv was running. She had been running for so long. They were after her. They were going to catch her. She didn't dare chance a look over her shoulder.

Her feet thundered against the pavement. Her breath was ragged. Each breath was never enough. Her energy was long gone. The ferals were gaining on her. With each step, they got closer, and it was only a matter of time before they caught her.

Elli let out another high-pitched wail, and Liv hugged her close. She had to keep running. If she stopped, they would both die.

But she didn't know where to go. She scanned the buildings around her. None of them looked familiar. She had no idea where she was. Each building could be harboring a horde of its own. She had no idea if there was somewhere safe nearby. She had to lose them.

Though the street ahead of her was clear, the road behind her was packed. She didn't need to look back to know that. Hundreds of footsteps pounded behind her. Their screams were a chorus that called for her flesh. They were bloody and broken. Inhuman now. They were feral. They would rip her to shreds, make her one of them.

Suddenly, her head was yanked back as a hand grabbed ahold of her hair. Liv swung around, ripping her head free as the hand took a chunk of hair with it. The feral was already in her face. Its disgusting teeth snapped furiously just inches from her nose.

With all her might, Liv kicked out, sending the feral sprawling to the ground. It was quickly overwhelmed by the others as they surged forward. Liv grabbed for her sledgehammer.

But it wasn't in its loop.

She backpedaled, trying to keep some distance, any distance, between herself and the horde. She found the hammer on her belt and yanked it out. In one motion, she smashed it into the side of a feral's head. The creature crumpled, and she swung again, this time catching a woman in the face. There was a terrible crunch as the hammer connected with bone. When the woman turned back, her jaw hung askew, her tongue lolling out of her mouth like a dog's.

Hands grabbed for her arms, her shoulders, her legs, her hair. Liv screamed, swinging the hammer with vicious desperation. It collided with another feral, catching him just behind the ear, and he crumpled to the ground. But more pushed forward.

Their hands were everywhere. They grabbed for her arms, her legs, her hair. Liv swung frantically, smashing the hammer down again and again. Ferals crumpled underneath its force, but she was no match for them. Teeth latched on to her shoulder and her arm. The pain began to radiate from everywhere, and she screamed.

Elli screamed with her. Fear and pain mixed to create a heartrending cry that only a child could produce.

And then she was gone.

Liv shrieked as the child was torn from her arms. She swung her hammer furiously, shoving her way through the ferals. She didn't care about their teeth or hands. She didn't care about herself. She could still hear Elli's cries somewhere amongst the moans and shrieks of the ferals. All she cared about was carving a path to her daughter.

The cries died and disappeared. Liv screamed, rage and fear and desperation all mixed into one.

The hands dragged her down, pulling her to the ground.

Liv sat up, gasping for breath. Her heart thundered in her ears, making her own breathing sound distant. She looked wildly around for ferals, their shrieks still echoing through her mind.

But there were none.

The room was quiet and empty though dark. It was unfamiliar. Liv began to panic. She didn't know where she was.

The memories flooded back. The running. The fighting. It had been real. Only the dying hadn't been.

Liv cast a glance down at the bed. Elli slept peacefully next to her. Her tiny mouth formed a sweet little O where her binky had fallen out. Her eyelashes were thick and dark against her pale cheeks. Her fawn brown, feather soft hair was tussled across her forehead. Her tiny chubby fingers gripped the pillow in her fist.

Her lips began moving, sucking on the binky that wasn't there.

Liv broke down. She clamped her hands over her mouth to stifle the sobs that escaped her lips.

They were safe.

She was safe.

Elli was safe.

The dream had been so real she was sure she would never see Elli again. She would never see the sweet little face that always looked up to her with so much love. Never feel the softness of her skin or the way her little hand would curl around Liv's finger.

Liv lay back down, pulling Elli close and snuggling against her. Elli's downy hair tickled her nose, but Liv didn't mind. In her sleep, Elli reached out, wrapping her arm around Liv.

Liv smiled. They were safe. After a hellish five days spent running and fighting for their lives, they were safe.

A scream rang through the farmhouse. Faintly, she could hear pounding reverberating through the walls. And the moans. They were muffled, but they were there.

Immediately, Liv's heart was racing again. Her eyes snapped open, and she sprang out of bed, snatching up the hammer that rested on the nightstand.

Liv stood perfectly still in the center of the room trying to calm her racing heart, so she could hear where the sounds were coming from.

Thump. Thump. Thump.

The glass in the window shook with each beat. Liv moved to the window and peered out through the blinds. Her heart stopped. Hundreds of ferals were lined up around the house in either direction. Were they surrounded?

Liv rushed to the door as quietly as she could. Their room was on the ground level. She couldn't risk drawing the attention of the horde.

Somewhere in the house, glass broke. Liv dropped to the floor, peering through the small crack between the door and the floor. No feet. Standing up, she slowly turned the knob, praying the old house wouldn't creak and give her away. Nothing in the hallway. At least, not yet.

Liv shut the door and raced back to the bed, scooping up Elli with one arm. Elli began to protest the sudden movement. Panic took over, and Liv shushed the child as quietly as she could, bouncing back and forth. Without opening her eyes, Elli settled again, and Liv breathed a sigh of relief.

Liv rushed to the door. She wanted to throw it open and run, but fear held her poised. The dream was still fresh in her mind. She had been running. Running from a horde while carrying Elli. The similarity paralyzed her.

With a concerted effort, she eased the door open and peered out in the hallway. They were there. They were in the living room at the end of the hall. Liv's breath hitched as she prepared to dart out of her room.

They had survived this long. She wasn't going to die now.

Liv cracked open the door. The ferals hadn't yet ventured further down the hallway. Each second seemed to take forever as she watched the ferals. They might see her at any moment.

Finally, when they were turned away from the hall, she darted out of her room and ran further down the hall. She counted the doors as she ran, praying she remembered the right room.

Fifth door on the right.

"Jordan!" she whispered. She knocked frantically on the door, trying to keep it quiet. "Jordan, let me in, please!"

The door swung open, and Jay grabbed Liv by the arm and pulled her into the room. He swung the door shut behind her, careful to latch it quietly.

"What are you doing?" Jordan whispered frantically.

"There are ferals in the house," Liv whispered back.

"Obviously!" Jordan snapped. "Why are you out of your room? And with Elli!" Jordan gave Liv a look that could have killed.

"We need to get up to the second floor," Liv explained. "We're as good as dead down here."

"They can't get in the windows upstairs," Jay agreed.

"Exactly!" Liv's voice rose just a bit, and she carefully brought it back down. "We can funnel them up the stairs and take them out a few at a time."

"All right," Jordan conceded. The stairs weren't far from their room. Two doors down. Though the farmhouse had an obscene number of rooms, it was far from a mansion.

"Let's go!" Jay picked up a hatchet and a few other items.

"Wait." Liv put up her hand to stop him. "We have to get the others."

"Are you crazy?" Jordan accused. "If we go door to door, those things will eat our faces off. I say we go upstairs and hope the others are smart enough to stay put."

"We cannot leave them down here. There are too damn many outside. Once we get the ferals riled up, they may start breaking windows to get in, and then the others will have no way out." Liv stared down her sister. They had always clashed. They were both stubborn, but Liv was not going to let this go. She wasn't going to leave anyone behind to get slaughtered.

"How many?" Jay asked.

"At least a hundred. Probably more."

"Jesus!" Jordan gasped.

"The hallway isn't wide. We can hold them back long enough to wake the others. They'll be able to fight too. We won't be alone." Liv set her shoulders back.

"All right," Jay nodded. "Let's go before more of them get in."

Liv thrust Elli into Jordan's arms. "Take her upstairs and start building a barricade. Make it passable but narrow."

"Liv!" Jordan clutched Elli.

"Don't argue with me right now!" Liv whispered with as much force as she could. "I need to know she's safe." Jordan had never been a fighter. She was strong-willed but shied away from blood and gore. If it came down to it though, she would defend Elli with her life.

Jay was already at the door. He cracked it open and peered out. After a moment, he nodded back to the others. They filed out. Jordan quickly rounded the corner to the stairs and disappeared out of sight. Liv and Jay ran down the hallway toward the living room, toward the first set of doors.

A feral shrieked. Angry. Hungry. Desperate.

Liv didn't look up. Jay was a big man. Tall and beefy. To many, he was intimidating, but he was a giant, goofy teddy bear. Most of the time. Now, he planted himself squarely in the entrance to the hallway and screamed back, challenging the might of the horde.

Liv slammed into the first door and threw it open. A man held a baseball bat tightly in his hands, his eyes wide as he took in Liv. Another man stood just behind him in the bedroom. Liv stood in shock for a moment as she stared at their identical faces before she sent up a silent thanks that they were up and ready.

"Get out now. A horde is here. Go help Jay." The man nodded, and Liv didn't wait to make sure he followed through. Liv didn't have time to hold everyone's hands. The best she could do was tell them to fight or get to safety.

In one leap, Liv was across the hall. The second door was locked. Liv banged on it hard.

"Wake up!" She screamed over the growing cries of the horde. "The horde is here. You have to move now!"

She spared a glance back at Jay and the men. Their silhouettes were almost lost amongst the horde in the dark.

"Get up! Now!" Liv shouted with all her might, hoping anyone awake would hear her. "Fight or die!"

She pounded furiously on the third door. Without waiting for a response, she hopped across the hall and pounded on the next one.

A mother pulled open the second door. Her child clung to her neck. Her eyes were wide as she took in what was happening.

7

"Go upstairs!" Liv shouted, pointing to the stairs. The woman nodded and scurried away.

More people were filtering into the hall. A few, too few, ran toward Jay and the trouble. Many more stood in the halls, paralyzed by their fear.

"Go! Go! Go! Upstairs!" Liv's voice boomed as she shooed the terrified herd of people in the right direction.

Liv spun back around. Another was fighting alongside Jay and the twins now, creating a wall of swinging weapons. They had lost some ground, but they all seemed to be unharmed. She dashed to the first door she could reach and peered inside. Empty. They should all be empty by now, but that didn't mean some petrified survivor couldn't be curled up in the corner. The ferals beat against the wall and the windows outside.

At each room, Liv checked inside before closing the door. They didn't need ferals coming at them from both sides.

With everyone else safely upstairs, they only had to worry about themselves now. Liv cast a glance up the stairs. She wanted to go up there with the others. Their plan seemed solid. But what if it wasn't? What if they led the ferals right back to everyone else?

"All right," Liv boomed over the horde. Her throat was starting to hurt from all the yelling. It had been dry when she woke up, but now it felt like sandpaper. "I want you guys to push forward on the count of three. Do whatever you have to but stay in line. Understand?" Jay gave her a quick sideways glance but nodded. The others nodded as well. "Once we reach the living room, we're going to form a circle. Backs inward. Do not spread out." Another quick round of nods.

"One…" The horde was frantic as ferals tried to climb over each other to reach them.

"Two…" There were already so many bodies on the floor.

"Three!" All shoved with all their might. The ferals in front of them toppled backward, taking down a few others directly behind them as well. The three men stepped and then began slashing at the monsters again.

"One…" The horde had already recollected itself. The ferals that were far enough behind not to be knocked over surged forward.

"Two…"

"Three!" They gave another massive shove. As the ferals hit the floor, they stepped forward again, this time lunging forward and taking out a few of the fallen ferals.

They were at the threshold to the living room. Liv swallowed the fear that rose up. This was where everything could go wrong if they weren't careful. "On three, push forward as fucking hard as you can. Then form up back to back. Got it!" Three nods.

"One…" Liv inched her way as close as she could without impeding their fighting.

"Two…" The living room was huge. It was a size that fit a house with almost fifty bedrooms. Liv hated the open space.

"Three!" The men leaned back and shoved with all their might. Several rows of ferals toppled backward. They lunged forward, dispatching the closest of the fallen before slamming their backs together. Liv vaulted over a dead body, landing right next to Jay and completing their pentagon.

"Do not separate!" Liv smashed her hammer against a head as one of the fallen ferals tried to rise. "Stick together!"

Teeth and hands were everywhere. Bloody mouths gnashed in her face. Liv kicked a feral in the knee and forced its leg to collapse before she smashed the hammer into its head. Another dove at her from the left. Jay's ax cleaved into its head, slicing a ribbon of flesh off its face.

Liv shoved back a feral without a right arm, bringing her hammer up and smashing it into another feral's forehead. They were surrounded on all sides now. There was no turning back.

Liv struck one feral in the jaw, sending it spinning to the floor. She immediately changed the direction on her swing, catching another feral in the side of the head with the hammer's claw.

The living room was starting to thin out. With a quick glance, Liv looked around the room. The front door was open, the frame splintered on the wall.

"We need to get to the door!" Liv said, relieved she didn't have to shout this time. "Fan out and push forward together." Jay and the other three men nodded.

"One. Two. Three!" Their pentagon unfurled into a single line. Now, they were all facing the door. The ferals were still pouring in without anything to hinder them.

"Outside! We have to get outside and decimate the rest of the horde, or they'll just keep coming!" Liv shattered the bones in the feral's face as it charged her.

"One. Two. Three!" They pushed forward, striking down the ferals in their way.

"One. Two. Three!" There weren't as many in the living room now. They could move more quickly.

"One. Two. Three!" They were almost to the door.

"One. Two. Three!" They struck down the ferals that managed to shove their way through the door. All that was left was for them to go out. Liv wondered how many more waited for them outside. The horde had seemed huge before, but they had struck down so many.

Somewhere else in the house, glass shattered and was quickly followed by a heavy thump.

"Out! Now! They're coming in the windows!"

"What about the others upstairs?" Jay asked.

Liv paused, thinking of Jordan and Elli upstairs. Jordan would protect her. Jordan loved Elli with all her heart. Liv shoved the thought away. "They can take care of themselves. They have plenty of people to fight the horde. Besides, if we create enough of a ruckus, the ferals should be drawn to us and not the house."

Jay nodded, his lips set into a grim line. "Then let's give them a show." With that, he let out the most ear-piercing shriek Liv had ever heard and charged out the door.

Liv sprinted after him, screaming until her throat was sore. The three other men followed behind her, adding their voices to the mad chorus.

Outside, they quickly formed into the back to back pentagon that had served them well in the living room. Liv lost track of how many ferals fell beneath her hammer. She had lost track inside, but she could no longer even guess.

A crack overhead made Liv jump. The feral directly in front of her jerked, his head twisting to the side in a spray of blood before he collapsed to the ground.

She glanced up to the second story windows. The barrel of a rifle pointed down at them, but she couldn't see his face. It didn't matter who it was, Liv was glad he was there.

A roar rose from the other end of the old farmhouse. Liv was already tense, and the added surprise didn't help.

Five figures sprinted around the side of the house. One of them ran right up to a feral, putting the barrel of a shotgun in its face before quickly pulling the trigger.

Reinforcements.

With renewed energy, the group hacked, slashed, and pummeled their way through the horde. The number of ferals outside the house quickly dwindled.

A feral was limping along the side of the house. His leg was bent unnaturally and crunched with every grotesque step he took. He snarled at Liv as she approached him. Though he tried to lunge for her, Liv kicked the bad leg out from beneath him and slammed the hammer down on the back of his head before he could even attempt to stand up.

Liv looked around, her heart still racing from the battle. The night was quiet once again. The yard was a mess. Bodies were scattered everywhere. It was hard to tell where one ended and the next one began.

As Liv moved to swipe some loose strands of hair from her forehead, she caught sight of her hands in the moonlight and gagged. They were covered in blood. A chunk of something clung persistently to the back of her wrist. She quickly swiped the chunk off her hand and wiped her hands on her pants. It didn't help much. Her pants were as much of a mess as the rest of her.

"Jesus," she whispered.

"Don't touch your face," she called to the others. "Eyes, nose, mouth…just don't touch anything…" The other looked down at themselves. Disgust played across all their faces in varying degrees.

Liv sighed and looked around again. They weren't done. Not by a long shot. The house had to be checked for ferals again. The bodies would need to be carried away soon. In the July heat, they would stink before the sun peaked in the sky. The house would need to be scoured clean. The yard…what could they do about all the blood and brains and small chunks in the yard?

Movement caught Liv's eye. Out at the tree line, ferals were still filtering in from the forest. There weren't many. Maybe a dozen that she could see, probably more still hidden by the tree lines, but they could manage that.

"Hey, uh…" Liv faltered, realizing she didn't know the names of the twins she had fought beside.

"Harvey and Daniel," one of the men supplied.

"Nice to meet you." Liv gave him a tired smile. She had seen the men around the farm but had not had a chance to speak with them yet. She extended her hand but quickly pulled it back as she remembered the bloody mess. "There are a few more ferals out by the trees. Would you go take care of them? If you think you need more people, take whomever you want; just make sure everything is clear."

Harvey nodded. Maybe it was Daniel. Liv inwardly cringed. She was terrible with names, and the identical twins would not be easy to pick apart.

"Sure thing," the other said. The two men spun in unison and loped off together.

"All right." Liv turned to the others. "They aren't the only ones who have work to do. Let's start getting those bodies out of the house and somewhere far…far away." Liv shuddered as she thought about the smell that would permeate the house.

A woman seated on the porch steps groaned without moving.

Liv rounded on her. "Are you hurt?"

The woman seemed startled by Liv's response. "N-no."

"Then what are you groaning about?" Liv snapped.

"It's the middle of the night," the woman snapped back angrily. "We're all exhausted. We worked all day to get seeds planted. We all want to go to bed."

"Yes. We all worked all day, but who do you think is going to come clean all this up?" Liv motioned to the bodies to her left, then turned and motioned to the rest that were to her right.

"I-I-I…"

"We are." Liv didn't let the woman continue. "We have been planting seeds from the ass crack of dawn until dusk because we are on our own. There aren't police officers who are going to come to investigate this. There aren't any morticians that are going to come to pick up the bodies. It is just us. If we want to survive, we are going to have to work for it."

Liv paused for a moment. The anger was swelling inside her, and it was a struggle to hold it back. It wasn't the woman's fault. It wasn't fair that they had been dealt this life. That everything had been so suddenly ripped away.

Liv massaged her temples wearily. "It sucks," she said.

"This whole situation sucks but look around you. Our whole home is a hot zone. There are blood and bodies everywhere, and it's all infectious. We need to get it cleaned up. Now. The longer it sits, the more of a risk we run."

"Is it even safe here anymore?" a man asked.

"Is it safe anywhere?" Max stepped in. "I may not know as well as some. I was fortunate enough to be here when shit hit the fan, but I've heard your stories. You've seen what it's like. Do you want to go back out there? To the Dead Zone?"

The man pushed the dirt around with his toe for a minute before replying. "You're right. It's probably not safe anywhere anymore. Maybe that's why settling down isn't a good idea. Maybe we should just keep moving." A few others nodded their agreement as a quiet murmur rippled through the gathered survivors.

"That's fine." Max nodded. "You're free to go whenever you like. So, who's staying?"

"Jordan and I are staying," Jay said.

"Elli and I are staying too." Liv was not about to go back out there.

Most people affirmed that they wouldn't be going anywhere. A few looked to the ground, staying silent.

"All right." Max nodded. "Those of you who are staying can start haulin' bodies." Max looked out at the dark farm. "Take them over by that shed." She pointed off into the darkness. The shed was more like a barn that Max used to store the large farm equipment when it wasn't being used. "That should hopefully be far enough from the house that it won't smell too bad while we get rid of the things."

"What do we do with all the bodies?" a man piped up. "It'll take weeks to dig enough holes for all of them."

Liv blinked. He was right. Dozens and dozens of bodies were strewn through the house and across the lawn.

Max's lips set into a grim line. "Burn 'em. Not sure if it's possible, but we don't need whatever infections they carry leeching into the soil anyhow."

"We should check all the rooms before we get started on clean up," Liv interjected before Max could dismiss the others. "Just in case any of the ferals got in through a window. I'm almost certain a few did."

Max nodded, her face almost seeming to age before Liv's eyes as she heaved a heavy sigh. "Of course. We should probably board up the windows on the lower floors as well." Max looked around at the group. "We'll suspend planting tomorrow. There is a lot of work that needs to be done."

Liv looked around one more time at all the bodies. In the last few days, the number of residents at Slag Stead had swelled from a handful to almost twenty. But their work kept piling up. More people meant more hands to work, but it also meant more mouths to feed and more crops to plant.

The night was still young. Liv guessed it wasn't much past eleven. They would have a long night ahead of them and an even longer day tomorrow.

DAY 10

Liv lay awake in bed. The sun had risen a while ago. Morning light peaked in through the blinds across the window. She couldn't be sure of the time because her room didn't have a clock, but the sun tended to rise around six o'clock, so it couldn't have been much later.

Six o'clock in the morning.

Liv wasn't usually up to see the sunrise, but she hadn't woken up. She had never really gone back to sleep. A few hours ago, Jay had sent Liv to bed for at least a few hours of sleep. Like the others, Liv had spent the night hauling bodies out of the house and into a truck that would carry them over to the shed. Others at the shed would unload the bodies and cut them up to be burned.

A shudder ran through Liv's body. She didn't enjoy hauling the bodies, but she would do that every day for the rest of her life to avoid burn duty. They could smell the fires at the house. The smell of smoke and charred flesh and hair permeated the entire farm. It couldn't be escaped. Even in her room, she could still smell it.

Outside, Liv could hear others working and swearing. With a sigh, Liv heaved herself up and sat on the edge of the bed. She had been lying in bed for a few hours. Sleep had never returned despite her exhaustion. Every time Liv had started to drift off to sleep, she had jolted awake, ready to fight off more ferals. It didn't make sense to keep lying in bed if she wasn't going to sleep. There was so much to be done.

Liv pulled on her clothes and dropped her sledgehammer into the loop on her belt. Its weight felt comforting at her side.

Liv pulled open the bedroom door and trudged down the hall. Before she even entered the living room, the smell hit her. Death and chemicals mixed together to create a noxious fume that permeated the entire house. Liv pulled her shirt up to cover her nose, though it didn't help much.

The living room was a disaster. The bodies were gone now, but blood was still everywhere. The furniture had been moved outside, so it could be inspected for any signs of contamination. Several people scrubbed at the floor with brushes, pink suds bubbling up as they cleaned.

There were splatters on the walls and ceilings too. Liv heaved a sigh and instantly regretted the action as she began to choke and cough on the fumes.

"How's it going?" Liv finally managed.

Ryland sat back with a sigh. "It's going." She cast a glance around the room, wincing at the mess that awaited them.

"Do you need more help?" Liv offered.

"Probably." She shrugged. "Don't we all, though. Why don't you go check with Max and see where they need you most?"

Liv ran a hand through her hair but gave up when her fingers got tangled in a mess of snarls. "Where is she?"

"Outside with the burn crew last I heard."

Liv winced. She didn't want to go near the fires. They were noxious enough even from a distance. Hopefully, she wouldn't get roped into helping them.

Liv reached for the doorknob, her hand absently pawing at a curtain. The door was gone. A sheet hung across the doorway in its place. Liv shook her head. The ferals had broken through last night. They would have to get it replaced before night fell again.

With an exasperated sigh, Liv pushed back the curtain, almost running into Max as she stepped through.

"Oh," Max exclaimed in surprise. "Just the person I was looking for."

"I'm sorry if I overslept," Liv apologized, even though she had only been in bed for a few hours. Even those few hours made her feel guilty. Others were working while she rested.

Max waved a dismissive hand. "Everyone has gotten a break here and there. I need to talk to you, though."

"Me?" Liv asked in shock.

"Yeah, meet me over at the barn. I'll be there in a minute." With that, Max stepped past Liv and into the house.

Liv frowned after the old crone. Why would Max want to talk to her?

Liv took a deep breath. The barn smelled musty. Alfalfa and dirt and a bit of manure but even that was a refreshing change from the smoke the fires put off.

There were a few others standing around the barn. Max had asked all of them to meet her. Jay was there, and so were the three men that had helped him hold back the ferals while Liv got the others to safety. Others had gathered in the barn as well.

"Anyone know why we're all here?" asked Jay.

Liv looked over the faces again. "It probably has to do with last night," she finally said. "I know we were in the midst of the ferals. What about you guys?" she asked the others.

The woman nodded, her bright blue hair falling into her face as she did. "Yup. Ryland and I managed to find Max when the horde reached the house." They were part of the group that came around the side of the house.

"I was on the second floor," the other man said. "I was sniping the ferals out the window."

"So, we were all involved in fending off the ferals." Liv looked at each person. Of the twenty-three survivors at Slag Stead, everyone here had been active in the fight last night.

"What does that mean for us?" Jay persisted. "Are we going to get an award or cookie or something?"

"Perhaps they are going to quarantine us." The man's voice was a deep baritone as he spoke. Seti crossed his arms over his chest. His dark brown eyes were piercing as he looked over the others. "We were all in close contact with the ferals last night. Maybe they want to make sure none of us were bitten."

Liv thought back to almost rubbing her eyes with her bloody hand. "Perhaps."

"Not me," the sniper spoke up again. "I was upstairs during the whole fight."

The room fell silent again as footsteps approached. Ryland stepped through the open barn door. She looked surprised for a moment to see so many other people.

"Welcome to the party!" Jay smiled. Ducking her head, Ryland joined the back of the group.

Max stepped in behind Ryland, squinting as she looked around the barn. "Good, you're all here." Max looked tired. The usual lines on her face had become deep groves. Her silvery gray hair had begun to come loose from its neat bun, creating a messy halo around her head.

They were all tired, though. Liv imagined she didn't look any better. Though she was clean from the previous night, she barely looked it. After putting on fresh clothes, she had slept in them, not wanting to get caught unprepared again. She hadn't brushed her hair when she had gotten out of bed, only pulled it back into a ponytail. It was a knotted messed from the scrubbing she had done last night.

"Please, have a seat." Max gestured to some bales of hay around the barn.

Liv mechanically walked over to one and sat down. Every muscle in her body was tense. She hated the news. She hated not knowing what the news was even more. She had liked surprises before the outbreak, but now they were full of terrifying possibilities.

"All right." Max plopped down on a bay of hale. "We've all been working real hard, and I want to thank you folks for that. I wasn't sure what would happen when I took in a bunch of strangers, but you folks have shown me that it was the right decision. Y'all are a bunch of hard workers...survivors." Maxine looked at each one of them in turn.

Liv knew there had be a but coming. Max was never this nice to anyone. Usually, she ran around and barked orders in between working on whatever had to get done.

"The crops are getting in the ground faster than I could have hoped. We should be...really well set come the fall and winter. It'll probably be rough until then, but we can make it." Max clasped her hands together nervously. "But we have been too focused on food."

Ava barked out a nervous laugh. "I don't know about everyone else, but I like food, and I like to eat. Isn't it a good thing that we've been so focused on the crops?"

"It is important." Max nodded her agreement. "However, there are other crucial things that we let slip through the cracks while we were busy making sure our bellies would be full."

"Like what?" Jay asked.

"Defense." The words slipped through Liv's lips before she could stop it.

"Exactly." Max looked up at Liv. "There is a lot more that needs doin' around here than just planting crops, and I plan on makin' sure it all gets done. The windows on the lower level should have been boarded up from day one, and we should have had people outside watchin' for more of the ferals. We were stupid, and stupid gets you killed. You got me?"

They all nodded back.

"Now, this is no one's fault. If anything, it's my fault. It's my farm. I should have made sure things got done." Max rubbed her temples with a shaky hand. "But from now on, we ain't going to be stupid. We're goin' to do this right because I'll be damned if I've survived this long only to die now."

"You want us to do patrols," Jay stated. Liv wasn't surprised when Maxine nodded. She had been dancing around the subject.

"We need someone to guard the farm." Max took a deep breath, blowing it out slowly. "Even if trouble hasn't come, and it obviously has, we need to make sure we see it before it sees us." Max paused before she continued. "We also need folks to run and get things we don't have from the Dead Zone."

"Why didn't you just ask?" Liv asked. "Why all of" — Liv gestured to the gathering— "this?"

"Because it's not fair to ask you folks to go out and face the monsters while the rest of us sit back here, comfy and safe." Max's jaw clenched as she spoke. "No one should have to face those things, and I hate the idea of asking y'all to do it because I'm too damn old to do it myself."

"Well, life isn't fair." Liv crossed her arms. "It's never been fair. Some people have always been lucky or gotten things handed to them while others worked hard and got nothing. Life has never been fair." Liv punctuated each word. "If it was, then none of us would be standing here right now. Whether it's fair or not, there is still work to be done."

Max nodded, her lips pressed into a thin line. "Fair enough." She heaved a heavy sigh. "If y'all agree to watch over the farm and fight off the ferals when they come, then you will be exempt from any other tasks around the farm. No planting. No harvesting. No mucking stalls. No washing laundry. Patrols will be your only duty, and in return, the rest of us will make sure your sheets are clean, your clothes are mended, and your food is hot."

"Why us?" Liv asked. "Why do you want us to be the farm's protection?"

Max laughed, a harsh throaty bark. "Come on now. Are you telling me you didn't walk in here and immediately figure out why each of you were here?"

Liv shifted. "We discussed it."

Max locked her gaze on Liv. "And what did you come up with?"

"We all fought off the horde last night."

"Exactly. Of the twenty-three people on this farm, you ten stepped up." Maxine hung her head for a moment, shaking it slightly. "Everyone should have stepped up. We're all damned survivors. We all fought our way here…'cept for me that is…but you ten stepped up and did what others did not. Made sure the others were safe and made sure the house was clear. Even culled off the rest of the horde."

"What…what else were we supposed to do?" Liv asked hesitantly.

Max shrugged. "Lay down and die? Hell if I know. But what do you think would have happened to everyone here if you folks hadn't stepped up and done what you did?" Before Liv or any of the others could say a word, Max continued. "We all would've been dead."

Liv blinked. Had they really been that instrumental in the survival of the farm last night?

"I need to get back to work." Max leaned back with a heavy sigh as she looked at the people she had gathered. "What'll it be?"

"I'll do it," Liv said without hesitating.

"Me, too," Jay agreed.

"I…" the man who had been sniping from the second story window hesitated. "I can't." He wouldn't look up from his boots. "I got here by being sneaky and quiet. I didn't get here by going toe to toe with the ferals. I won't survive that."

"So did I." Anger burned hot in Liv's veins as she took a step toward the man. "I came here with a baby on my back. Do you think I ran through the streets fighting every feral who would try me? You can't just opt out of survival."

"I'm sorry," the man whispered.

"I'll do it." Ava nodded to Liv as she glared daggers at the man.

"I can't either," another man chimed in, one from the group Max had led.

"Me neither," another chimed in. Liv's heart began to sink. What would they do without people to protect the farm?

"Stop." Max held up her hands, frustration plain on her face. "You folks who have…opted out. What if…" Her gaze drifted to the rafters as she tried to figure out how to salvage the meeting.

"What if we break up into two groups?" Liv offered. "One group will stay at the farm and patrol the grounds for ferals. If a horde comes, the patrols can call for backup. The other group will go out into the Dead Zone and find supplies we need."

The sniper chewed on his lip for a moment. "I think I could do that." The other two dissenters nodded their agreement.

"I'll go with the raiding party." Liv didn't like the idea of going out into the Dead Zone, but someone had to do it. If it would help the farm, then it would help Ellie. She had to do everything she could. Others around her nodded their agreement.

"Good." Max gave them a curt nod. "I'm glad you are all so willing to stick your neck out for us." Max turned and caught Liv's gaze. "You'll be in charge of this band of merry men." She gestured to the raiders.

Liv blinked at Max. "What?"

"You heard me." Max groaned as she pushed herself up. "Last night, when the pressure was on and lives were at risk, you kept your cool. You got everyone organized and rallied the troops to take back the farm. If that's not a leader, then I don't know what is."

"I-I-I don't know anything about tactics," Liv managed, looking to the others. No one stepped forward to take charge. Instead, they turned to her with hopeful faces.

Max smiled. "I think you'll do just fine." The words hardly seemed encouraging to Liv. Just fine. Would that be good enough to keep everyone alive?

"Oh," Max said as if struck by an afterthought. "One more thing. I already have a list of things the farm is short on. The farm had enough cleaning supplies to deal with day to day cleaning, but the clean up last night has wiped us out. We could also use some more gas for the equipment among other things."

"We'll do it." Liv nodded. "I'm not very familiar with the area. Do you know where we might go to find the cleaning supplies?"

"I've got a list of some places you can check." Max waved off the question.

Liv leaned her head on the truck's passenger window. The gentle bumping of the road was almost enough to put her to sleep. Almost.

It had been relatively easy to find the cleaning supplies. Liv had been surprised. They had gone to a local funeral home. The thought of all the forgotten bodies of loved ones rotting away had churned her gut initially. They had been lucky, though. The funeral home had been empty. The bodies had been locked away out of sight, and they hadn't investigated if there were any there at all.

The cleaning supplies had all been stacked neatly in a back room, gallons and gallons of antiseptic spray just waiting for them.

They had also found medical instruments, scalpels, suture needles, hypodermic needles, aspirators, and a gurney. Though the mortician had used them for embalming, the tools were standard medical instruments. No one was sick at Slag Stead. Yet. But it was only a matter of time. They would come in handy.

With their first set of items checked off, they headed back out to get the gas. Gas was easy to find. It was everywhere. Hundreds of cars had been left to rot on the roads when their owners had been attacked and subsequently infected. However, siphoning the amount of gas they needed would take time. A lot of time. They could at least try a gas station first. Perhaps the pumps would still work. The electricity wasn't out everywhere yet. While many places had lost power, there were still isolated pockets where the electrical grid had stayed intact.

There was only one gas station between the funeral home and Hawk Point, a Phillips 66 on the eastern side of the town. Hawk Point was a small town, barely more than a cluster of houses really. The gas station had been almost empty when they had passed as they headed to the funeral home.

As they neared, Liv signaled Jay to slow. The gas station was just as barren as before. A few ferals milled around the pumps. Liv counted three. They could handle that, even if a few more were around that she hadn't seen.

"Ok. Pull up to the pump. We're going to tackle the ferals at once. We don't want to give them a chance to scream and draw in others. Ryland and Seti, take the one closest to the pumps. Corbin and Connor, take the one by the silver truck. Ava and I will get the one by the doors. Ramsey, you jump out and check the pumps. See if they are still working. Jay, you keep the truck running for now in case we all screw this up. Got it?" Liv unbuckled her seatbelt as she prepared to bail out of the truck.

The others nodded. With that, the truck lurched forward, speeding toward the gas station. Liv grabbed ahold of the door handle to steady herself, and Jay yanked hard on the wheel and pulled into the station.

The truck wasn't even fully stopped before her door was open. Her feet hit the ground, and she sprinted toward the convenience store. The gas station was small with front doors that were no more than fifteen steps from the truck. The feral whipped around. Liv's sledgehammer was ready. The creature took a step toward her, its mouth opening. Too late. The head of the sledgehammer smashed into the feral's face, pushing it back until it hit the brick wall of the convenience store with an audible crack. Liv pulled back the sledgehammer, and the feral slid to the ground. Ava darted in, her knife sinking into the creature's eye.

Liv spun to check on the others. The ferals were down. They hadn't made a sound. Liv breathed a sigh of relief.

"It looks like this place still has power," Ramsey announced, picking up the nozzle to the pump.

Liv briskly walked back to the truck, her eyes scanning their surroundings. "Well, let's get the barrels filled and get home. I'm tired of being out in the open."

Ramsey handed her the nozzle and carefully hopped into the bed of the pickup, where four large drums sat. Ramsey carefully picked his way through the drums and situated himself on the edge of the truck. Liv handed the nozzle back and pushed the pay inside button. A quiet hiss as the gas moved through the hose.

The area was empty. In front of the gas station, a sign proclaimed the price of gas. $2.99 for a gallon of diesel fuel. Gas prices had been steadily climbing before the outbreak. Now, they had bottomed out at the low price of free to those willing to venture through the hordes of ferals.

"Well, we might as well go inside and see if there is any food left. We're going to be here for a while." The drums wouldn't fill quickly. Eighty gallons of gasoline would take some time to pump.

Seti stayed outside, watching over Ramsey as the others went inside. The large glass doors were locked. Jay pulled out his hatchet and punched a small hole in the glass next to the handles. Liv cringed and looked around as the glass cluttered to the floor. No screams came. No running feet. Jay pulled open the door and ushered them inside.

"Stay together," Liv whispered hurriedly as the others entered. "We should clear the rooms before we spread out." It didn't seem like there were many rooms to clear. The store was open. Any feral inside would have been attracted to the sound of breaking glass. The bathrooms were around the back side of the building, separate from the main store. The only places that really needed to be checked were behind the fridges and the back room.

Liv carefully peered down the few aisles as they moved through the store. The store was relatively untouched. A few stands had been knocked over, but most things still sat where they had been. The shelves were still filled with bags of chips, candy, and jerky.

Jay pushed open the door to the back room. It was pitch black inside. As the lights flickered on, the room appeared to be much smaller than Liv had imagined. The gas station itself was small, but she had thought they would need somewhere to store food before it went on the shelves. Apparently not, the back room was barely a closet stuffed with boxes.

"Well, I guess that settles that." Jay let the door close behind him. "Who's hungry?"

Liv was hungry. They all turned to mingle in the rows of food. There were a lot of options. None of them very healthy, but food was food. Liv snatched a bag of jerky off one of the shelves and tore it open. The meat inside would have been prepared and packaged well before the outbreak.

As Liv bit into the first piece, the delicious salt and pepper flavor washed over her tongue. She chewed on the tough meat for a moment. As Liv pulled out a large piece and struggled to bite it in half, the unbidden image came to mind of how similar she must look to a feral trying to strip the flesh from an arm or a leg. Suddenly, Liv's stomach revolted. She dropped the bag and spat out the jerky. The taste soured in her mouth.

"You all right?" Ryland asked, frowning.

"Yeah." Liv wiped her mouth on her sleeve. "It was just...a mind thing," she stammered.

With a sigh, Liv turned back to the shelves, her appetite completely gone. Even if she couldn't eat now, the heavily processed foods could be stockpiled for the winter. They needed everything they could take.

The fridges were still stocked with all kinds of drink, so Liv reached for a blue and black energy drink. She used to drink the things in college all the time, and she really needed the extra energy now. Since the electricity was still on, the fridge was still cold. When Liv opened the glass door, cold air wafted out, washing over her. For a moment, she simply stood in front of the open fridge door, luxuriating in the cold air. The drink was deliciously cold as she chugged it down. The sweltering Missouri heat had not been kind to them, and the added layers of protective clothing didn't help. The cooler was like a little slice of heaven.

"Man." Jay stood at another open fridge door, his eyes closed as he relished the cold air. "Beer is just not going to be the same warm."

Liv eyed him. "No beer right now. You can take it back if you want, though."

"I know. I know." Jay threw her a goofy smile. "It's just a shame to see all this going to waste."

"We'll take some back now. We can come back tomorrow when the trucks are empty and load up," Liv suggested.

A loud bang sounded from outside, startling Liv.

"What was that?" Ava asked.

Liv dropped the can in her hand and sprinted for the door. Outside, one of the large drums lay on the ground near the truck. Seti ran over and picked it up as Ramsey looked on from the truck bed.

Liv rushed over to the truck. "What happened?" Before Ramsey could answer, the howls echoed from the side streets. A chill ran down Liv's spine.

"Shit!"

"How many do you think are coming?" Ryland asked.

"I-I-I don't know." The howls were growing in number as they got closer.

"Should we stay or leave?" Ava was eyeing the streets, trying to decide where they were most likely to come from.

"How much fuel do we have?" Liv turned to Ramsey.

"Two full barrels." Ramsey shook his head. "I was switching to the third."

Liv gritted her teeth. From what Max had told her, they only had enough fuel to run the farming equipment today. Tomorrow, they would be out of luck if they didn't bring home more. Two barrels seemed like a lot, but how long would it last? "Circle around the truck," she growled. "We're going to hold them off. If things even start looking a little too dicey, we'll cut and run."

The first feral came around the corner of a house. Its head whipped back and forth. Dried blood dripped down the man's chin and matted his short beard. His shirt hung in tatters around his neck. The flesh had been ripped away from his side, leaving the shiny white ribs exposed. As his eyes fell on them, he shrieked and broke into an all-out sprint. A few more rounded the corner, trailing behind him.

Three. They could deal with three.

Jay stepped forward, his hatchet connecting with the side of the man's head. The feral went limp, rolling across the ground as he fell.

Liv's eyes roved over the streets around them. A few more ferals appeared, responding to the calls of the others. She wanted to run, tell the others to hop in the cars and take off. But they couldn't; they needed the gas.

A woman ran at Liv. Half her face had been peeled back, along with a good portion of her scalp, but the skin wasn't red or scabbed. New, knotted scar tissue covered her wounds. The woman's lips peeled back in an animalistic snarl as her arms and legs pumped. Her eyes were locked on Liv.

As the feral neared, Liv pulled back her sledgehammer and stepped forward, swinging it with all her might. The sledgehammer smashed into the woman's face. Her head snapped around with a terrible crunch, and the feral fell to the ground.

Liv looked around for the others. They were taking care of the last few ferals. A few still stood ready, but they were handling it. Liv smiled and breathed a sigh of relief.

Jay stepped toward a feral that had crawled around the side of the gas station. It pulled itself along the ground with its arms. Its legs were gone. Only its spine poked out from the bottom of its shirt.

"Leave it!" Liv shouted to him. She didn't want them to break rank unless they had to. The creature was slow. It would be a while before it reached them.

A pack of seven ferals slid out from a side street a few blocks up the street. Almost in unison, they threw their heads back and howled. Goosebumps rippled across Liv's skin. She had gotten used to a lot of things, but she would never be able to get used to that.

The pack thinned out as they ran. The ferals all ran at different speeds. The fastest pulled ahead of the others, while those who were slow, either before the change or due to injury, lagged behind.

Seti let the first feral pass him, stepping out of its path just as it reached for him. As the creature turned to grab him, he smashed his mace into the side of its head. Ryland sliced clean through another feral's neck before it could grab hold of Seti.

The girl wielded a heavy two-handed broadsword. Ryland had shown up for the excursion in a full suit of armor, the metal gleaming in the light. Now, as she swung her sword with her face contorted in a vicious snarl as she cut down the ferals, the shy girl was gone, and she looked like a warrior princess. For a moment, Liv marveled at the beauty of the old weapon. Ryland wore a primal snarl as swung the gleaming sword. She made it look so easy.

The pack hadn't stood a chance. Bodies lay around the truck like dropped dolls. Liv slammed her sledgehammer on the feral's decapitated head with a shudder. Connor wrestled another to the ground, spearing it through the eye with a knife.

A heavy thunk resounded behind Liv, and she spun toward the truck. The legless feral sat on the hood. As Liv watched, it scurried up over the cab. Its eyes locked on Ramsey. Before Liv could utter a word, the creature launched itself, slamming into Ramsey. The man cried out as the two toppled out of the bed of the truck, landing hard on the ground.

Liv raised her sledgehammer and swung. The head connected with the feral's side, flinging the monster off of Ramsey. There was so much blood already. It spread out in a pool around Ramsey, flowing freely from his neck. Liv turned back to the feral as it righted itself. The creature snarled at her through a mutilated and broken jaw, its lips and teeth gleaming with a fresh coat of blood. Liv slammed her sledgehammer down on its head.

Liv spun back to Ramsey, dropping beside him. The man spluttered and coughed, blood flecking his lips. The feral had torn a large hole in his neck. Blood didn't just ooze out of the wound; it squirted in tiny damning jets.

"Shit! Shit! Shit!" Liv yanked off her jacket, quickly rolling it up and pressing it to his neck.

"What happened?" Jay asked, shoving down a feral and slamming his hatchet into its forehead.

"I-I-I don't know." Liv shook her head. "We have to go now! Help me get him into the car."

Jay hesitated, his eyes darting between Liv and Ramsey. "Liv…"

"I know," she snarled back at him. "I know what's going to happen, but I won't leave him here. We'll put him down when he changes. The instant he changes." When. Not if. When.

Jay nodded and motioned for Seti to help him. Together, the two men lifted Ramsey into the back of the SUV that held their haul from the funeral home. Liv leaped into the back with him, maintaining the pressure on his neck the best she could.

"Go!" she screamed as Jay jumped into the driver's seat.

"You put him down the instant he changes." Jay's voice was flat as he spoke.

"The instant he changes," Liv agreed. She pulled her hunting knife out of the sheath on her thigh and tucked it into the seat where she could reach it easily.

"Ramsey." Liv patted his face gently, each pat getting a little firmer. Finally, the man's eyes rolled open. "We're going home," Liv said, forcing a smile to her face. "You're going to be fine. Can you keep your eyes open for me?" Even though she tried to keep her voice level and calm, she could hear the panicked edge to it.

Even as Ramsey nodded, his eyes rolled back and closed.

"Hey, stay with me!" Liv felt along the other side of his neck for a pulse. She found it. It was weak and thready but

33

there. "Come on, Ramsey. Wake up." Liv rubbed his chest hard as she tried to rouse the dying man.

Liv caught Seti's gaze. He usually wore a rather stoic expression, but now his lips turned down ever so slightly.

"Who does he have waiting back at Slag Stead?" Liv asked, her hand trembling as she reached for her knife.

"A sister…I think," Seti replied.

"A sister," Jay confirmed. "She's the girl with one arm that's been helping to keep the house in order." Liv's stomach sank.

The SUV slid around a corner, throwing Liv against the front seat. As her jacket fell to the floor, blood began to spurt from Ramsey's neck again. The stream was weaker than before, more like a dribble.

"Hurry up!" Liv barked at Jay as the truck bumped along the gravel road. They were only a few minutes from Slag Stead. Just a few more minutes and Ramsey could say goodbye to his sister.

"Ramsey, wake up!" Liv patted his face, her touch hard enough to almost be a slap. His eyes didn't even flutter. "Wake up!" Liv couldn't feel his pulse anymore. It had been weak before, but she couldn't find even a hint of it. "Damn it!"

Ramsey's eyes snapped open and immediately latched on to Liv. There was nothing in them. They were just empty.

Without thinking, Liv raised the knife. Ramsey's mouth opened, a weak growl emanating from his throat. Liv brought down the knife, jamming it into his temple. A shock ran through his body just before he went still.

Liv leaned back and looked out the window. The farmhouse sat at the end of a winding gravel road. Her stomach knotted as it came into view. Ramsey's head lay in her lap, and Liv could feel the blood seeping through her pants. It coated her hands and splattered her shirt, marring everything inside the car.

As the car stopped, Jay leaned forward, resting his head on the steering wheel. Seti just stayed in his seat, staring straight ahead. They were lost in their own thoughts. The truck pulled up beside them. Liv finally pushed her door open and slid out from underneath Ramsey's body. She could see the others' faces fall as she climbed out alone.

"Liv!" Liv spun toward the voice. Jordan was running toward her, worry etching deep lines in her face. "Oh my god, Liv! What happened to you? Where's Jay?" Jordan looked around quickly before taking in the gory spectacle. Her eyes roved over Liv's blood-soaked pants, the splatters on her shirt, and her bloody hands.

"Jay is fine." Liv gestured wearily to the front seat. Jordan sighed with relief.

"What happened?" Jordan persisted. "Are you hurt? Where are you hurt?"

Liv shook her head. "It's not mine." Liv could feel tears threatening to come to the surface. She choked them back, determined to stay strong.

"Who's is it? A feral? Is everyone all right?"

"No." Liv's voice was barely a whisper as took a deep breath to steady herself. More people were gathering around them by the second. Their concerned looks threatened to dissolve her. Liv spotted Maxine in the crowd. The old crone's shoulders sagged as they locked eyes. "It's Ramsey's."

"Oh god!" Jordan's hands flew to her mouth.

Liv heard the screen door slam closed. Emma stood on the top step of the porch. Her ruddy hair had been pulled back into a bun. The apron around her waist was messy from cooking all day. She still held a dishtowel in one hand, in her only hand.

As Liv took a few steps toward the girl, all the color drained from her face. Her smile fell. Tears began to trickle down her cheeks.

"Where's my brother?" Emma asked feebly. Her eyes fell on Liv, growing wide before she spun, retreating into the house.

Liv looked down at herself. She was covered in blood all the way from her knees to her stomach. Ramsey's blood.

Bile rose in Liv's throat, and she immediately started pulling off her gore covered jacket. Underneath lay a patchwork of magazines and duct tape. The patchwork looked slapped together but worked well to protect her vulnerable flesh. One by one, she cut the freshest layer of tape and let the patchwork fall away.

Liv moved toward the front door, determined to wash off.

"Don't you even think about setting foot inside my house," Max's hard voice cut through the air. Flecks of brains still covered Liv's boots. Her pants were soaked in blood. She was a walking contagion.

"We need to wash up. We should set up a station outside, so we can wash off. Can you get us a big bucket and some bleach?"

Max nodded and hurried away. She returned with Randall, the two of them carrying a large basin that would be used to give water to horses. They set up the basin near the hose. Liv poured bleach into the water as the basin began to fill. The solution would dry out their skin, but the diluted bleach would kill any kind of germ or bacteria they might be carrying.

With a sigh, Liv sat down, pulled off her boots, and began to scrub.

DAY 13

Even under the shade of the porch, it was sweltering. Liv's heavy clothes didn't help either. The leather jacket and long pants covered everything but meant she couldn't get any relief from the heat and humidity. The sun had begun to set, but it didn't seem to do much good.

Ryland strolled out of the house. She smiled and waved to Liv. Her armor gleamed in the dying light. The metal was scratched, but Ryland had polished it almost like new again. Liv stood up from the porch swing and joined her as they jogged down the steps.

Liv was glad she had taken the night shift. The thought of running around all day wearing all her gear was awful. She shouldn't have even had to go on the patrol. The patrols had claimed they needed more people until they could recruit others. Liv had volunteered for a shift to help. She had made the choice, but it didn't mean she was happy about it.

"So how do you want to do this?" Ryland asked.

Liv thought for a moment. They would be walking around the farm all night on patrol. They weren't like security guards before the outbreak. Ferals wouldn't watch for routine.

"Why don't we start at that shed?" Liv pointed to a small shed that stored the farm's small equipment. The shed was the closest building to the tree line. "We can use it as a marker."

Ryland nodded. "Sounds good." Their pace was brisk as they headed out. There was a lot of ground to cover.

Liv watched Ryland out of the corner of her eye. She hardly knew the woman. Ryland had been at Slag Stead when Liv had arrived. She was quiet and mostly kept to herself. However, she didn't seem entirely shy. Her auburn hair was pulled back into a tight bun. She seemed relaxed as they walked, her hand resting on the hilt of her sword.

The sword. The one that she wielded so effortlessly. Along with her armor, it made the girl stand out amongst the hodgepodge of protective clothing the others wore.

Liv wanted to ask about the sword. She had wanted to ask since they had all been brought together a few days ago. Everyone else's weapons seemed bland and boring by comparison.

"So" —Liv started as the silence grew uncomfortable— "how are you doing?" Liv inwardly cringed. She had never been terribly social. She had her friends, and she loved them dearly, but she wouldn't go out of her way to make new ones.

Ryland nibbled on her lip as she mulled over her answer. "I think I'm doing ok," she finally replied after carefully considering her answer. "Don't get me wrong. This is all still…a bit shocking. Weird. Two weeks ago, I sat at a desk and filed insurance claims. Today, I'm strutting around a farm with a sword at my hip…it's just…unbelievable."

"Yeah, if you don't mind me asking, how did an insurance adjuster end up with a sword?" Liv asked, seizing the opportunity.

"I liked to go to Ren Faires." Ryland shrugged, a flush creeping across her cheeks. "I started going when I was in high school. During college, I started making my own outfits. One of the friends I made there was into metal work." Her eyes glazed over a bit as she got lost in her memories. "He helped me make this...or I should say, he made it and I helped a bit."

"Did you take fencing lessons?"

"No. Not to mention, fencing doesn't really translate to practical sword fighting." Ryland shook her head. "I just thought it would look cool. Before the outbreak, I was building a lady knight costume." She knocked on her chest, the metal chest plate clinking.

"Then how are you so good with a sword?" Liv asked, no longer hiding her amazement and envy.

Ryland shrugged. "You don't have to be good when it comes to the ferals. They don't try to block attacks or disarm you. They just charge. It leaves them pretty vulnerable."

"That is honestly really cool." A broad smile spread across Liv's face.

Ryland smiled back, her eyes lighting up. "I really liked going to the Ren Faires. Everyone was weird, but they were all so happy. You could be whomever you wanted. I wasn't an insurance adjuster who hated her job. I was a princess or knight or a barmaid." Ryland fell silent for a moment. "I wonder how everyone else is doing. Those people were resourceful. I hope they made it through the outbreak all right."

Liv wanted to say something comforting, to say that her friends would be fine, but chances were that they were dead. It felt wrong to give her empty platitudes. "I'm sorry, Ryland," she whispered. The words sounded hollow and pathetic. When Liv looked up, there were tears glistening in Ryland's eyes.

"It's all right. I mean it's not, but I know what the world has turned into. I know what their chances are." Ryland sighed. "Call me Ry. No one calls me Ryland except my parents...so I guess no one calls me Ryland now."

They fell into silence again. Crickets chirped around them, silencing as the pair neared and singing again once they had passed.

"So," Ryland started, "how are you holding up?"

Liv regretted asking Ryland the question. She should have known it would come back to her. Liv tried to think of something to say.

Liv's shoulders slumped. "I've been having nightmares. I can't escape the hordes; even in my sleep, they come after me." She opted for an honest answer. Everyone was dealing with the apocalypse. Everyone was grieving and scared, but they didn't have to be alone in it.

Ryland nodded. "That makes sense."

Liv shook her head. "It's just...a lot. I miss Colin. My parents are...dead." They weren't dead. Or at least they hadn't stopped moving. Liv knew they were out there in the world somewhere, hunting, just like the rest of the ferals. "And to be honest, I don't know how I feel being in charge of...this little group of ours."

Ryland shrugged. "I can't say that I would want the job." She smiled at Liv. "You're honestly doing great, though."

Liv barked a laugh. "Great. Right." She sobered as the memory of Ramsey's eyes opening and staring blankly back at her resurfaced.

"You are." There was a hard edge to Ryland's voice. "What happened with Ramsey was tragic...but anyone would have made the same calls. We needed the fuel. There weren't that many of the ferals. We were doing great...until we weren't."

Liv nodded.

"Can I ask?" Ryland asked slowly. When Liv nodded, she continued, "What happened with Ramsey? At the gas station? It just all happened so quickly."

Liv shook her head. "I don't know." The scene replayed in her mind. "This feral…didn't have any legs…but it managed to climb up onto the truck. It leaped on top of him. Knocked him over."

Ryland nodded.

"It's just…it's weird," Liv continued. That night had been bugging her ever since. "The creature was so slow at first…and then it was just there."

"Could there have been two?" Ryland suggested.

Liv rolled the thought around. Could there have been two? Maybe. "No," she finally said. "It was the same one."

"Then how did it get on top of the truck without us seeing it?" Ryland asked.

"I don't know," Liv shook her head. "I've been thinking about that for the past three days."

Ry was silent for a moment as she thought. "Do you really think this is the end of days?"

"For us? Maybe. For the world…" Liv chewed on her lip. "The world will just keep going, with or without us."

Ry walked on in silence. "There was all kinds of stuff all over the news during the first few days. A scientist came on with the doomsday clock and told everyone that this was Midnight. It always stuck out to me. All the other newscasters were so distraught and upset and rightly so, but this man was so calm, like he was talking about the weather instead of the extinction of his own species."

"I didn't see that one. Elli and I didn't have access to TV too much. We hardly ever knew where we were until we got here."

"Be glad. The scientist killed himself. Most of the other channels were filled with hordes roaming the streets and breaking into buildings. Newscasters got killed on live TV. We already knew it was bad; we didn't need to see the scope it took." Ry's brow creased into a frown. "It still feels like midnight, like the end."

Liv swallowed around the lump in her throat. "Maybe it was the end, and this is the beginning of something else."

The trees all looked the same. Dead leaves crunched underfoot even as they tried to silence their steps. Liv and Ry had been walking circles around the farm for hours. Each circle was bigger than the last as they worked their way outward, slowly combing for ferals.

Their walk had been quiet. Occasionally, they would spook a bird into flight, but they hadn't seen a single feral during their patrol.

Liv liked walking in the woods at night. Moonlight filtered through the trees, leaving them just barely enough light to see where they were going. The smell of rotting wood and leaves permeated the air. It was quiet and soothing. The patrol was the closest thing she had done to relaxing since the outbreak.

A shift in the light caught Liv's eye, and she held out her arm to stop Ry. She stared hard into the dark, willing the ill-defined shadows to become shapes. A figure shifted, falling against a tree and sliding to the ground.

"Feral," Liv breathed, pointing at the figure.

Liv inched forward. The creature was still as it sat against the tree, its head hanging against its chest. The man was dirty and covered in blood. The feral must have been sleeping and fallen over. Liv had seen it before. Sometimes, they crumpled to the ground. Sometimes, they would fall like a log, but most of the time, they stayed standing all night until the sun woke them.

Together, Liv and Ry crept forward, hiding behind a bush as they observed the creature. As Ry drew her sword, a twig snapped beneath her boot, and the feral's head snapped up. His head swung back and forth, looking for the source of the sound. Ry advanced forward to dispatch the creature, but Liv stuck out her arm again, shaking her head. With a nod, Ry stilled, awaiting Liv's command.

"Speak." Liv's voice came out loud and clear, making the man jump, but he didn't say anything as he looked around wildly. If the man uttered one word, any word, it would mean he wasn't a feral but a survivor. "Speak," Liv commanded again.

The man's hand went to his hip, and Liv unholstered her own Glock. He drew a pistol, pointing it vaguely in their direction.

"Who's there? Show yourself." His voice cracked as he spoke.

Liv wasn't sure if she was relieved that he was human. Ferals were simple. They attacked. They killed. Humans could hide their intentions. Liv scanned the woods looking for any signs that this man wasn't alone. That they were being lured into a trap. The flickering moonlight was no longer soft and soothing. It was menacing, hiding foes in every dark corner.

"What do we do?" Ry whispered, her voice pitched low.

Liv nibbled on her lip. "You stay down. Keep me covered. If anything goes wrong, kill him."

Liv offered Ry the Glock and drew her sledgehammer. She took a deep breath, willing herself to look as big and intimidating as she could.

"If I step out, are you going to shoot me?" Liv kept her voice level.

The man shifted slightly, aiming the gun directly at where Liv hid. Her heart thundered in her chest as she waited for him to pull the trigger. "That depends on you."

With one final deep breath, Liv rose. Ry reached for her arm to pull her back down, but Liv quickly stepped through the bush just out of her reach.

"You can see me now." Her fingers clenched tight around the handle of the sledgehammer. "Why don't you put down the gun?" She wouldn't be fast enough if he decided to shoot her, but the weapon brought her comfort.

The longer Liv stared at him, the more she could see. The dark circles under his eyes that weren't just shadows in the dark. His face was gaunt. He was hungry. He had been hungry for a while. His eyes were hollow and haunted. He twitched at every sound, expecting monsters to materialize before him.

Liv's gaze fell to the gun that was still pointed at her chest. It shook as he held it. The effort of holding up the weapon sapped the last of his strength, and he relented. His arms dropped to his sides, and he holstered the weapon.

"It looks like you could use some help," Liv said gently. The man leaned his head back against the tree, not acknowledging her words. "Where are you headed?" She crouched down in front of him, bringing her face level with his.

"A farm."

Liv's eyebrows raised a fraction before she brought her reaction under control. "What's the name of the farm?"

"I don't remember," he growled in frustration.

"That's all right." Liv struggled with how to keep this man talking, how to get him to trust her. "Are you looking for someone?" The man nodded. "Who?"

He sighed, his head sagging down to his chest. "A woman named Olivia Bennett. She has a child with her. A daughter."

Liv straightened, a frown creasing her face. Who was this man? Was he one of Colin's coworkers? Did she know him? She looked him over again, inspecting every part of his face, but she couldn't remember ever meeting him.

Be quick. Be quiet. Be safe.

The voice rang through her head. The kind voice that had helped her through the first few days and pushed her to continue onward to Slag Stead. The voice she had encouraged to join her. The same voice she was talking to now.

"Are you Officer Ward?" Liv asked slowly.

The man started at hearing his own name. "Yes…" he said slowly.

"My name is Olivia Bennett." A broad smile spread across Liv's face. "Welcome to Slag Stead, Officer." Liv extended her hand to him.

For a moment, Wyatt only stared at her hand in shock. Liv's smile faltered as her hand hung in the air. Slowly, she pulled it back.

Liv looked around in the woods again. When she had spoken to Officer Ward last, he had been trapped in the Cottleville Police Station with a few others. No one else was around. No one had come with him.

No one else had survived.

"Come on." She gently took him by the arm. "You must be exhausted. Why don't we get you back to the house, so you can rest?"

"Are you real?" Wyatt's hand shot out, and he gripped her arm.

Liv let out a nervous laugh. "I sure hope so! I'd be rather disappointed to find out I wasn't." His hold on her arm loosened as he accepted this answer.

Liv turned and beckoned to the bushes she had emerged from. Ry stepped out, and together, they helped Wyatt up. He stumbled as he stood, his legs stiff and sore.

"I'm glad you're all right, Olivia," Wyatt whispered as they slowly made their way through the trees. They crashed through the underbrush, no longer trying to silence their steps.

"And I'm glad you're here." Liv squeezed his arm gently. He felt so weak as they helped him through the underbrush. He tripped over fallen branches and roots, barely keeping on his feet. "By the way, you can call me Liv. Everyone else does."

"Nice to finally meet you in person. Call me Wyatt…I'm not an officer anymore."

The tree line stopped abruptly and opened into a large field full of knee-length grass, the farmhouse planted directly in the center. The house bent in the middle, curving in the shape of an L. Vines had grown up the sides of the house on one wing but left the old brick exposed on the other. The old building was shrouded in darkness. The house had a generator, but they needed to conserve all the fuel they could for necessities like cooking.

"We need to talk to Max before we get you settled in," Liv whispered. "She owns the farm, and she insists on meeting all the survivors we bring in."

"Do you bring in many?" Wyatt asked curiously.

"We've had a few." Liv nodded, her breathing was labored as she held him up. "Max is a big person, personality wise. She might seem kind of…harsh, but don't worry. She wouldn't take all of us in if she wasn't a good person."

"Yeah," Ry chimed in. "She might seem like an old hag at first, but you'll like her once you get to know her better." Liv and Ry cackled.

"I'm sorry," Liv continued, reigning in her laughter. "There is a bit of a routine we have to go through before we can get you really settled in. You'll need to be cleaned up and looked over for infection by another male after meeting with Max. I know you're probably tired, but it's for everyone's safety. I'm sure it seems like a lot to take in, but Max insists on it, and I think it's a good idea."

"Seems reasonable." Wyatt nodded. "You guys really have things all figured out."

"Hardly." Liv chuckled. "But we're trying."

As they neared the house, Ry ran ahead and opened the door. Wyatt held on to the railing as Liv helped him up the steps. As soon as they were inside, Ry disappeared down one of the dark hallways.

"Here." Liv motioned for Wyatt to sit on a bench by the door. "As soon as we hear Max, you need to stand. Without my help. Stand as tall and strong as you can," she whispered quickly. "Everyone has a place here, but you need to make a good impression on Max."

Liv danced from foot to foot as they waited. This meeting with Max was so important, but Wyatt seemed so weak now. Max wouldn't turn him away. At least she hadn't turned anyone away yet, but that didn't mean she wouldn't. Liv didn't know how long he had been trapped in the Cottleville Police Station. Perhaps he had been starving since the beginning. He would need time to heal, but she wanted him to get the best start possible.

It wasn't just Max's judgment she was concerned about. She was nervous about Wyatt's judgment of the farm. They had all accepted the rules, but would they seem odd to a stranger? They had accepted the realities of what the world was becoming. Would they seem crazy for changing so quickly?

47

As Wyatt, glanced around the living room, Liv became acutely aware of all its faults. It was rather bare. The furniture had all been pushed to the edges. Nothing was left in the center. No rug or coffee table. A red stain on the floor caught her eye. It was light and had been scrubbed nearly clean, but it was still there. The door frame was cracked in a few places. One of the windows was missing the glass behind the boards. Would he deem them too lax with their security? Would he think this place was unsafe?

"I'm comin'. I'm comin'." A woman's sharp voice rang through the house. Liv blew out a nervous breath and frantically motioned for Wyatt to stand. He stood up as quickly as he could and straightened his clothes. There wasn't much that could be done for him. Grime covered every inch of his skin, blood splatters punctuating the dirt and mud. He smelled like he hadn't bathed in a while.

Liv smiled to herself as she watched him frantically try to wipe off some of the dirt. She hadn't looked any better when she had arrived.

"What do we have here?" Wyatt's head snapped up. Max marched down the hallway from the east wing of the house. The grooves in her face grew deeper as she looked over him.

"Max, this is Wyatt Ward. He's a police officer from Cottleville. He helped me get Ellie out of the city," Liv introduced them.

Wyatt offered Max his hand, but she only stared at it dubiously. "Why didn't you show up here with Liv?" the crone asked.

"He wasn't—" Max shot Liv a silencing glare, and Liv ducked her head.

Max looked back to Wyatt. The man cleared his throat nervously. "I wasn't with Liv during the outbreak. We got in contact through a radio. I gave her some advice for staying safe."

"You look ill." Her eyes roved over Wyatt from head to toe and back again, taking in every speck of dirt and blood. "Were you bitten?" Max's lip curled as she said the words.

"No, ma'am." Wyatt ducked his head, embarrassed by his own filth. "Just tired…and dirty."

Max nodded a few times. "Certainly. Get yourself cleaned up. Get checked out and go to bed."

Max spun on her heel and marched back down the hallway. "And don't wake me again! If you drag in any more strays, they can wait until morning," she hollered grouchily as she retreated.

"Wyatt, this is Jay." He stood quietly to the side as Max had spoken with Wyatt. "He's my sister's boyfriend. He will take you to the showers. You can wash up, and then he'll inspect you for any bites or scratches that might be infected. This is all part of the protocol and meant to keep everyone here safe. Any newcomers must undergo inspection before they can be allowed to roam the farm on their own. Is that all right?"

Wyatt nodded.

"When you're done, we'll get you something to eat and show you to your room," Liv called after them as Jay led Wyatt away.

Liv fussed around the kitchen. It was late, but her shift on patrol wasn't nearly over. She had managed to beg Ava to take her place after promising to take her next shift. Wyatt and Jay had been gone for a long time. She couldn't help but wonder what that meant. Had Jay found something? A bite? A scratch?

Liv jumped when someone cleared their throat. Wyatt stood in the doorway wearing a fresh set of clothing. He looked so different from the person she had seen just an hour earlier. His skin still glistened from the shower, all the dirt washed away. His new clothes were wrinkled but clean. He looked less tired, less beaten down. There was even more life in his eyes.

"All good? Liv smiled, turning back to the plate she was preparing.

"Better than I've felt in weeks." The stool scraped across the floor as he pulled it out and sat down at the small kitchen island.

"I figured you'd be hungry." Liv turned back to him, presenting the heaping plate. The food was cold but fresh. "We don't have much meat around here, but we've got a lot of veggies." She placed the plate in front of him. There was a large pile of candied carrots, a salad made with spinach and tomatoes, a large slice of cheese, a few hard-boiled eggs, and a roll.

Liv pulled out the stool next to Wyatt and sat down. Even the counter was warm from the summer heat.

"Thank you." Wyatt's voice cracked, and he cleared his throat. "It looks delicious." Wyatt took a bite of the salad, chewing it slowly. It wasn't the ravenous hunger that Liv had expected.

"I'm really glad you made it out here." She toyed with an extra roll she had grabbed, picking off pieces but not really eating much. "I wondered what happened to you, but my radio died sometime around day five."

"I'm glad you made it out here, too." Wyatt took another bite, letting the food roll around in his mouth. It tasted delicious and fresh compared to the canned and packaged food he had been eating.

"Is everything all right?" Liv asked. It was a stupid question. He had just come from the Dead Zone. "If you don't like the food, I can see what else we have." The words rushed out. She had never been good at comforting those in crisis. He had been through something terrible. The world had ended. His own world had ended. Words just weren't enough.

"It's fine." Wyatt smiled and set down his fork. "It's just…I guess this feels like a dream. After being in the station…after going home…after everything. It doesn't feel like any place should be safe now. It doesn't feel real."

Home. Who had he been looking for at home? Liv swallowed hard. Whoever it had been, he hadn't found them. Not alive at least or they would have been here now. Liv wasn't sure if she should ask. What was the protocol for asking about family and friends when most of them had probably died horrifically? Would it reopen fresh wounds? Would it be a welcome chance to talk about those he had loved?

"I'm not going to ask you about what you've been through. I'm sure it was terrible. Worse than terrible." Liv's voice broke, and she cleared her throat. "But if you want to talk about it, I'm here. You really helped me pull myself back together when I needed someone." She pressed her lips into a thin line. "If I can repay the gesture, I'd be more than happy to do so."

"Thank you." Wyatt smiled at her, broad and genuine. "I'll keep that in mind."

"You don't have to pretend to be all right here." Liv blew out a long breath as she carefully selected her words. "We've had our share of trouble." She ran a hand through her hair. "But this farm really is a nice place. It does feel like a dream sometimes, like I might wake up back in some house still fighting my way across the city. The feeling is going away. Slowly, but it's fading." Liv glanced over at him. "It's really the best thing I could have hoped for. I know getting here is rough, though." Her eyes glazed over as she was swept up in her own memories. Jen. Corey. Her mom and dad. The little neighbor boy. After a moment, she shook herself and continued, "We're not perfect, but the people here are good people. We're trying to move forward together. I hope you'll find it as welcoming as I have."

Wyatt pushed the carrots around. His mouth opened and closed a few times before he was able to speak. "How is your daughter doing?"

Liv smiled. "Elli is doing really good, all things considered. Things are pretty normal here for her. She runs around the house. She can play outside in the yard. She has people doting on her all day." Liv looked down at her roll, a small smile spreading across her lips. Though Liv saw Elli less than ever, the child was probably more spoiled than she had been before the outbreak. Nana Eve, an ancient woman, who had managed to find the Slag with her family, doted on her all day. Elli was always under her watchful eyes. She always had a lap for her to sit on, a book to read, a game to play with her. "I think she knows things are different now. I don't think she knows how different...but I'm kind of grateful for that. I'm glad she doesn't really understand how scary all of this is."

Wyatt smiled. "Kids are resilient. They can survive anything..." his words trailed off. A haunted look washed over him as he stared off into space. Wyatt shook his head and tried to wipe away the memories.

"I'm sorry." Liv's voice was barely a whisper. "I know you've lost folks, and I am just really sorry." Liv squeezed his arms. "But I'm glad you're here now."

Wyatt's shoulders sagged. "We've all lost folks." He shrugged, trying to be nonchalant, but he continued to stare straight ahead.

Liv nodded. "We have, but it doesn't make it hurt less." She touched the rings that dangled from a long chain under her shirt. Her mother's wedding ring and her own.

She hadn't given up on Colin. Not yet. It hadn't even been a full two weeks since the outbreak. He would come home. He would find them here.

DAY 18

"What's on the list today?" Ava asked.

"The usual. Food, gas, stuff for the fence. If any other necessities catch our eye, then we can snatch those up, too." Liv shrugged. This was hardly routine yet, but they were getting there. The list rarely varied. They always needed the same things. For now, the houses in Hawk Point held most of what they needed. Sooner or later, though, they would need to make those things on their own.

"Necessities." Jay made air quotes with a smirk. "I could use some necessities."

"I mean toothpaste and soap," Liv said flatly.

Ry gave Jay a light shove as she passed. "Some of us could use some soap more than others." Her nose wrinkled as she sniffed the air around him.

"Hey! I don't smell any worse than the rest of you," Jay protested.

"We all smell pretty bad," Liv muttered. She felt disgusting. They had been rationing soap and shampoo since the outbreak, but it hadn't lasted. While Max had stocked up on seeds and canned food, the soap had been disappointingly understocked. It was on her list of things to grab today. It was always on her list. Liv hated feeling this dirty and hated being dirty in general.

"I was thinking we'd scope out Walmart in Troy," Liv suggested. "It would have everything we need."

"Including a swift and grisly death." Ava leaned against the long dining room table.

"I agree," Seti said, his deep voice resonating through the room. "That place has to be crawling with ferals. Everyone would have flocked there during the Midnight Days. They're probably all still there."

"I know. I know." Liv held up her hands defensively. "But we've got" —Liv did some quick calculations in her head— "eleven new survivors in the last week alone. Raiding neighborhoods isn't going to cut it much longer. We need bigger resources, or we're going to have to go out more. Even then, if we keep getting more survivors, I don't know if that will be enough to keep up."

The others fell silent. It was wonderful to have new people on the farm. More faces, more hands, but more mouths to feed. Their food was dwindling faster each day. If they didn't do something, they wouldn't make it to the first harvest at the end of fall.

"Either way, it can't hurt to check. If it's too overrun, we'll…we'll find something else," Liv said. The others nodded. "All right, then let's get going. We're burning daylight."

The group filed outside to their vehicles, the same large SUV and truck they had taken out the last two times.

As Liv walked out to the car, she saw Wyatt at the edge of the field. He moved along one of the rows and pulled weeds. Liv threw her gear into the passenger seat and jogged out to Wyatt.

"Hey," she called. Wyatt stood up, stretched, and waved back to her. They had spoken a few times since the night he arrived, but he was always quiet, and it was hard to hold a conversation for very long. "Some of us are heading out to go find some supplies. Want to come with?"

Wyatt looked around at the field. He finally shook his head. "I can't."

"If you're worried about the field, we can get someone to fill in for you," Liv explained. "I know you've just come back from...the Dead Zone." Liv swept her hand and gestured to the rest of the world. "We could really use you. As a police officer, I'm sure your training could really help. The rest of us are more or less making this up as we go."

"To be honest, I would rather go with you." Wyatt straightened up and rubbed the back of his neck. "I don't know anyone else here. Don't get me wrong, I know we don't know each other very well, but so much has changed recently, so it's kind of nice to be around someone else that is familiar."

Liv smiled. "Awesome. Ok. We're leaving now, so go get changed and meet us out at the cars."

Liv was tense as they rolled through Troy. They had circled around the outskirts of the small city to avoid attracting attention from the ferals. Now, they were approaching Walmart. It was everything they needed. If there was any possible way to get in, they had to take it. The supplies would make all their lives so much easier.

"What do you guys want to grab first?" Jay asked excitedly. "I'm thinking about a nice big box of Lucky Charms. That sounds amazing right now."

"Let's not get ahead of ourselves," Liv murmured. Her eyes hadn't left the window. She wanted to see it the instant it was in sight.

"Oh, come on." Jay rolled his eyes. "This was your idea."

"Yeah, but I didn't say it would actually work, just that it couldn't hurt to look." Liv nibbled on her lip. "I've always been a 'plan for the worst and hope for the best' kind of gal. I'm not expecting the place to be a ghost town." Quite the opposite. She expected to find the place packed with thousands of ferals just waiting to rip them to shreds.

"I want a freakin' Dr. Pepper." Connor turned around in his seat to join their conversation. "Hell, I just want a soda."

Liv smirked. "I want a coffee. I would kill for a cup of coffee." Her last cup of coffee had been on the second day of the outbreak in a random house in the suburbs. It seemed like a lifetime ago.

Jay groaned. "Oh, my god! Yes!"

As they rounded the corner, Liv's heart sank. She had known what to expect, but it was even worse than she had imagined. Cars lined the streets. In numerous places, they had smashed together, creating a tangled mess of metal. The parking lot was a massive meshwork of vehicles, none going the same direction, none parked in the parking spots. They were jammed into every spare opening on the asphalt. Between it all were thousands of ferals. They wandered listlessly between the cars, bumping into the vehicles and each other. Some simply stood, waiting for the food to come to them as they swayed to a rhythm that only the ferals knew.

"Jesus!" Ava breathed as Connor brought the car to a stop. They were still a little way down the street.

"Well…" Jay said slowly. "What's plan B?" Liv's eyes continuously roved over the large building surrounded by thousands of ferals.

"Could we get in the back?" Connor asked.

"Probably not. There are probably hundreds more inside." Liv eyes were wide as she took in the enormity of the horde. She had known this was what they would find, but she couldn't stop herself from hoping.

"Probably." Wyatt nodded in agreement. "Could we draw them off? If we could pull some of them away, maybe we could clear out the inside from the back. If we could just get into the storeroom, that would have plenty of supplies."

Liv nodded. "We need a plan, though. There are too many to charge in blindly. Why don't we go scout some neighborhoods for now? We'll come up with a plan tonight and try it tomorrow or in a few days."

Jay's shoulders slumped as the others relaxed back in their seats. Liv pulled out a map. "Why don't we try here, Wingate Drive? It's on the edges of the main city. There will probably be less ferals. We'll check the houses and bring back whatever we can find."

Connor nodded. "Sounds like a plan." He swung the car around. "Want me to circle around the way we came?"

"Yeah." Liv's shoulders slumped as she continued looking over her map and making notes. "Let's not draw any attention to ourselves if we can help it."

Liv looked up and watched Walmart as the car pulled away. She gripped the edges of the map tightly until the building fell out of sight. She had never seen so many in one place. It made sense that people would flock to the store during the outbreak. The ferals would have followed, drawn in by the masses and made worse by those who were infected but hadn't changed.

The car was silent as they took the long way back around. Liv stared aimlessly out the window, trying not to let the scene get to her. It was hard. They need a break or just some luck. It didn't seem like they could get either.

"Hey," Connor said nervously, "I think there is someone behind us."

Liv sat bolt upright and spun around in her seat. "Where?"

"They're pretty far back, but a speck keeps appearing on the horizon." Connor clutched the steering wheel tightly as he glanced back in the rearview mirror.

Liv clamored over her seat to the back window. Just on the horizon was a dot. Maybe it was a car. As she sat in the back, the speck disappeared. Liv continued to watch intently, her nose almost pressed against the window. Sure enough, a few moments later, the speck reappeared.

"What do we do?"

Liv had no idea. If they were being followed, it meant there were other survivors in the area, but she wasn't sure how to feel about them. They hadn't acted. They hadn't attacked. They were simply following the raiders. Liv looked at Wyatt.

"I don't like that they are following us without trying to make contact." His voice was hard when he spoke.

"Me either," Liv agreed. "Take a turn. Not toward the farm." Liv scrambled back over the seats and snatched up the map, quickly tracing their route. "Up ahead, turn left. Let's see if they follow us. Radio the others ahead of us."

Ava snatched up the radio. The devices were cheap kids' toys, but they kept the cars in communication while they were moving.

Connor turned hard onto a dirt road. Liv's head swiveled back to the rear window. The speck had morphed into a definite car shape as it drew nearer. She cursed their lack of cover. Missouri was so flat. They had nowhere to hide out here. The other car would see that they had turned, and if they wanted to follow, they would.

Sure enough, the car turned to follow the same road they had.

"Crap," Liv muttered. They had to figure out what to do. They couldn't go home. Not until they knew that the other survivors could be trusted.

"Guys," Ava's uttered word made Liv's head snap up. Ahead of them, a plume of dust followed a car that that was blasting down the road ahead of them.

"Shit!"

"What do we do?" Connor asked, panic rising in his voice.

Liv quickly traced their road on the map. There weren't any more side roads between them and the car ahead of them.

"Should I go into the fields?" Connor asked.

"No!" Liv almost shouted. "There could be things there that we can't see. We'd wreck the car and be stuck."

The radio crackled in Ava's hand. The car ahead of them was bearing down on them quickly. The car behind had nearly caught up.

Liv took a deep breath. "Just stop. We'll see what they want."

"What?" Ava snapped.

"I could try going around them," Connor suggested.

"I don't like this." Wyatt's voice was calm but hard. He scooted closer to the window, picking up the AR-15. He wouldn't be able to hit much with the car flying down the roads like this but, maybe he could get close enough to keep them back.

"We can't go around them. We have two cars. Even if the first car managed to do it, the second one probably wouldn't get away with it. Just stop. We're boxed in. We don't have a choice," Liv reasoned.

The car slowed and finally came to a stop. At first, Liv thought the approaching vehicles were just going to ram right into them, and she braced for impact. They roared up the road and slammed on the brakes at the last second, skidding to a halt just a few feet away. Several men piled out of the cars in front and behind them.

Liv's heart thrummed in her ears. They had taken in a lot of survivors at the farm. Some were resilient. Some were angry. Some were broken. She had never been afraid of them, but she was afraid now.

"Come on out," one of the men hollered. He was tall and beefy with a shaved head. "We just want to talk."

"Absolutely not," Wyatt said firmly. "This doesn't feel like a talking scenario." He flipped off the safety. Faint clicks echoed through the vehicle as others followed suite.

"They don't have weapons," Liv pointed out, "no visible guns at least."

"It doesn't mean they don't have them," Wyatt shot back.

"No, but they aren't waving them around yet. They could be. They could have killed us all by now." Liv sucked in a breath through her teeth and pushed open her door.

"Wait," Wyatt hissed. He tried to grab her as she hopped out the door but missed.

"You wanted to talk?" Liv put up her hands and walked slowly around the car. Another door opened on the other side, and Wyatt climbed out, his face tense but expressionless. Several of the strangers scrambled for their weapons.

"Whoa! Whoa!" Liv threw her hands up frantically. "We're just talking, but you guys have to admit you've come on a bit strong here. We're just being cautious." Liv's heart thudded hard against her ribs as she tried to de-escalate the situation. The strangers didn't put down their weapons but didn't point them at the raiders either.

One of the men nodded. "What were you doing in town?" he demanded.

Liv frowned. "Looking for food, medicine, some soap, and maybe other survivors. What else would we be doing?"

"You need to look elsewhere," the man said curtly as he folded his arms across his chest.

"Like where?" Liv demanded. "We don't have much gas either. We need to make it last, and we need food."

"Stay away from Highway 47 and stay away from Walmart."

Liv nodded. "I see. You think you can get in there."

"You think we can't," the man snarled. Liv saw the slight movement as Wyatt tensed. He didn't raise his AR, but he was ready. All it would take was a flick of his wrist and the situation would become a bloodbath.

Liv took a deep breath and reeled in her own frustration. "I don't think either of us can," she said honestly. "There are probably thousands of ferals crawling all over that place. It's too many for either of us to take on alone, but maybe we could do it together." The man's eyebrows rose over his sunglasses in surprise. "That store is packed to the brim with supplies that we both need, and there is more than plenty to go around. If we work together, we could both prosper. Or we could be selfish, and both our groups will starve…" Liv let the words hang in the air for a moment. "I'm willing to work together if you are."

The man with the shaved head glanced back toward his companions uncertainly. After a moment, they huddled together and whispered among themselves. Liv could feel her shoulders relax. If they were talking about it, it meant they were at least considering the proposition.

Finally, they turned back toward Liv. "We agree," the man said slowly, "that we would all be stronger together. However, we won't do this with just anyone. We need proof that you will keep your word."

"We can't rush into this. We need a plan. Why don't we meet someplace and decide on the best approach to clearing out the ferals?" Liv nodded. "You pick the location."

The man nodded. "Sure. Our colony. One week from now."

"Sounds good." Liv forced a smile across her face. Their turf meant their advantage, and she wasn't thrilled with that.

"And do not approach Walmart," the man said sternly. "That will be considered a break in our agreement."

"All right," Liv agreed. "We won't approach it without a prior agreement by both groups. I assume the same rule applies to your group as well."

The man grunted and pulled a piece of paper out of his wallet and began to scribble on it. "You can find us here." He handed over the paper, and Liv looked over the directions. It was a location a bit south of Walmart.

"All right. See you in a week."

"See you in a week," the man replied, his voice flat. The other group turned back toward their vehicles and began to climb in.

Liv could feel her limbs start shaking as she walked back to the SUV. She took a deep breath and tried to calm herself as adrenaline ran rampant through her veins. As soon as the door was closed, Liv let out a long sigh, slouching back into her seat.

"That was terrifying," Connor remarked.

"You think?" Liv asked, running her shaky fingers through her hair. "We're meeting them in a week. They want to try to work together, though. Which sounds…terrifying too."

"You're kidding?"

"No, that…that went better than I expected," Liv admitted.

"What do we do now?" Ava asked. "Do we just go about our day?"

"No." Liv shook her head. "We need to go back to the Slag and let the others know about this group."

"Got it." Connor clenched his jaw. They all sat silently in the SUV and watched the other vehicles pull away, waiting until they were long gone before leaving.

"I don't like the idea of going to their colony." Wyatt crossed his arms over his chest. "It's not safe. You should have insisted on meeting at a third location. Someplace neutral."

"I know. I don't think they would have gone for it, though." Liv shook her head. "They were on edge at first. They didn't expect us to offer an alliance to them. They expected a fight. I wanted to give them the path of least resistance to show them that we can be trusted."

Wyatt pressed his lips into a thin line. "They may not be so trustworthy."

"I know." Liv's eyes flashed deviously. "It doesn't mean we won't go to the meeting armed and ready. My mother used to always say: plan for the worst and hope for the best. That's exactly what we're going to do."

When they arrived home, everyone piled out of the vehicles. They had talked about what to do on the entire circuitous drive back to the farm. Everyone had something to do or someone to find. They needed to act fast. They had returned home early and without the supplies that they set out to find. It wouldn't be long before rumors started flying around the farm.

"Liv!" Jordan exclaimed as Liv stepped through the front door, her face scrunched into a scowl. "Liv! Why are you guys back so early? Who got hurt? Where is Jay?" Elli was on Jordan's hip as she rushed over.

"Everything is fine," Liv reassured Jordan.

"You're lying," Jordan snapped. "I can tell when you're lying. What happened?"

Liv massaged her eye as it began to twitch. "Nothing bad happened. That is not a lie." Liv planted a kiss on Elli's forehead as the child reached for her. "I can't talk now, though." She smiled at Jordan. "Trust me. Please. Just stay calm. Everything is fine. I'll fill you in later, but right now, I have to go talk to Max."

Jordan rubbed the back of her neck. "I don't like you going out there." Her words weren't angry when she spoke, just scared. "It's too dangerous. I've only just gotten you back...and I don't want to lose you."

"I know." Liv sighed, pulling her sister into a hug. "I know, but someone has to go." Liv hugged Jordan. "I love you."

"I love you, too," Jordan whispered back.

With that, Liv turned and walked through the hallway. She had to find Max. Liv jogged past the long hallway filled with doors. The house had ten bedrooms off each wing on both the upper and lower floors. Forty rooms total. Liv had been amazed when she had seen it all the first time. The rooms were small, barely big enough for a small bed and a dresser. Jordan had told her that the house had been a boarding school at one time. Eventually, it had closed, and Max's family had bought the property decades ago.

Instead of going upstairs, Liv turned and went downstairs into the cellar. The large room was a maze of shelves filled with cans, jars, and bags of food.

"Max!" Liv called out.

"Over here," came the gruff reply. Liv followed the voice to a back corner where Max stood with a notebook and pen, counting the jars on the shelf. "Well, I didn't expect to see you back so soon." Max's brows knit together in a frown.

"Everything is fine, but we need to talk."

Max pursed her lips. "At the barn?" Liv nodded. "Get Emma to finish counting. I'll head out there."

Liv had been receiving stares since she arrived back at the farm. Everyone was curious. They needed to wrap up this conversation quickly and figure out how to tell the others, so they wouldn't incite a panic.

Liv shoved open the large barn door and stepped inside. She glanced around and took a head count before shutting the door behind her.

"So, what is all the fuss about?" Max asked as soon as the door was closed.

Liv straightened her clothes and smoothed her hair, suddenly aware of all the eyes on her. "We found another group of survivors while we were out."

Max rolled her eyes. "We take in survivors all the time. That hardly seems like big news."

"They are their own group like us," Wyatt said. "They weren't exactly friendly toward us."

"Though not outright hostile either," Liv continued. "It was...tense. They didn't trust us. No question there. However, they never outright threatened us either."

Wyatt pinched the bridge of his nose. "That's true, but I wouldn't trust them."

"They followed us after we left Walmart." Liv shifted. "That place is a disaster. It's absolutely crawling with ferals. Thousands of them."

Max's eyes widen. "Thousands?"

Liv nodded. "There is really no way in right now."

"And these folks followed you from there? They were watching the place."

"I assume so. Their base is probably close by. I assume they have been scoping it out and trying to get in since the outbreak. When we went to check it out, we must have...encroached on their territory or something."

Max scoffed. "Territory. It's no more theirs than ours."

Liv nodded. "We spoke with them briefly. They," Liv was trying to tell the story as it had happened, but was afraid recounting it would seem scarier for those who hadn't been there, "cut us off and forced us to stop. I proposed that we work together." Max's eyebrows shot up, but Liv hurried to continue. "If we work with them, we may be able to clear out Walmart, and then we can both have access to it. Individually, there is just no way we can take care of that many ferals."

"No," Max said flatly. "Absolutely not. We are not working with those people. We don't know who they are or what their intentions are. Their actions are already questionable at best."

"Now, hold up." Liv rested her hands on her hips. "We have taken in every survivor we have come across. We don't know them any better than these folks. You didn't know a thing about me when I got here."

"Jay vouched for you," Max snapped. "That was good enough for me."

"Who vouched for Ramsey and Emma?" The room was silent. "Nobody," Liv answered her owned question. "Nobody knew them when they got here. Ramsey was brave. Emma has been one of the hardest damn workers we have. None of us would have clean clothes without her. Why didn't we turn them away?" Liv pushed the old woman. Max's jaw worked back and forth as she mulled over Liv's words. "We do this every day. The only difference is we need them now."

"This is different," Max said. "It is too risky. You'd be walking right into the lion's den. It would put all of us in danger."

"Then what do we do? Ignore them? They are in the same area. We can't pretend they aren't here because they are. We have to share resources with them. If we piss them off, it could lead to a turf war, and we definitely don't need that. If we make friends, we could have new allies. Allies that could help us when we need it most." Liv purposefully made her voice level and calm. They needed to think about this rationally. All of them. She didn't know if she was right, but she knew they had to look at the big picture, not just the immediate future.

"Liv's right," Wyatt broke the silence. Liv spun to face him, surprised to hear him arguing for the partnership when he had been so adamantly against it. "The rules don't apply anymore, not as we knew them at least." He rubbed his head, blowing out a long breath. "And that can mean a lot of different things, but she is right. They could have taken us out today, and no one would have known, but they didn't. I don't see what point it would serve to wait. They may not be the most inviting folks, but it might be worth looking into. Right now, allies are an asset we don't have and one that we probably need."

Max's brows pulled together as she absently scratched at her wrist.

"It makes sense," Kraus nodded. He was in charge of the horses. The young man's family had worked with Max for years. Though the man was barely into his thirties, he worked magnificently with the horses. When the outbreak had occurred, his family had been overrun. He had come here as a last resort, and Max had welcomed him in as she would her own child if she had any. "It couldn't hurt to play nice until there is a reason not to do so."

"Or we could just keep to ourselves and mind our own business," Max muttered.

"No, we can't. Before the outbreak, we could mind our own business and keep to ourselves. If we do that now, we'll die. We need doctors, mechanics, hell even just people to work in the field and make sure the crops are growing. If we don't work together, we will die together." Liv crossed her arms, ready to fight with Max.

"This is too dangerous," Max replied, equally as stubborn. "You will be walking into the lion's den. You don't know what these people are thinking."

"We are already in the lion's den. It is all around us. Everything outside of this farm is a Dead Zone. The ferals are everywhere. If we don't work together, they will overrun us, one way or another."

For a moment, Liv and Max stared each other down, each holding to their ideals.

"I don't go out like you folks do." Max gestured to Liv and the rest of the raiders. "I don't see it every day. Hell, I ain't seen a feral since the outbreak until they was at our door." She chewed on her lip as she thought for a moment. "I don't like this. Not one bit. I still say it's different takin' in a few survivors here and there. However, if you seem to think speakin' with these other folks is what's best, I'll trust you." She nodded, more to herself than anyone else.

"Thank you." Liv nodded respectfully.

"To be honest, there are too many decisions to be made now. Too many people for me to be makin' decisions for everyone." Max looked around at the others. "I think it's time we changed things. I won't be rulin' over y'all with an iron fist."

Kraus snorted. "You don't need a fist. You can kill people with a look."

Max glared at the man. "Lucky for you, I'm not much of the killin' type." She turned her attention back to the rest of the group. "There is too much that needs doin' now for me to keep track of it all. Most of you here are already takin' on responsibilities for keepin' this farm afloat. I think it's time we made it official." Everyone looked at each other curiously. "Everyone here has their place. Everyone here has a job. Everyone here should have a voice. I think we should figure out a better way to run things."

"Like an election?" Ava asked.

"Maybe not an election exactly." Max shook her head. "I don't know if we could have a true democracy here but at least some way for everyone to have their own say."

Wyatt rubbed his head thoughtfully. "I'm all for giving the power to the people, but it could get a little jumbled if everyone can't agree."

"What about breaking everyone up by job?" Liv asked. "Our lives revolve around what we do here. If we separated everyone by their job and had them pick someone to speak for them, those leaders would know their group best. They would know their wants and needs best."

"That sounds an awful lot like what we were doing before and look how that shit turned out." Ava rolled her eyes.

Liv nodded. "We aren't a state, though. And the leaders don't gain anything by holding the position. Nobody is getting paid. The only thing they get is the burden of everyone else's survival, and that is pretty...daunting if you ask me."

As the others hurried off, the raiders huddled together in the barn. Since they had all been part of the conversation, they thought it was best to sit down and make their decision.

"So how do we want to go about this?" Connor asked.

"Why don't we start with nominations?" Liv suggested. "If anyone here thinks someone would make a good representative, then just say so."

"I nominate Liv," Ryland said quickly. Liv blinked back at the woman. "I think you've done a good job leading us and keeping us safe. I think you know what we need and what we need to do."

Liv's heart raced. She wasn't sure she wanted to be everyone's voice. True, she had already technically been in charge of the raiders, but it was more by default. A part of her had hoped that they would choose someone else.

"All right," Liv said slowly, careful to keep her expression composed. "I would like to nominate Wyatt." Blatant shock came across Wyatt's face. "As a police officer, he knows more about tactics than I do. He was trained to deal with difficult decisions. I think he would make an excellent leader for the raiders."

A few of the others around Liv nodded in agreement.

"Thank you for the vote of confidence." Wyatt smiled.

Liv smiled back. "Well, it's true." She turned back to the others. "Anyone else have someone they would like to nominate?" No one else offered a suggestion. The raiders weren't a large group. There were only seven of them. "All right. I guess then we need a vote. All those in favor of Wyatt, please raise your hand."

Seti raised his hand up discreetly. "Sorry, Liv," he said earnestly. "You've done a good job, but you made a good point."

"No hard feelings." Liv raised her hands in a placating gesture. "I think you're right." She raised her own hand. Connor slowly raised his hand as well.

"That makes three votes for Wyatt." Liv swallowed around the lump in her throat. "All those in favor of me, please raise your hand."

Jay's hand shot up. It was quickly followed by Ry and Ava. Finally, Wyatt raised his hand as well, giving Liv a sheepish grin.

Liv nodded. "Four votes for me." Though her voice was calm, inside she was terrified. She didn't want to let these people down. She didn't want to be in charge. She didn't want to get them killed. "I guess that makes me the speaker for our group."

"Aw, come on. You've got this." Jay clapped Liv on the shoulder. "And if you get us all killed, no one will be around to complain." He laughed at his own joke.

"That really doesn't make me feel any better," she replied dryly. Liv took a deep breath. "Thank you for your confidence in me. I won't let you down." The others smiled back at her.

"Well, we have work to do, and I should probably go speak with the other representatives." As they began to disperse, Wyatt ran up to Liv, falling in step with her as she walked back to the house.

"Congratulations," he said good-naturedly. "You have a knack for reading people. I think you're going to do a good job leading our group." Liv looked at him out of the corner of her eye, trying to gauge just how much to say. Wyatt nibbled on his lip. "…but you aren't happy about it?"

Liv sighed. "Not entirely. It's just," Liv's eyes darted back and forth as she searched for the right word, "a lot of responsibility. I don't feel like I know what I'm doing. For the most part, I'm just working on instinct and common sense."

"Those will do a lot to help you," Wyatt pointed out.

"Yeah, we've survived so far." Liv laughed darkly. "But that's the thing. I don't want to get anyone killed." She stopped, her lips pressing into a thin line. "Anyone else killed." Jen and Corey's final moments surfaced in her mind.

Wyatt was silent for a moment. "Anyone else?"

"On our first run, we lost Ramsey. I made the call to stay and try to gather supplies when some ferals came in." Liv replayed the events in her head. She had lost count of how many times she had done that. She knew all her mistakes by heart. She had replayed the exact moment he had changed over and over again. "If we had left, he would still be here."

"Maybe. Maybe not." Wyatt shrugged. "Clearly everyone else doesn't think you are to blame. I doubt they would have such faith in you if they did."

"It's just…scary."

"I know." Wyatt nodded. "I do. When we were at the station, there were so many people. They were all depending on us to protect them and keep them safe…"

Liv looked up at Wyatt. She could see the weight this put on him. The weight of their expectations. The weight of his own failure. It was the very thing she feared.

"But this is the world we live in. It was always the world we lived in. Even before the outbreak, people died even if you did everything right. Now…now, there are just more chances for things to go wrong. That doesn't mean when it happens that it's your fault." Wyatt's words were slow and deliberate.

"Do you really believe that?" Liv asked.

Wyatt scratched his head in thought. "Yeah. Yeah, I do." Liv nodded. She wasn't sure yet, but it did make her feel better. "Besides, I'm not going anywhere. I can always help teach you guys some of the things I was taught," Wyatt offered.

"Actually, I wanted to talk to you about that." Wyatt cocked his head toward her as he listened. "I have a gun, but I can't say I've ever used one. It was more of a last resort. Would you help me practice?"

Wyatt swallowed hard. "Sure."

DAY 24

Liv sat on the porch, hiding from the awful noon sun. She was steaming in her own clothes. They had spent all morning hauling in the chain link and fence posts from another run to the Dead Zone. She was looking forward to crawling in bed when Elli went down for a nap.

"Hey!" a voice called from behind her. Liv swiveled toward the door to see a young man walking out. He was Max's nephew. For the life of her, Liv could not remember his name. She was terrible with names, and she'd had to learn too many recently to keep them all straight.

"Hey," Liv replied. "What's up?"

"Well," the man flushed a bit, his hair falling across his face as he tried to hide it. "The night you came in, you said your radio died." Liv nodded. He had knocked on her door to welcome her to the farm and had seen it sitting out on the bed. "I've been tinkering with it, but I couldn't do much without a way to charge it, but that CB you guys brought in a few days ago was just what it needed!"

"The CB?" Liv asked.

"Yeah. Most radios now have the same or similar connecting cords. The CB had the same cords as this one, so I hooked it up and was able to charge it. Do you want it back?"

"Nah." Liv waved her hand at him. "The only person I was contacting with it is here now. Besides, you fixed it. You can keep it." The boy smiled again. "Do you mind me asking...what's your name again?"

"Ralph," he replied. "There are a lot of people to keep track of here now." Ralph looked at the radio for a minute. "Want to scan some of the channels for a minute? See if anyone is out there," he offered. They had only met one other group of survivors, but there had to be more out there.

Didn't there?

"Sure," she said. Ralph plopped down on the steps next to her. He immediately turned on the radio and quiet static emitted from it. He played with the dial, and the static grew louder. Slowly, he cranked another knob. The static rose and fell as he scanned across the channels.

There were no other sounds. No voices calling out for help. No music to fill the void. Just nothing.

Liv didn't like it. It made her feel alone. The world was so vast, and it was so unnatural for it to be so quiet. Ralph's shoulder slumped as well.

"Wait," Liv cried out. She had heard something in the static for a brief moment. "Go back really slowly."

The light returned to Ralph's eyes as well. His tongue poked out from between his lips, and he concentrated on turning the knob back as slowly as he could.

More static. Then suddenly, a garbled voice began to come through. Liv jumped, grabbing Ralph's shoulder in excitement. As he continued to slowly tweak the dial, the voice became clearer.

"…a new book would be nice…or a board game. Why don't people keep board games anymore? I'd be fine playing by myself. Maybe I'll try to go a few streets over today and see if I can find something out there. It'll probably just be nice to get out." The speaker let out a loud, harsh bark of laughter. "Who am I kidding? I hate going out. I did before, and that hasn't changed."

"There's someone out there!" Ralph exclaimed excitedly. "Sh-should we say something? We should say something shouldn't we?"

Liv nibbled on her lip and thought as the speaker continued to ramble.

"…Every time I go out is a nightmare. Those things are everywhere. I've only had to deal with a few luckily…but…" the speaker trailed off with a long sigh. "I can't stay cooped up here forever."

Finally, Liv nodded. "Go ahead."

"H-hello?" Ralph said tentatively. "Can you hear us?"

"Yes!" the speaker shouted. In an instant, the voice transformed from tired and defeated to exuberant. "Yes, I can hear you. God damn! It is so fucking good to hear you. Oh, shit! Excuse my language. I've been talking to myself for…a couple weeks now, so the filter is pretty much gone."

Ralph's smile spread from ear to ear. "No worries. We're glad to hear you too."

"Jesus Christ, man! I thought for sure I was all alone. You said 'we.' How many do you have with you?" The man spoke quickly. His words tumbled out so fast that they slurred together in his excitement.

"Uhhhh." Ralph looked to Liv for an answer.

She mentally tallied everyone. "Thirty-four. I think."

"Thirty-four of us," Ralph told the voice on the radio.

"Hot fucking damn!" The radio fell silent again.

After the silence had spanned for a few moments, Ralph called out again. "Hello? Are you still there?"

"Yeah! Sorry. Sorry." The speaker's voice was shaky. "I...uh... dropped my mic. That's amazing!"

"So you are by yourself?" Ralph asked.

"Yeah. I'm a 911 dispatcher at the Lincoln County call center. When the outbreak started, initially I was sending police and EMTs out to calls, but that didn't last long...so I stayed here to try to direct folks to safe areas."

"Where are there safe areas?" Ralph asked. "Are there more people out there?"

"There was one at city hall, but I haven't heard from them in sixteen days." The man's voice grew heavy. "Oh Jesus!" he cried suddenly, startling both Liv and Randy. "Where are my manners? My name is Henry. It sure is nice to meet you."

"Hi, Henry. My name is Ralph, and a woman named Liv is sitting here with me listening to the conversation."

"Wonderful! Really wonderful to meet you guys. Listen," Henry started nervously, "do you guys mind me asking where you are? It would be really, really, really nice to be around some other folks."

Ralph looked to Liv before replying.

"Tell him the direction but not a specific location or name," Liv whispered. She wasn't sure why she was whispering. The transmitter wasn't pressed, and Henry wouldn't hear them even if they shouted.

Ralph nodded and pressed the transmitter. "We're on a farm to the east of Troy."

"I see. Are you close to Troy?"

"Reasonably."

"Would you folks by chance mind picking me up? I don't have much to offer in exchange for my stay with you, but I can make myself useful if I have to," Henry pleaded.

Liv gestured for Ralph to give her the radio. "Here at the farm, everyone has a job. No one gets a free ride. We all work so everyone's needs are met. Does that sound like something you could do?"

"Darlin', I would cut off my own right hand for a friendly face right now. Pulling my weight isn't asking too much."

"It seems quiet enough," Jay said as the large suburban rolled to a stop a few blocks away from the call center.

Liv nodded. There were only a few ferals in this neighborhood. Henry had told them that he hadn't seen many, and there were none hanging around the call center, but they had to be sure. "Let's still walk in. Wyatt, Ry, and I will walk in and scope the place out. Jay, you and Ava hang back here. We'll call over the walkies if it's clear."

Jay nodded back.

"Got it." Ava slouched down in her seat.

Liv pushed open her door. Instead of slamming it, she gently latched it. The area seemed clear, but they wanted to avoid drawing any unwanted attention.

Without hesitation, Liv darted across the street toward a house. Even if there weren't any ferals in sight, she didn't like being out in the open.

The neighborhood was quiet. Only their footsteps broke the silence. When the call center came into view, Liv relaxed. The area was clear as Henry had promised.

"This guy could not have picked a better place to set up," Ry whispered. "I wonder where all the ferals went."

Liv shook her head. "As long as they aren't around, I couldn't care less."

They strode across the street and up to the square brown building. It was rather plain with no markings. There were two large glass doors at the front. Desks were tossed haphazardly to the side just inside the doors.

"Radio the others and tell them to bring the car around," Liv told Ry as she pulled out her own radio. "Henry," Liv whispered into the radio, "we're outside the front doors."

After a few moments, there was movement behind the doors. A man peeked around the corner and scurried forward to unlock the door.

"Where is the car?" Henry whispered. His face was gaunt, and there were dark circles underneath his eyes. His arms were skinny. The man hadn't been eating much. Perhaps he hadn't been sleeping much either.

"It's coming," Liv affirmed. "They should be here any second."

Henry nodded, his eyes darting around nervously. "Thank you for coming to get me."

"It's not a problem." Liv smiled. "We'll get you back to the farm in no time. You can get rested and get to know everyone there."

"Do you have anything you want to take with you?" Wyatt asked.

"I didn't have much with me when the outbreak happened, but I have a few things." Henry shook his head and motioned to a backpack and a small box of food. "I don't have much food to share," he said nervously.

"We have plenty back at the farm." Liv rested a reassuring hand on his shoulder. She could feel the bones poking against his skin. At that moment, the suburban roared up to the building and came to a quick stop.

"Come on!" Jay leaped out of the driver's seat and pulled open the rear door.

"That's our queue!" Liv shoved through the glass door and beckoned to Henry. The man hesitated for a moment. "Come on!" Liv motioned more urgently. "The sound of the car will attract the ferals. We have to go now."

Finally, Henry turned and grabbed his things. Together, they hustled out of the door. A few ferals ran up the street from behind the car, their howls echoing down the street.

"Get in the car!" Liv barked. Wyatt took up a position next to Liv as the ferals approached. Liv pulled her sledgehammer from its loop on her belt.

Before the first feral could reach them, she stepped forward and swung. The sledgehammer connected with the feral man's shoulder, slamming him into the ground. Liv raised the sledgehammer again, bringing it down on the man's head. His head collapsed with a sickening crunch.

As another approached, Liv stepped to the side, allowing the feral woman to stumble past her. The feral pivoted as Wyatt stepped up behind her. He swung his baseball bat and connected squarely with her temple, leaving the woman in a crumpled heap on the ground.

Liv sighed and looked around. More were coming.

"That was awesome," Henry exclaimed.

As Liv turned to face him, her blood chilled. A feral came around the corner of the dispatch building and dashed toward him.

"Henry!" Liv shrieked.

The man's eyes went wide a split second before the feral slammed into him, pinning him against the side of the suburban. Suddenly, there was chaos as all the raiders converged on the pair. The feral man leaned in, black bile spewing from his mouth and coating Henry's face.

Jay was the first to reach him. He grabbed the feral by the back of the neck, slamming a screwdriver into the creature's ear.

"Oh my god!" Henry retched as it swiped at the goop on his face. It dripped down his face and the front of his shirt.

Shit. Shit. Shit. Liv's mind spun as she reached Henry. The bile was thick and chunky as it clung to his face and shirt.

"What the fuck?" Henry cried.

"Stop talking!" Liv bellowed as she grabbed ahold of him. "And keep your eyes closed."

"Here." Wyatt thrust his shirt into Liv's hands, and she frantically began to wipe the goop off Henry's face.

"Water!" Liv barked. "Get me some water!" Jay produced some of the bottles from the suburban.

The goop was everywhere. It clung to Henry's skin and left behind a sticky film, even when Liv wiped it away.

"Guys!" Ry called. Liv's head snapped around as she looked for the female feral. She stood in a swath of fallen ferals, her sword out and bloodied. "We're starting to attract more attention." As she spoke, more ferals moved into the street, attracted by the noise they were making. They threw their heads back and shrieked, running toward the raiders.

"We need to go. Now." Liv pushed Henry into the suburban. "Everyone get in. We're leaving." The raiders piled in the car, the door not even closed before Jay peeled away.

"What the hell was that thing?" Henry asked, pulling at the slime on his face.

"I don't know." Liv shook her head. "I've never seen a feral do that before."

"What's going to happen to me?"

Liv bit her lip. "I don't know." She wanted to give him answers, but she didn't have any. The ferals had never thrown up before. They attacked and bit. However, their saliva was infectious. That could mean the vomit was infectious too.

"Liv, just what are we going to do with him?" Ry asked. She hadn't thought that far ahead yet. "If he's infected, he could pose a risk to the rest of the farm."

"We probably shouldn't bring him back," Jay added.

"Please, don't leave me out here like this!" Henry clutched his backpack in front of him.

Liv laid a hand on Henry's arm to calm him. "We won't," she told him firmly then turned back to the rest of the raiders. "We don't know that he is infected yet. We'll take him back to the farm and quarantine him. If he changes, we'll deal with it then."

"Isn't that a little risky?" Ava asked. "What if he changes and gets loose?"

Liv shook her head. Henry was starting to panic, and she couldn't blame him. "We'll take him back and quarantine him. I've done it before." Liv didn't miss the questioning look she got from Wyatt. "It will work. We need to make sure he will change before we do anything. Statistically, there are always some people who are immune." The words sounded hollow to Liv's ears. No one had been immune. Not yet.

Wyatt nodded. "Agreed. We can't just go tossing people out left and right if they might be immune. Then we're pretty much killing them ourselves."

"Besides," Liv added, "if people know they are safe if they are infected, they'll be more likely to admit it and go to quarantine. We wouldn't want anyone to become infected, hide it, and wake up with a nasty surprise for all of us."

Ava shivered. "All right, point taken."

It was exactly what she had feared.

Henry leaned over the side of the bed, spewing black bile into the bucket Liv hastily shoved under his chin. His words were already scrambled. Whenever he tried to speak, weird cryptic messages would come from his lips. Liv had babbled on for a long time, filling the air and giving Henry company. She had talked about books she liked, video games she had played before the outbreak, animals, and weird facts she had picked up here and there. Really, she had just continued on with whatever mindless chatter she could.

Henry had fallen asleep some time ago. Now, Liv just sat and watched his chest rise and fall.

There was a quiet knock at the door, and Wyatt poked his head through, looking around before entering. "How's he doing?"

"He's changing." Liv slouched back in her chair with a sigh. "It shouldn't be too long now."

Wyatt's lips turned down into a frown. "I'm sorry."

"Me, too." Liv shook her head. He had been by himself for so long. It was terrible to think that his rescue was ripped from his hands at the very last second.

"Mind if I keep you company?" Wyatt asked.

"Not at all." Liv pulled a second chair closer. "Can't sleep?"

"No." Wyatt shook his head. "Sleeping isn't something I do much of anymore."

"Me neither," Liv agreed. They were silent for a moment. They were watching a man die before their eyes when, just hours earlier, he had been fine. "So how are you liking the farm?"

"It's nice," Wyatt said. "It's a big change, but it's nice. Everyone seems so…together."

Liv nodded. "I can't say I don't miss my alone time, though."

Wyatt chuckled. "Yeah, I do miss that."

"So, Wyatt, what did you do for fun before the outbreak? I've been chatting with Henry about books and video games, and I feel like I'm about out of things to say."

"I didn't really have much free time," Wyatt said thoughtfully. "Between working twelve-hour shifts and my family, it just wasn't really a thing." He smiled wistfully. "I liked going to the zoo with my son. He liked the giraffes."

The world seemed to slow. She had never known he had a family of his own. Her heart sank. If they weren't here with him now, it meant one of two things. They were missing, like Colin, or they were dead, like her parents. Probably dead since he was here. The night of his arrival suddenly came into sharp focus. She had found a broken man in the woods.

Liv swallowed around the lump in her throat. "We never got to take Elli to the zoo. Colin and I were always…so busy." Liv sighed.

Wyatt nodded. "Yeah, we were too. I wouldn't have spent nearly so much time at work if I had known…"

Liv could see the tears that welled up in Wyatt's eyes. "I am so sorry." Liv's voice was barely a whisper.

Wyatt smiled gratefully at her. "We've all been through a lot recently."

"But that doesn't make it any easier."

"No…no it doesn't." Wyatt stared down at his hands. "What else can we do besides keep moving forward?"

"It's fight or die," Liv repeated Wyatt's own words. He had said them to her over the radio while she had still been fighting her way to the Slag. At the time, he had been her only connection to the outside world.

Wyatt smiled. "Man, doesn't that seem like a lifetime ago?"

Liv let out a dry laugh. "Yeah, it does."

Suddenly, Henry started coughing. Liv sat up straight in her chair. Before she could do anything else, Henry leaned forward, vomiting gummy bile down the front of his shirt and on to the bed.

Liv jumped up, grabbing the bucket. "Go get me some rags and water!" she told Wyatt frantically as Henry continued to cough. Wyatt disappeared out the door and returned a few moments later with a large basin of water from the kitchen.

Henry retched again, and Liv held the bucket beneath his chin. More of the black bile came up, plopping into the basin. With that, the coughs began to settle, and Henry's eyes opened.

"Hi," Liv said to him, her voice unusually gentle. She set the bucket down, careful to keep her distance in case he started spewing again.

"How...how...how..." His brow furrowed as he tried to get the words out, but they wouldn't come.

"It's all right," Liv said reassuringly. "We aren't going anywhere."

Henry closed his eyes, focusing hard. "Now...now...kill..." He growled in frustration. "Kill, kill, kill...now. Kill...me...now..." He relaxed again. "Precious." He looked up to her, his sunken, hollow eyes pleading with her.

Liv's heart raced. *Kill him?* She had killed the ferals, but she had never killed a human. Henry was different, though.

He was changing. He would become a feral. Wouldn't he? Was there still a chance he could come back from the disease?

"You want me to kill you? Because you are changing?" Liv asked nervously. Henry nodded slowly.

"I can do it," Wyatt offered, placing a hand on Liv's arm.

"No." Liv shook her head. "I can do it." *Could she?*

Liv turned and looked around the room, her thoughts swirling around in her brain like an angry swarm of bees. Could she kill someone? Henry was dying. Not just dying, but dying horribly. The disease was stripping away every bit of who he was. He had already lost his ability to talk, and he was rapidly losing his memories. Soon, there would be nothing left but the disease.

Would she want to stay alive until the end? To forget every happy memory? To forget Elli and Colin?

No. Maybe not. Maybe she would wait it out, but at the very least, she could understand why someone would want to die rather than let the disease ravage them.

The Glock felt heavy on her hip. She had only drawn it once before when she had been desperate. The ferals clawing at her back. Pressing her into the pavement as they tried to bite through her armor. The memory made her shudder.

Finally, Liv took a deep breath. "All right." She nodded.

Her heart thundered in her ears as she walked stiffly toward Henry's bed. "Don't worry." She sat on the edge next to him. She could see the fear in his eyes. "Are you sure?" she asked him again.

His eyes drifted closed, and he nodded.

She flicked the safety off but left the gun still holstered. "It won't hurt," she promised, bringing her left hand up to his forehead. Her fingers lightly traced along his skin, and he relaxed back against his pillow. Her parents had done this for her as a child, and she did it for Elli as well. It felt wonderful and soothing. Henry's face relaxed in a peacefulness that she had never seen on his face.

Liv hadn't been sure he would feel the soft touch. The disease killed the nerves in the skin, making them immune to both pain and pleasure indiscriminately. She was glad to offer him a final moment of peace.

Slowly, she drew the gun, careful not to shift or make a sound. She brought the gun up alongside his temple. As she slowly put pressure on the trigger, she withdrew her other hand.

A loud pop erupted through the room and startled Liv. Henry's body jerked before sagging back against the pillow, his head lolling to the side.

Jay burst through the door, his eyes wild as he looked for the threat. "You all right?!"

Liv pressed her lips together. *No.* "Yes, but I should probably go wash up. Can you take care of him?" She motioned to Henry's body.

"Sure thing." Jay nodded. Liv stood and walked to the door. Her limbs felt mechanical as they moved without thought.

She paused at the door. "I would toss the sheets. I doubt the bile will come out of them." She didn't wait for Jay to acknowledge her. She knew he had heard. Instead, she left the room and headed for the showers.

DAY 26

The man with the shaved head was already waiting for them at the meetup location. He leaned against the hood of his car, looking out at the post office parking lot as if he had been waiting all day. Two other cars flanked his. Men who had been milling around jumped to attention as the raiders pulled into the lot.

Wyatt gripped the steering wheel so tight his knuckles turned white. Liv tapped her foot anxiously. The others fidgeted in the back.

"This can't be their colony," Wyatt said as he glanced around. There weren't any signs of the ferals in the area. The place had been cleared out at some point, though it simply could have been earlier in the day.

Liv nodded as she nibbled on her lip. "I doubt those guys were postal workers before the outbreak. Maybe they holed up here during the outbreak. I don't think many people would have flocked to the post office in the first few days. It would have been a calm and quiet place to hide." Her head swiveled from side to side as she looked around. "But you're right. I don't think this is where they are staying. There aren't any reinforcements to the nearby buildings. Everything was like it would have been before."

Wyatt pulled the cars to a stop on the opposite side of the parking lot. Jay pulled the second car up alongside them.

"Ready to do this?" Ava's voice crackled through the radio in Liv's hand. Wyatt glanced at Liv out of the corner of his eye. "I'm not sure this is the right choice anymore."

"I guess there's no chance that I could convince you to leave now?" Wyatt asked.

"Maybe not." Liv sucked in a deep breath. She didn't look at him but stared straight out of the windshield at the unfamiliar vehicles and people. "We need this. We need their help...and we need to know that there are others out there like us. That we aren't alone." Liv finally tore her gaze away from the windshield. "In four weeks, we've only seen the odd few survivors that have shown up at the farm. It feels like we are the last outpost. So many of the safe havens didn't last, but maybe some of them did."

Wyatt swallowed around the lump in his throat but managed to nod. "You're right," he said. "Are you ready?"

"No." Liv nervously straightened her clothes and checked her weapons. "But let's do this." She pushed open her door and hopped out.

"Hello!" Liv called, waving as the other group exited their own vehicles. The man with the shaved head didn't return her wave. He seemed to have a perpetual scowl plastered across his face. As the two groups neared each other, they slowed, leaving some distance between themselves.

"Thank you for coming," the man said, though the flatness in his voice sounded as if he couldn't have cared less.

"We're glad to be here." Liv shifted uncomfortably when the man made no move to instruct them further.

"Are we just going to stand around here chatting?" Wyatt asked. "I'm sure you understand. We don't exactly like standing out in the open if we don't have to. Can we move this inside?"

The man looked down at the ground and rubbed the back of his head. "We have to move on first."

"What? Why?" Wyatt snapped. Liv took a few cautious steps back, as the group of raiders moved closer together for protection.

"The isn't our colony. The buildings here haven't been cleared yet, so I wouldn't settle in," the man explained. "We can head to our colony now. We just didn't want to give total strangers our location. We had to know we could trust you before we let you know where our people are."

"How do you know that you can trust us?" Liv asked.

The man shrugged. "To be honest, I still don't know if we can, but you folks didn't try to follow us last week. You didn't try to stake out the meet-up beyond normal precautionary measures, and you didn't go near Walmart." He ran a hand over his bare head. "We don't have much to go off, but it seems like a good start."

Liv stared hard at the man. "And how do we know we can trust you? You've now lied to us. How do we know you won't do it again?"

The man's mouth open and closed a few times. "You don't," he finally said. "Nothing I can say will alleviate that fear."

Liv regarded the group for another moment. "Fair enough. Here's the deal going forward. When we get to your colony, we get to keep our weapons. All of them." The man opened his mouth to protest, but Liv held up her hand to silence them. "This is not up for debate. You said, so far, we have shown ourselves to be trustworthy. You have not, and I will not endanger my people. We keep our weapons, or this alliance ends right here, right now."

The man shifted uncomfortably before nodding. "Weapons stay holstered at all times at the colony. Any hands on weapons will be considered an aggressive act and will be met with the same."

Liv nodded. "Fair enough. The exception being if any ferals show up, of course."

"Of course. We wouldn't ask you to stand around and die."

"So where are we going?" Wyatt asked slowly.

"You can follow us. It's not like we have to worry about being separated by traffic now," the man said.

"Why won't you tell us?" Liv growled. "We'll be there soon anyway."

The man crossed his arms over his chest. "Call it another insurance policy. I don't tell you until we're there and you can't cut and run back to your group with our location."

"No, we agreed—"

"No, you listen to me," the man snapped. Wyatt's hand inched toward the pistol at his hip. "I have well over a hundred folks who are depending on my judgment for protection, and I will not let them down. You can come with us and see for yourselves, or you can go home, and we will end this."

Over a hundred? Liv's mind spun. It was more than double the number of people at the Slag. How could they be hiding so many people in town?

"Give us a moment." Liv's voice was calm when she spoke.

She motioned the raiders toward her, and they all huddled together. Wyatt joined the group, carefully positioning himself so he could keep an eye on the others.

"I want you all to understand that we might be walking into a trap if we do this," Liv whispered.

"They lied to us again." Wyatt pointed out, flexing his fingers on the steering wheel. "What's to say they aren't lying now? We could be walking right into some gang's headquarters."

Liv nodded in agreement. "I don't like liars. That doesn't sit well with me…but if he does have so many people in his care, it makes sense why he would be so cautious."

"If they were a gang, I don't think they would have played this game for so long." Seti scratched his chin as he spoke. "They would have just attacked us from the get-go."

"And they certainly wouldn't let us carry in our weapons if it was a trap," Jay added.

"Agreed." Liv glanced to Wyatt. Wyatt simply shook his head and sighed. People had been unpredictable before the outbreak. Now that the rules were gone, there was no telling what they would do.

Liv pressed her lips into a thin line. "Let's go. We could use their help clearing out Walmart but keep on your guard. Until we know for sure, treat this like it's a trap." The group nodded and broke up.

Liv turned to the man with the shaved head. "What's your name?"

The man frowned at her question. "Jackson."

"My name is Liv." She suddenly strode across the gap between them and extended her hand. The man stepped back, surprised by her action, but Liv stood firm with her hand out. After a moment, Jackson took her hand and shook it firmly.

"It's nice to meet you," he said slowly.

"It's nice to meet you too."

"Why don't you folks jump back in your cars, and we'll take you back to our colony. For security reasons, I'll have one of my cars bring up the tail."

Liv looked him over before responding. "We'll see you there."

Liv spun to face the raiders. "Let's go. We're burning daylight!"

Wyatt followed Liv back to their vehicles, matching her brisk walk, and they climbed in. Liv let out a long, slow breath as she buckled her seatbelt.

"Everything will be fine," Wyatt said as he pulled out of the parking spot and fell in line behind Jackson's car.

Liv let out a short, barking laugh. "I don't know about that."

"I do." Out of the corner of his eye, Wyatt could see Liv turn toward him.

"How?"

"I think he's just being cautious. While we talked with him, he seemed defensive but not...sneaky. His words were carefully thought out. His actions, though mistrustful, are measured. He's used to being on the edge. This is no different."

Liv's chest felt tight, each bump in the road tightening it a little more. "I hope you're right. As exciting as it is to find out there are other people out there, it's terrifying not knowing what we are walking into. I want to think the people that are left are good. That they want to pick up the pieces and work together...but realistically, I don't think they'll all be like that."

Wyatt nodded. "We'll be at a disadvantage going in, but I think this is the right decision."

Liv's lips turned up in a small smile that quickly faded. She picked up the walkie-talkie. "All right, guys. We're friendly walking into this place but stay on guard. Watch for anything that seems off. And, for the love of God, keep your hands off your guns. The last thing we need is a misunderstanding."

"Got it, boss," Jay replied.

It was only a few minutes before they reached Jackson's complex. They turned onto a small private road that led up a hill. The small road was lined with cars that had been turned on their sides and pushed together. The barrier stretched all the way down the road to a large warehouse. The side of the warehouse was nothing but a large white brick wall. No windows. No doors. No signs. Jackson's car turned, circling the building to the other side.

"I wonder how long it took them to get this in place," Liv mused aloud as she took in their defenses.

"If they really do have over a hundred people, they probably could have done it in just a few days." Wyatt put the car in park. "Ready to go in?"

"Let's just get this over with." Liv laid her hand on the handle but didn't open it. "You know, before all this, I was pretty much a hermit. I didn't go out much and preferred staying in to spending the night out." She rubbed her face wearily. "That hasn't changed. All this interacting with other people has just left me drained. I'm ready to go home and go to bed. I always thought the apocalypse would be quieter than this."

Wyatt chuckled. "Well, get ready. I think we're going to have a lot more interacting to do before we leave."

Liv groaned, opened her door, and swung her feet out.

"Welcome to Collier, folks." Jackson seemed much more relaxed back in his own territory.

Liv wore a smile on her face, but it was fake. It was a small smile, barely an upturn of her lips. The smile didn't reach her eyes.

"The barrier was impressive," Liv said, the compliment genuine.

"Agreed." Wyatt nodded. "It must work wonders for funneling the ferals."

Jackson beamed. "That is our pride and joy. We check for weak spots but having it in place makes it a lot easier to watch the place."

"Does it go all the way around?" Liv asked, though she already knew the answer.

Jackson nodded. "Sure does. It was one hell of a task to get it done, but we've all slept better since it was put up." Jackson took one last look at the patchwork of cars before turning back to the raiders. "Well, why don't we head inside? I can't say it's anything impressive, but it suits us."

On this side of the building, a set of double doors was set into the brick. A big sign read: "Collier Manufacturers" in plain black letters above the door. The name wasn't familiar to Liv, though she hadn't expected it to be.

"This building looks like it was made as a stronghold," Ava commented, her eyes wandering across the sparsely decorated interior. "There aren't any low windows, only a few doors. How did you find it?" Once white linoleum covered the floor; years of grime had turned it a grayish beige. The countertop that separated the employees from the customers was warped and cracked. A few chairs that sat against the wall seemed like they had been new in the '70s.

"I worked down the street every day before the outbreak. I saw it a few times. When everyone started eating each other, it seemed like as good a place as any to hole up."

"What did you do before the outbreak?" Jay asked offhand.

Jackson tensed for a moment. "I was a parole officer."

Now it all made sense. All the caution that Jackson had taken was second nature to him from the time he had spent with parolees before the outbreak. He was cautious by necessity, and the apocalypse had only enforced these habits.

Jackson pulled open another set of double doors and motioned for them to go inside. As Wyatt stepped in, he immediately tensed. The entire building was silent and dark. Shadows flickering at the end of a hallway, moving between shelves of boxes that went up to the ceiling without making a sound.

"Where are all the folks you said would be here?" Wyatt bristled.

"They're here," Jackson replied, his voice steady but low. He sauntered through the entryway and deeper into the darkness.

Liv cast a glance toward Wyatt, her brow furrowed.

Wyatt regretted his words from earlier. This seemed like a trap. A hundred people should make noise. A lot of noise. Following Jackson deeper into the building hardly seemed like a good idea.

Liv turned and followed the man, her steps rigid and her back straight. Her eyes darted back and forth, though her head barely moved. They needed to leave. Wyatt ground his teeth together, resisting the impulse to lay his hand on his sidearm. He quickly followed Liv with the other raiders trailing behind him. He was acutely aware of Jackson's men following behind their group. They were surrounded on both sides.

Their footsteps echoed off the empty hallway as they pushed deeper into the building. At the other end of the corridor was another set of double doors.

"Right through here." Jackson stepped out into the large open room. Before even stepping into the room, Liv could see the people.

The room opened up into a giant cavern broken up by shelves stacked high with boxes. Sleeping bags and blankets were arranged in neat rows with paths between each one. People bustled around the room. Their footsteps didn't make a sound. Nothing clanked. No one spoke a word. Despite the people, the room was utterly silent.

As they entered, everyone stopped and turned toward them. Liv's breath caught in her chest as so many eyes turned toward her like the eyes of a horde. The group paused. For a moment, the people morphed. No longer people, but ferals with missing limbs and bloodied faces. They eyed her hungrily.

Liv shook her head, and the people were once again people. After a moment, they returned to their business. One group washed clothes in old wash tubs, their motions slow and controlled. Others prepared food with the same precise movements. In the whole room, no one made a sound.

"We've stayed hidden because of sound discipline." Jackson turned back to the raiders. A few of the survivors turned to glare at Jackson. His voice seemed to boom through the eerily silent room. "Remaining quiet has meant we go unnoticed both by the living and the dead."

Wyatt's eyes danced across the room. There were so many people here. Before the outbreak, the sight would not have been uncommon. It would have been a small number at a mall, but now, it was almost magical.

The more she looked, the more the magic evaporated. The people looked skittish. Afraid. The survivors at the Slag smiled and laughed. They complained loudly about the heat and the sun. They gritted their teeth and worked hard for their survival and then relished the spare moments when they came. These people looked defeated. They were existing, but only just.

"What…" Liv looked around the room, trying to take it all in. "How is it possible for all of these people to stay this quiet?"

"Noise discipline is strictly enforced," Jackson said simply. "Speaking is forbidden except when it is absolutely necessary. We have practiced tasks to ensure that they are done in such a way as to minimize our noise and make sure we all remain safe."

"Yes, but…" Liv's mouth opened and closed a few times as she struggled to find the right words. "What do your people do? This looks miserable."

"We are surviving," Jackson growled. "Or have you forgotten that the world is dying around us?"

"No one has forgotten that," Wyatt snapped. "We've all had our lives turned upside down. We've all suffered."

Jackson took a breath to collect himself. "Controlling our noise and making sure we carefully monitor ourselves is what has allowed us to survive when others perished. What did your people do?"

"We regrouped and started rebuilding outside of town," Jay cut in. "These people here seem more like prisoners than people who are lucky to be alive."

"They are lucky," Jackson snapped. "We have cared for everyone who could get here, regardless of what they've done."

"What they've done?" Liv echoed.

"Most of these survivors are parolees and their families." Liv looked over the group again, shifting uncomfortably. "Make no mistake. They have all fought and worked hard to be here." Jackson's shoulders slumped, and for a minute, the man looked years older. "If they refuse to work or adhere to the rules, they don't get to stay."

"Don't get to stay?" Liv hated the way she parroted Jackson's words.

"Yes." Jackson nodded slowly. "We had a few that could not work for the greater good, so we had to throw them out." The words were not said lightly. The weight they bore on Jackson's shoulders was evident.

"At the Slag, everyone must work for their keep as well." Liv nodded, stepping toward Jackson. "We have been lucky enough not to have to worry about rule breakers."

Jackson nodded and motioned for them to follow him deeper into the large room. "We do everything in here, cooking, washing, sleeping. I'll admit it's not the most ideal situation, and there is absolutely no privacy, but it's worked for us."

The room was dark, mostly lit by battery-powered lanterns and what light trickled in through the high windows. As she looked over the people though, she noticed their faces looked gaunt. If it were only a few folks, it might be mistaken for a stern look, but each face showed the same signs.

"Why don't we move somewhere private to hash out the details of our alliance?" Liv suggested.

"We have an office at the back of the warehouse, but those rooms will be darker, and there aren't any windows," Jackson noted.

"That's fine. Is there anyone else you'd like to bring in with you?"

Jackson nodded. "Riley. Smith." Jackson motioned two men over that had been following the raiders. "Why don't you show these folk to the conference rooms while I gather the others?"

The raiders followed the men to the back of the cavernous room. Liv was aware of how loud her footsteps sounded in the utter silence. The raiders sounded like a herd of buffalo charging through the room.

Riley opened the door to an office. The space was small and cramped. The desk was buried in forms that no one would ever file. Soda cans were littered among the papers. The chair behind the desk was rickety, more duct tape than chair. The carpet was old and stained.

Liv turned to the man, Riley, after the last of the raiders had entered. "Would you mind giving us a moment of privacy?"

"I really shouldn't..." Riley furrowed his brow. He was there to watch them. He couldn't do that if they were given privacy.

"Just two minutes," Liv insisted. "You can stay right outside the door. I just want to make sure my people are all on the same page." She flashed him a smile. After a moment of consideration, Riley nodded, closing the door behind him.

"What the hell?" Jay asked after the door closed. Liv motioned for him to be quiet, sure that Riley had heard him outside the door.

"Yeah, those people are being treated like prisoners," Ava jumped in. "What the hell is Jackson doing?"

Liv held up her hands in a placating gesture. "This is how these people have survived. They didn't have a farm to run to. They didn't have a way to get out of town." They had this place and they had to make it work.

Wyatt nodded. "The fact that the parole officers are still here is a wonder at all. My station had half of its officers disappear when the outbreak started. They didn't have to stay behind and protect these people, and chances are they gave up protecting others to do it."

The room grew silent.

"Ok," Liv started. "They are keeping these people alive. Worst case scenario, it doesn't look like these people are being held prisoner. They are free to leave. It may seem odd, but if this helped them survive, then I think we need to step back." The raiders exchanged glances, and slowly, they all nodded in agreement.

A quiet knock echoed through the room.

"Come in," Liv called, with a sing-song wit to her voice, as her nerves got the better of her.

"I'm not intruding?" Jackson poked his head into the room.

"Not at all!" Liv smiled. "We were just making sure everyone was in agreement and we wanted to continue moving forward."

"I assume by the fact that you are still here that you would like to pursue an alliance then."

"Correct."

"Good." Jackson opened the door fully and stepped in, a few other men right behind him.

"Folks, this is Harris. He's my second in command here. He was also a parole officer across the way before the outbreak. For now, I seem to be the one in charge." Jackson's smile was sad as he introduced the others. The deep grooves in his face were formed by both laughter and stress. "Riley has told me you are slightly uncomfortable with how we do things around here."

Liv's mouth opened and closed as she struggled for a response.

"Don't worry," Jackson held up his hand dismissively. "It's an odd lifestyle. I get it." He leaned against the table. "I just want to make sure we aren't going to have any issues. I can't say it's the way I imagined myself living, but it works."

"If you don't like the way you're doing things now, then why don't you do something different?" Ava asked, her voice unusually quiet.

"Changes mean risk. Right now, risk can mean death." Jackson rubbed his temple wearily. "Most of these people are good people that made stupid choices. They're parolees and their families. They came to us for help during the outbreak. They were afraid of getting sent back to jail if they missed their appointments."

"Why didn't you send them to a shelter?" Wyatt asked.

Jackson looked Wyatt up and down. "Are you an officer?"

"Was."

"What was your experience with shelters?" Wyatt balked at the question. "Exactly," Jackson muttered. "The chaos descended too quickly for us to do much of anything, so we tried to guide these people through it as best as we could. At first, we thought it was just a matter of hunkering down until it blew over. But…days passed and then a few weeks…and here we are. It's just a way of life now."

The room fell silent. Wyatt didn't like talking about the outbreak. He didn't like thinking about his own failures, the losses he had suffered.

"Everyone survived how they had to. I broke into houses to find someplace safe for my daughter and me. I can't say it's something I ever imagined doing," Liv finally said. "We all did what we had to do."

The group nodded collectively. All around her, Liv could see the thousand-yard stare as everyone thought back on the midnight days and the things they had to do to survive.

She's just a child!

"We've done ok here." Jackson stood up straight. "However, the one thing we are lacking is food. We managed to scrape together some supplies. We're swimming in car parts, but with the sheer number of people we have, nothing lasts long. We need to get into that Walmart. Our people need the food."

Liv nodded. "The Slag has plenty of room for growing crops. Most of our people work the fields from sun up to sun down, but it'll be a few more months before the first of the crops are ready for harvest. It would make a huge difference for us as well."

"The place is crawling with infected," Jackson stated. "Everyone and their mother went there to stock up when the outbreak happened. It's a hornet's nest just waiting to be kicked."

"As many as there are outside, they must be packed in tight on the inside as well," Wyatt added. "There are easily a couple thousand in the building and the surrounding parking lot."

Jackson nodded. "We can't take on those numbers. Even if we had a tank, they could bury us with their sheer numbers."

"So, what do we do?" Jay asked. "If we can't fight them all, we have to reduce their numbers somehow."

"What if we draw some of them off?" Liv asked.

Jackson frowned as he thought. "I see what you're getting at, but how would you execute such an idea? Anything that would draw the infected from the store would probably draw in more from the surrounding area."

Liv leaned back against the wall, nibbling on her lip as she thought. "It would probably have to be more of a long-haul game. We could draw them off a bit at a time. A few more every couple of days until their numbers thinned out enough that we could clear out the rest."

"We could drive by. Blast the horns a few times. Lead away the ones that follow," Wyatt chimed in. "Take them in some direction that wouldn't lead them to either of our colonies."

"If we stayed in the vehicles and never really stopped, it would reduce the risk to our people." Jackson nodded.

"But what about the ones inside?" Ava asked. "We couldn't draw them off."

Jackson grimaced. "We'll have to get our hands dirty at some point, but if we could clear out the parking lot, it would bring the numbers down significantly." He scratched his chin. "Any idea how long something like that might take?" He looked to Liv.

Liv shook her head. "I've never tried it. Once we did the first few rounds of draw offs, we might be able to get a good estimate. We'd need to see how many follow the car and how their numbers swell with those being drawn into the sound before I could make a guess."

"Based on the sheer numbers outside the building, my guess would be a month or two before we could get inside," Jackson mumbled.

Liv nodded in agreement. "It would take a while. This would all have to be done while still doing what we must to survive in the meantime."

"It seems like a solid plan," Jackson said thoughtfully, "but it doesn't address our immediate concern."

"How bad is your situation?" Wyatt asked.

The room was silent as Jackson debated how much to divulge to the strangers. Finally, he sighed. "At the current rate, we'll be entirely out of supplies in two weeks. We could stretch it to a month if we cut rations in half, but people would be hungry."

"That still may not give you enough time." Liv rubbed her hands over her face. "What are you guys doing to supplement your rations?"

"We've gone out a few times, but most of the stores are either heavily guarded by the infected or picked clean." Harris looked down at the floor.

"What about the nearby houses?" Liv asked.

"What about them?" Jackson asked.

"Have you checked them?" Liv shifted, crossing her arms.

Jackson grimaced. "We aren't criminals," he spat.

"No, but you'll be dead if you don't start improvising," Liv snapped back. "You've gotten these people this far. If y'all want to last longer, you're going to have to do something different. The stores are train wrecks, but the houses usually don't have more than a few ferals at a time."

"Those are people's homes," an accusatory tone crept into Harris's voice.

"No, they aren't." Liv rounded on Harris. "The people who lived there have either abandoned them or they're dead. I'm not suggesting you run in, ransack the place, kill any survivors, and burn the place to the ground. If it's empty, it's empty. Nobody is using those things, and they are just going to sit there and rot. So you can stick to principles and rules that no longer apply and starve. Or you can survive. That's up to you."

Jackson eyed Liv for a moment, his gaze boring into her, but Liv didn't back down. She held her head high, refusing to think she was a criminal for her actions. Finally, the man nodded. "Fair enough. I assume this is what you folks have been doing."

Liv nodded. "It's a bit more time consuming, but you can also find a lot of other things you might need, like toothpaste or blankets." Liv hesitated, and Wyatt could see indecision wore across her face for a brief moment. "By the looks of your people, you need something now, though."

Jackson jumped up. "Don't you dare accuse me of—"

"I haven't accused you of anything!" Liv cut Jackson off. She stood up straight to him as he towered over her. "This is the end of the world. Shit is hard. Nothing is assured. That doesn't mean you aren't trying, just that things are a whole hell of a lot harder. Your people can't fight well if they are hungry. And if they are distracted by their bellies, they are just going to get themselves and others killed."

Jackson stared down Liv for a second before taking a deep breath. "All right."

"We have some extra supplies for now." Jackson visibly perked at the words. "You seem to have an excess of vehicles and parts. Does that mean you also have quite a bit of fuel?"

Jackson nodded. "We emptied all the cars before we turned them on their sides for the wall."

"We don't have much to spare, mostly dried goods like corn, beans, and rice. But we would be willing to trade for some fuel."

Jackson eyed Liv skeptically. "Why?" he asked.

"Operating the machinery at the Slag requires a lot of fuel. Running around to gather supplies takes up more as well. It would do a great deal to ease our burden if we had a reserve," Liv stated simply. Jackson pressed his lips into a thin line. "I'll grant you that the food isn't anything special, but it could probably go a long way to bulking up what you have and making it last longer, giving your people a bit more."

"Of course, it could." Jackson rubbed his chin, still eyeing Liv as if he was trying to figure out the catch. "All you want is fuel?"

"Fuel is one of the things we most commonly have to scavenge. That and medical supplies." Liv nodded. "I really don't know what we'll do once the fuel starts going bad."

Jackson grimaced. "Diesel will last a lot longer, but I guess that's a bridge we'll cross once we get to it."

Liv nodded. "Do we have a deal?" She stuck out her hand to Jackson.

Jackson sighed and took her hand. "We have a deal."

DAY 28

Wyatt pulled the car to a stop in front of the farmhouse. The sun was just starting to crest the horizon and lighten the sky. After driving past Walmart, honking the car's horn to draw off some of the horde, they had spent the rest of the night gathering more supplies. Liv had insisted on grabbing every bit of food they could find. While they needed to stock up for the eventual winter, Wyatt knew she was thinking about the survivors at Collier. She wanted to be able to help them if they needed more supplies.

They both hopped out and threw open the door to the back. It was packed to the brim with food. Only canned and dried. Fresh food was rotting, and they didn't dare open the fridges after they had been so long without power.

"Mama!" The shriek greeted them, and Liv whirled around. Elli streaked through the tall grass making a beeline straight for Liv as Nana Eve watched from the porch. The elderly woman had come in with another family. Her close-cropped hair was solid white, and wrinkles creased every inch of her face. She was too old to work the fields. But she made herself useful by keeping an eye on the children.

"Hello, my baby!" Liv bent down, scooping up the child in a big hug, planting a kiss on her forehead.

"I love you." Elli locked her arms tight around Liv.

"I love you too, baby."

A vice took hold of Wyatt's heart. His own son had only been about a year older than Elli. He had been a precious and happy child, who always wanted to snuggle. He had seen the same scene play out hundreds of times between Ben and Sarah.

"You play?" Elli asked, laying her tiny hand on Liv's cheek.

"Not yet, baby. I have to help get everything inside." Before Liv could even finish speaking, tears welled up in Elli's eyes.

Wyatt swallowed around the lump in his throat and walked over to Liv. "Hey, the seven of us can get things inside if you want to spend some time with Elli," he offered.

"Oh, I couldn't leave you guys to finish hauling everything in by yourselves." Liv shook her head.

"Sure, you can," Jay shouted from the back of his own car. "We've got this. Go frolic or something. You'll just owe us all a beer later." Liv rolled her eyes.

"Go," Wyatt urged. "We'll get this done."

"Thank you." Liv reached out and squeezed his arm before turning and heading toward Nana Eve.

Wyatt watched them go for a moment before turning back to the vehicle. Everything was wedged in tight. They had packed both of the vehicles to the brim. His arms ached just thinking about all the trips back and forth he would have to make. He carefully worked the first box out from where it was wedged in between the other boxes and the ceiling of the car. Wyatt hefted the box and marched to the kitchen.

"Took you guys long enough." Max was leaning against the counter as he entered.

"Pft! Next time, you can go sneak around the ferals all night. I'll stay here and sleep."

"Did you find everything?" Max ignored his suggestion.

"Nearly everything." Wyatt deposited the box on the floor.

"Where's Liv?" Max scowled as the others filed in carrying their own boxes. For a moment, Wyatt thought he could see the fear in the old woman's eyes. Though Max lived to hassle everyone on the farm, she had a kind heart. She had taken them all in after the outbreak and organized everyone.

"Elli caught sight of her as we came in. I told her to go spend some time with her daughter."

Max nodded. "Just as long as she doesn't go soft and get lazy."

This time, Wyatt laughed outright. "I don't think that's going to happen."

With that, he turned and walked back out to the car. One box at a time, they brought in the boxes. They were filled with whatever would fit without any rhyme or reason to their contents. When they were out in the Dead Zone, they simply tried to grab what they needed as quickly and quietly as they could. Max and a few others sorted through the contents of their trips once they got home and made sure everything was put away properly.

The car was nearly empty, and Wyatt could hear his bed calling to him. A peel of laughter sounded behind him, and Wyatt set down his box for a moment. More children had joined Liv and Ellie. The farm didn't have many. Only four. Two boys who had come in with their father and a little girl who had come in with her much older sister. And Elli.

Children had easily fallen victim to the ferals. Parents had fallen just as quickly as they had desperately tried to protect their little ones. Almost overnight, children had become a rarity, both a gift and a curse.

Wyatt watched them as they ran around in the grass playing tag. The children smiled and laughed, shrieking as the one who was 'it' neared. Around him, Wyatt noticed others had stopped to watch the scene. Small smiles lit their faces as they watched the children simply be children.

Suddenly, Elli disappeared into the grass. Not even a second later, she let out a wail, stopping the other children in their places. Liv scooped her up as the other children rushed in. Wyatt's heart lurched as the innocent scene was suddenly broken.

The little girl cried, and Liv pulled her in close with a hug. The older boy enveloped the smaller one in his arms, whispering to him.

After a moment, Nana Eve appeared, ushering the other children inside. Liv stood, walking toward the cars with Elli on her hip.

"Everything all right?" Wyatt asked.

"Yeah, just a little tumble," Liv replied nonchalantly. Elli clung to Liv's shirt, her tiny fists clutching wads of the fabric. Elli eyed Wyatt over her shoulder.

"Hi, ma'am." Wyatt smiled at her. "Did you have fun?" Elli nodded, a large yawn erupting across her face. Wyatt laughed. "You must be sleepy now."

"No!" Ellie stated adamantly.

Sarah laughed. Wyatt's eyes snapped up. Sarah stood before him, just as he remembered her. Her long mahogany hair shone in the morning sun. Ben sat on her hip, nuzzling his mother's shoulder as he rubbed his eyes sleepily.

"He would never admit he was tired."

111

Wyatt just stared blankly at Sarah. She couldn't be here. It wasn't her. She was dead.

Sarah frowned. "Is everything all right, hon? You don't look well."

"Yeah," Wyatt said slowly, taking a small step back. "I think I'm just tired."

Movement caught his attention. Jay was pulling more boxes out of the car. But it wasn't Jay anymore. Bites covered his body. His ear had been ripped from the side of his head and hung only by a small flap of skin. Blood drenched the front of his tattered clothes. Ry limped toward the front steps on a twisted and mangled leg.

All around him, the farm was changing. It wasn't the farm. It was his neighborhood. The home that he and Sarah had purchased. The home that he left behind when his family had been taken by the outbreak.

"Are you sure?"

Before his eyes, they began to change. The skin broke on Sarah's neck, a bite spontaneously erupting. Blood oozed from the wound, staining her shirt. The black spider-web of infection rippled across her face, and her skin turned gray.

"Wyatt?" Sarah's voice slurred into a growl. Wyatt reached for the gun at his hip, waiting for the monsters to spring upon him. Sarah turned, thrusting Ben at the feral that had been Ry.

"No!" Wyatt shouted, reaching for Ben.

"Wyatt!" He turned back toward Sarah. Her flesh had turned to the putrid green from when he had last seen her. The bite no longer oozed but had clotted. The flesh around it was infected and foul. Her clothes were matted with blood. She reached out to him, her hand missing two of its fingers, and he flinched away from her touch.

"Wyatt!" Liv's voice boomed from Sarah's rotting mouth. "Close your eyes." He was shaking. How had she seemed so real? How had he not realized?

"Take a deep breath." Liv's voice was gentle but commanding. Her hand slid into his. It wasn't the dead flesh he had expected to feel. Her fingers were warm and soft. Callouses dotted her hands from the work they had been doing. She squeezed his hand, and he squeezed back, grounding himself with the contact.

Finally, he opened one eye then the other. Liv stood before him, her brow furrowed in concern.

"Come on." She gently tugged him away from the car. She caught Ry's arm, whispering something before moving on. She gently led him toward the barn.

His arms and legs were shaking as they walked. Sarah had seemed so real. How had she not been real?

"What happened?" Liv finally asked when they reached the side of the barn. Her voice was gentle, pitched low so others wouldn't hear.

"I…I don't know." Wyatt's fingers shook, and he ran them through his hair. "One minute we were talking. I remember us talking…but then it wasn't you. You were Sarah."

"Your wife?"

Wyatt nodded, plopping down on a long log that had been set aside for firewood but never chopped. "She looked like nothing had happened…at first." He clasped his hands together to stop the shaking. "And then I was back in my neighborhood, and everyone started turning into ferals…Sarah started…she…" Wyatt swallowed down the bile that rose in his throat. "She became the thing that I saw last."

Liv sat down on the log next to him. "Jesus." She was silent for a long time. "Do you…want to talk about what happened? To your family."

Wyatt rung his hands together. "What is there to talk about? By the time I got out of the police station, they were gone. They were probably among the first few to die."

"And you found them at your home?" Wyatt nodded. "Jesus," Liv breathed.

"It's no different than what everyone else has been through. Everyone has seen their share of monsters. Everyone has lost someone," Wyatt said adamantly.

"But that doesn't make it easier." Liv turned to look at him. "I cannot imagine what you must be going through…to have lost your wife and son all at once."

Wyatt looked down at his feet, no longer able to hold her gaze as it pierced his soul. He didn't know what to say. For the most part, he tried to shut out any thought of his family, any thought of his life before.

Liv threaded her arm around his. "I am sorry," she said firmly. "I truly am. I can't imagine how hard it must be to carry that burden with you and keep moving forward."

Wyatt let out a short laugh, startling Liv. "That was actually the easiest part." Liv gave him a questioning look. "Moving forward. Do you remember trying to call me on the radio about five days after the outbreak?"

Liv nodded. "I had just reached the Slag. I wanted you to know we were safe."

Wyatt snorted and shook his head. "That's not what I thought. Some of the radio towers must have gone down because your message cut out…a lot. I thought you were trapped. I thought you needed my help…so I picked up and I left. I thought…" He stumbled over his words. "I thought, maybe if I could save you and Elli, it would make up for not saving Sarah and Ben."

Liv's mouth opened and closed as she tried to think of something to say. "You just left? Because of me?" Liv stammered in disbelief.

"I thought you needed me. The idea that there was someone out there that I could still save helped me get back up." A smile crossed Wyatt's face quickly before disappearing again.

"Thank you," Liv said quietly, "for coming to my rescue."

"You didn't need me. You never really did." Wyatt shrugged. "You rescued me."

DAY 30

The neighborhood was quiet. A breeze rustled the leaves on the large trees that dotted many of the front yards. A few cars still sat in driveways. It looked like everyone was at school or at work, where they should be. Not like the apocalyptic mess that most of the world had been left in.

The Slag had seen a large influx of survivors in the last few days. A group of fifteen survivors had stumbled across the farm, quickly followed by a group of three and another group of six. Almost overnight, their community had almost doubled in size. This meant the house had become incredibly crowded. Even the barn was running out of space for people to sleep. Jay and Jordan had moved into Liv and Elli's room, sleeping on blankets on the floor. Every free space had been taken.

Suddenly, they were running low on everything. They not only needed food to feed the extra mouths, but clothes, blankets, soap, and other necessities. They were in dire need of almost everything. The raiders had been making trips nonstop for the last forty-eight hours as they tried to replenish their supplies. The day they could get into Walmart could not come fast enough. They had done another drive-by before their supply run. The horde's numbers were slowly dwindling, but there were still more than she liked.

"All right." Liv heaved herself off the curb. She was tired. Beyond tired. But there would be time to rest after this run. "Let's split up and get this over with. I'm done with the Dead Zone." The other raiders mumbled their agreement. "Pick a house and stick to your pairs. Be safe. You know the drill. Don't make me explain it again." She felt compelled to tell them the same things every time they were on a run, as if her saying the words kept them safe. If she didn't say them, it would be her fault if someone was killed. Logically, she knew it wasn't true, but she still said the same thing every time.

This was their third run. In the last two days, they had refined their ability to comb through a neighborhood down to a science.

"Which one?" Wyatt asked.

"This one looks as good as any." Liv motioned to the house they were standing in front of.

Liv stood off to the side of the door as Wyatt beat his fist hard against the door. For a few minutes, they stood silently, not even breathing as they listened for movement inside. Nothing returned but silence. Wyatt tried the doorknob, and it turned. His lips pressed into a thin line. Unlocked doors usually meant undead owners.

He gave the door a shove, letting it slam against the wall. The two stood in the doorway for an extra moment, waiting. The house remained silent.

"After you." Wyatt gestured for Liv to enter.

"Oh, you're so kind." Liv's eyes roved back and forth across the room as she darted in the door. The interior was darkened but not pitch black. Large windows on the other side allowed light to filter in through sheer curtains. The house was neat, everything in its place. Nothing had been knocked over. Nothing seemed missing. That was promising. Hopefully, they would find everything they needed.

"It's weird," Liv commented as she looked over the living room. "It's weird how normal everything looks in some places, and other places are just utterly destroyed."

"Like these people might come home at any moment and catch us creeping around."

"Yeah." Liv nodded, peering into the kitchen. Everything downstairs was clear. Liv pulled open one of the cabinets, and her heart sank. It was utterly bare, except for a thick layer of dust on the empty shelves.

"Well, this place may not be as untouched as we thought," she sighed. Wyatt raised a questioning eyebrow at her. "The cupboards are empty." Liv motioned back to the kitchen.

Wyatt shrugged. "I'm sure—" His words were halted midsentence as a soft shuffling sounded from upstairs. "You hear that?"

"Yep. Got one upstairs." Wyatt was already ahead of her. He crept slowly up the stairs, carefully twisting his body to keep the top in sight.

At the top of the stairs, he raised his bat, tapping it against the landing. More shuffling came from behind a closed door.

"Shush. Please. Shush." The voice was hushed and frantic.

Wyatt and Liv exchanged a glance. Wyatt took the last few steps two at a time and approached the door. He reached out, gently knocking.

"Hello," Wyatt called out tentatively. "Is someone in there?"

The shuffling resumed.

"Hello," Wyatt called again. "We aren't here to hurt you. If you're in there, please come out."

"Go away!" a woman shrieked. Wyatt jumped back as her shrill voice cut through the air.

"Ma'am, we aren't here to hurt you." Wyatt kept his voice measured as he tried to reassure the woman. "There are several of us out here. We're just gathering supplies. If you would talk to us, maybe we could help you."

"I said go away," the woman shrieked with the same intensity.

"What should I do?" Wyatt mouthed to Liv.

Liv nibbled on her lip. If someone didn't want their help, they couldn't do anything, even if they wanted to.

"It's all right, honey. It's all right. Mommy will protect you. It's ok." The quiet words weren't meant for them. The woman repeated the words over and over.

Liv motioned for Wyatt to step aside. "Hello." Like Wyatt, her voice was purposefully level. "Ma'am, my name is Olivia. Will you talk to me?"

The room was quiet. At least it was an improvement.

"Ma'am, we're sorry if we scared you. Some of us are just out looking for things we need. We didn't know you were here. We won't take anything of yours." Liv paused again.

"It's all right," the woman said weakly. "I was trying to be quiet, so you wouldn't know we were here."

"That's smart." Liv nodded, even though the woman couldn't see her. "But ma'am, we have a large colony. We've taken in a lot of other survivors over the past month. We would love to bring you back with us. The farm is safe. We're running a bit short on supplies right now, but that's why we're out looking through empty houses."

"I…I…I don't know. I don't know you." Her voice shook as she struggled to decide.

"Ma'am, it sounded like you were talking to someone when we knocked. Do you have a child with you?"

There was another long pause before the woman spoke again. "Yes. My daughter."

"A daughter." Liv smiled, resting her forehead against the door. "I have a daughter. She's going to be two soon. She's back at the farm. There are lots of people there that help care for her. Nana Eve watches the children. She's...she's kind of like everyone's grandma now. My daughter is well-fed. She gets to play outside. She's got most of the adults wrapped around her finger." Liv chuckled. "But even in this world, what it has become, she is happy."

The woman had fallen silent again. The silence drew on, and after a while, she wasn't sure if the woman was going to respond.

"That sounds like a lovely place. I know my daughter would love to have someone to play with."

"We have a few other children that live there. Not many, but they are all getting the best we can offer them, and I think we're doing pretty good." Liv looked to Wyatt.

There was more shuffling behind the door. The footsteps were slow as they approached. A heavy piece of furniture scraped across the floor as the woman moved it out of the way. A lock clicked, and the woman opened the door an inch and peered out.

"Hello." Liv smiled at the woman. She couldn't have bathed in weeks. Her eyes were wide and wild, and her skin was gaunt. "My name is Liv."

"Hello." The woman looked over Liv. "I'm Susan. I just...I just need to gather a few things before we go."

"Take your time," Liv said patiently. "Would you like some help?"

The woman nibbled on her lip. "That would be fine." The woman opened the door, so Liv could enter.

"Do you mind if my partner watches over us?" Liv gestured to Wyatt. "His name is Wyatt. He used to be a police officer." The woman regarded Wyatt for a moment before nodding.

As Liv stepped into the room, the stench hit her. Decay mixed with rotting food, sweat, and human waste. The room was a disaster. Liv sucked a breath in through her teeth as she took it all in. Trash was piled in the corners. Wrappers, cans, dirty dishes, soiled clothes. A bucket sat on the other side of the bed. A lid sealed the top, but it didn't contain the smell.

The closet doors had been removed and set to the side. Inside the closest, a little girl was bound and gagged. Her clothes were dirty and stained with blood. Her wrists were held above her head, attached to the bar that usually held clothes. Her eyes had been blindfolded, but the instant Liv stepped into the room, her head whipped around. A growl emanated through the gag tied across her mouth.

"Oh god," Liv whispered.

"What?" Wyatt stepped into the room, recoiling as the smell hit him. As his gaze fell upon the little girl, he reflexively pulled out his sidearm.

"No!" shrieked the woman, throwing herself between Liv, Wyatt, and the child.

"Get out of the way," Wyatt growled.

"No! Don't hurt her!" The woman sobbed. "She's just sick. She needs help. Surely, you can help her at your farm." The woman's eyes were filled with a hopeful light that made Liv's heart break.

"There is no help for her." Wyatt's tone was low and dangerous. "She's infected. The only thing we can do is put her out of her misery."

"No!" The woman wailed, wrapping her arms around the child. The girl began to writhe in the woman's grip, her teeth gnashing at the gag.

"Step out of the way," Wyatt demanded. "That thing is not your daughter anymore. She'll kill you if she gets the chance."

"She's just not herself right now." The woman switched to pleading. "She just needs help, and she'll get better."

"No, she—"

"Wyatt." Liv laid her hand on his arm. He didn't take his gaze off the child. "Wyatt," Liv said more firmly. "Put your gun down and wait for me in the hall." He still didn't respond, his eyes locked on the thrashing child. "Now!" Liv bellowed.

Wyatt pressed his lips into a thin line before angrily shaking his head. "I will be right outside the door. If she gets free..." He let his words trail off.

Liv shooed him from the room. She took a couple of steps toward the woman but carefully kept her distance.

"I am sorry." She truly meant it. She would never have gotten the woman's hopes up if she had known. "But your daughter cannot come to the farm. She would be a danger to everyone there, and we cannot allow that." Her voice was gentle as she spoke.

"No! No, please! You have to take us with you! You have to help her!"

"We can't. If there is a way, we don't know how." Liv's gaze fell to the floor as the woman began to sob once again. How many parents out there were just like this woman? Clinging to a hope that their child could be cured? Driven mad by their loss.

"You have to help us! She needs help," the woman screamed angrily through her tears.

"She cannot come back to the farm. I will not put my daughter or any of the others who have entrusted their safety to me in danger. You can come with us, but she must stay behind."

"I won't leave her! What kind of monster would that make me?" The woman shook as she spoke. Every muscle vibrated as the anger and adrenaline hit her. "You are a monster!"

Liv closed her eyes, steadying herself with a deep breath. "I am sorry. We'll leave some rations in the kitchen to help you." Liv turned toward the door.

"You can't leave us here!" The woman screamed the words at Liv's back over and over again.

Liv forced herself to place one foot in front of the other as she continued out the door and down the stairs.

"What was that?" Wyatt snarled once they were outside.

"What was what?" Liv shot back.

"Why in the hell would you leave that woman with a feral?" Wyatt gestured back at the house. "She is clinging to a hope that isn't real, and one day that child will get loose and rip her to shreds."

"That woman has nothing left to hold onto besides false hope. Without that child, she won't survive either. How can you of all people not see that?" Liv stared hard at him.

"No! Don't you throw that at me!" Wyatt reared back. "No. I did what needed to be done. I put my son out of his misery. She needs to do the same. That child shouldn't even be walking around. That thing is not a child anymore."

"You did what was right for you," Liv said evenly. "We have no right to make that decision for her."

123

"And what happens when that feral gets loose and kills her? We could have stopped that. That will be our fault. Your fault."

"That woman has to find her own will to live. We can't force her. We can't kill her child and expect her to thank us. If that child kills her, then so be it." Liv swallowed around the lump in her throat. She probably was leaving this woman to die. "She has made her decision."

Wyatt took a deep breath, pulling a hand across his face. "I…I'm sorry. I kind of lost my cool for a minute. It just…it just doesn't seem right."

"I know but thank you for the apology." Liv shook her head. "It's not right. When I saw that child, I knew things were going to go south. I just couldn't react quickly enough."

"It was…something else," Wyatt agreed.

"I could have gone my whole life without having to see that," Liv said solemnly.

"Yeah." Wyatt nodded. "I'd rather not deal with it again either."

***

Liv wiped the sweat off her face. She had been sweating all day. The Missouri sun in July was not forgiving, but the cars were almost full. They had maybe one or two more houses to go through before they could call it quits and go home. The other car was already completely full. They were so close to the end she could almost taste it.

"What was that?" Ry straightened, her head whipping back and forth.

"What?" Liv frowned.

"Everyone, shut up!" Ry barked. All of the raiders abruptly fell silent, listening for the sound Ry had heard.

"Mommy!" The wail was faint.

Liv and Ry made eye contact. Ryland's eyes were wide in disbelief. "I heard it, too." Liv grabbed her sledgehammer from where it leaned against the vehicle. "Come on." Liv moved in the direction that she thought the cry had come from.

"Mommy!" The wail came from down a side street. Liv stalked down the street, her eyes darting everywhere as her feet carried her forward without thought.

"Anything?" Ry whispered from beside her.

"No." The street was entirely empty.

"Could it be coming from inside one of the houses?"

Liv looked around. They hadn't been able to move through these houses yet. "Maybe."

"Mooooommy!" The cry warbled piteously. Liv's head whipped around. It came from another street just a few houses down. The cry was coming from there. Liv looked back over her shoulder. The others had gathered near her.

"Follow me." She mouthed the words.

Liv crept around the side of the house, forcing herself to move slowly despite her instinct to run to the child. At the end of the row, she once again peeked around the corner, peering down the lane of joined backyards. Ferals drifted between the houses, their movements lazy and listless. Liv frowned. How had they not heard the cry?

"Mommy!" They were getting closer. Liv darted across the gap in the houses, sprinting down the length of the next house. She pulled up short at the corner, quickly peering around the side.

A child walked down the sidewalk. His back to Liv.

"Mommy!" The boy's voice cracked as he cried out again.

"There he is!" Daniel whispered. "Why are we standing here?"

"Something doesn't feel right." Liv peeked around the corner at the boy again. His clothes were dirty, and his feet were bare, but he looked no different than any other survivor who lived alone in the Dead Zone. "There are ferals in the backyards that should be able to hear him and get to him, but they aren't doing anything."

"Let's just creep forward until we can get close enough to grab him quickly and quietly," Wyatt whispered.

"Screw that."

"No!" Liv lunged, trying to grab ahold of Daniel, but the man darted out of reach before she could even react. Liv abandoned her cover, following him.

Daniel ran up on the boy at full tilt, scooping him up in his arms without missing a beat. The boy let out a deep guttural roar as he twisted in Daniel's arms.

He's a feral. Goosebumps rippled across Liv's sweaty flesh as her feet pounded against the pavement. *How can that be?*

Daniel released the boy, but he had already locked his small arms around him. He buried his face in Daniel's neck. Daniel let out a shrill scream as the boy ripped a chunk of tendons and flesh from his neck. The pair crumpled to a heap on the ground.

Liv pulled the sledgehammer back as she approached and swung with everything she had. The weapon slammed into the boy's side, catapulting him off of Daniel. Liv dropped down next to the fallen raider, pressing hard against the wound.

The boy picked himself up, wobbling slightly. He looked up, his eyes locking on Liv and Daniel. "Mommy!" The single word came out as a shrieking war cry.

"Put him down!" Liv screamed.

The high shriek of the responding ferals made the hairs rise on the back on Liv's arms. The creatures flooded in from between the houses, seeming to appear out of nowhere as they surged into the street.

Wyatt didn't stop as he approached the boy. His baseball bat slammed into the side of the boy's head, sending him spinning across the ground.

The ferals were everywhere. So many had appeared so quickly. Where could they all have come from?

"Fall back!" Liv screamed over the howls of the horde. Wyatt was already by her side. "Get him!" Liv gestured to Daniel. "I'll cover us." Wyatt scooped up Daniel effortlessly.

Liv swung her sledgehammer as a feral man lunged at her. His lips had been ripped away, leaving him with a perpetual snarl. The sledgehammer caught him in the temple, shattering his skull.

Another woman reached for Wyatt with fingers that were worn down to the bone. Liv slammed into the woman with her shoulder, sending the feral sprawling. Liv swung the sledgehammer over her head, bringing it down squarely on the woman's crown. Her skull cracked open, spilling blood and brains onto the road.

Liv looked around wildly. The other raiders were closing in. They came together in a loose circle, depending on each other to keep their backs protected as the horde pressed in on them.

Ry's sword whipped through the air, decapitating a feral as he charged her. The man stumbled forward a few more steps before collapsing to the ground.

Another feral rushed in at Liv. She swung her sledgehammer, but the monster was too quick. The heavy head passed harmlessly over the feral. Without a thought, Liv stuck out her forearm. The feral clamped down with all his might, his teeth gnashing hungrily at her jacket. Liv sucked in a breath and dropped her sledgehammer. She snatched the knife from its sheath and jammed it through the feral's eye, yanking it back as he dropped to the ground.

A path opened up across the yards as the horde surged forward.

"Go!" Liv screamed.

As one, the raiders charged forward into the closing gap. A feral lunged, his teeth chomping furiously. Liv swung, hitting him in the shoulder. They didn't all have to be put down for good. They just needed to clear a path.

Liv rounded the first corner. The next street was more open than the last. There were ferals rushing in from all sides, drawn in by the sounds of the fight, but not nearly as many.

"Just get to the cars!"

As they plowed ahead, a feral charged straight for Liv. She leaned forward, not slowing. As they collided, Liv threw her shoulder into the monster.

They turned the last corner. The cars were in sight. Liv could hear the horde behind them. The sound of dozens of feet echoed off the houses. Their shrieks melded into one cry of rage.

Liv put everything she had into the final sprint, pulling ahead of Wyatt. She slammed into the side of the car and yanked open the back door, before throwing herself in.

"Get in!" Wyatt shoved Daniel in the back door. Liv clamped her hand around the wound on the man's neck. He was already pale. The deep red of the blood stood more starkly against the pallor of his skin. His hair was plastered to the edges of his face.

Wyatt threw himself into the driver's seat and jammed the key into the ignition just as the first feral slammed into the car. Harvey dove into the passenger's seat, twisting around to watch Liv and his brother.

Did everyone else make it? She could barely make out four other heads in the other car. The second car peeled away, its tires screeching as it threw off the ferals that had already clustered around it. Wyatt slammed on the gas, throwing Liv back in her seat.

"How far are we from the farm?"

The delicate black veins snaked across Daniel's face. His breathing was quick and shallow.

He's not going to make it.

"Twenty minutes." The car rocked as Wyatt took a turn too quickly.

"Shit," Liv whispered.

"How is he?" Wyatt's gaze flicked to the rearview mirror momentarily. Harvey watched them silently. His face was almost as pale as Daniel's.

Liv didn't respond. Instead, she turned her attention to Daniel.

"Daniel." Liv patted the man's cheek. "Daniel, open your eyes." Her gloved fingers left bloody marks where they touched his cheek.

Daniel's eyes flicked open lazily, as if it took all the effort in the world. His lips moved, but nothing came out.

"It's all right." Liv tried to sound reassuring, but her voiced cracked as she spoke. "We're taking you home. We'll be there soon."

"No." The word wasn't even a whisper.

Liv's breath came in short gasps. The blood that oozed from Daniel's neck had slowed to a trickle.

"Just hang on," Liv insisted.

"No." Daniel's voice was firmer, but the word pained him. "Too late. It's too late. Too late. It's too late. Too late." He kept repeating the words over and over.

Suddenly, he gasped, his fingers digging painfully into Liv's arm. He slowly released the breath, his fingers relaxing. His eyes were still open as he stared off at Harvey.

"Daniel!" Liv rubbed his sternum, trying desperately to rouse him.

"Liv…" Wyatt warned.

"I know!" barked Liv, laying her hand on her pistol.

Daniel's eyes fluttered open. For a moment, they were unfocused and disoriented. Liv didn't even breathe. Then they locked on her.

"Too late!" screamed Daniel, his voice warping in a way only the ferals' could. He suddenly sprang into action, reaching for Liv with fingers curled into claws.

Liv grabbed Daniel's throat, holding him back as she pulled out the pistol. She pressed the barrel against Daniel's temple and pulled the trigger. The crack of the weapon drowned out Daniel's vicious snarls and snapping teeth. Then, everything fell silent. Daniel flopped down, his head falling into Liv's lap.

Liv sucked in a deep breath. A muffled cry escaped Harvey's lips. For a moment, they locked eyes. Tears slipped down his cheeks. Then, suddenly, Harvey spun in his seat, lurching forward without a word.

"You all right?" Wyatt's eyes darted to the rearview mirror.

"Fine." Liv gently placed Daniel's head across her lap. She leaned back against the seat and closed her eyes.

She had lost so many friends since the outbreak. Friends she had known for years. Friends she had only just met. Neighbors she had known all her life. Family that couldn't be replaced. At some point, she had thought it would get easier. That the loss would become a normal part of life. But none had been easier than the last. Each one reminded her that her world was growing smaller. That her own days were numbered and that they were probably fewer than she had ever thought.

"So, what the hell happened out there?" Max sat at the head of the dining room table. When they arrived home, Liv and Wyatt had gathered the other head members of the Slag.

Liv ran her hands through her hair. "We heard a boy crying out for his mother. We went to investigate and found him a few streets over, but he wasn't a boy; he was a feral."

"Not possible," Randall scoffed, leaning back in his chair. Randall was Max's long-term partner. Though they had never been married, they had lived together for thirty years. The burly man never said much outside of his work. He was in charge of the fields. He ensured the crops were rotated properly and that the proper seeds were planted.

"Excuse me," Liv snapped, rounding on Randall. "I wasn't aware that you were there."

"The ferals don't speak," Randall defended himself. "They grunt and wail like animals, but they don't speak."

"Not until today. The boy was not human." Liv's eyes darted back and forth as she replayed the scene in her mind. Could the boy have been just a frightened child? Had he just been traumatized by the outbreak? Had they overreacted? No. "The boy was feral, and he spoke. He didn't say much, just 'mommy' over and over again. It was more like a parrot than actual speech."

"Could the boy have simply been in shock?" Kraus didn't sound like he believed the question himself.

"No." Liv shook her head adamantly. "When Daniel approached him, he reacted as a feral."

"But what if he was just acting?" Kraus pressed. "People can get all sorts of messed up. What if he was just…crazy? The kid thought he was a feral and therefore acted like one."

"No!" Liv slammed her hands down on the table, making a few of the others jump. "You weren't there. He wasn't just some poor, messed up kid. He was feral. He screamed like a feral. He reacted like a feral. His bite was infectious. Daniel died. If the boy had been human, Daniel wouldn't have changed."

"He was feral," Wyatt reinforced Liv's words more calmly. "Daniel began changing after being bitten. Of everything else that should leave no question about it."

"Daniel's wound was on the neck." Liv took a deep breath to compose herself. "It missed the major blood vessels, but it was severe. He showed all the signs of rapid onset infection, including the black veins that occur as the infection spreads toward the brain." The room was silent as the others allowed Liv's words to sink in. "There was one key difference," Liv continued. "Like the boy, when he succumbed to the infection, Daniel continued to repeat the same words."

"Words? You mean multiple words?" Max clarified, leaning forward.

"Too late." Liv nodded. "He kept repeating it over and over, even when he attacked."

"He became a talking feral as well," Kraus muttered. "That means whatever caused the boy to talk is transmissible."

"Exactly. I think it's a mutation in the virus. If it's a mutation, then it can be spread from one host to the next." Liv looked pointedly at the others around the table.

"That isn't all," Wyatt continued slowly.

"Jesus." Kraus leaned back in his chair. "What else is there?"

"Looking back on the incident with the boy, there was other behavior we found odd. This could be incidental, but we think it's something that should be thought about." Max motioned for Wyatt to go on. "Up until the boy attacked Daniel, there were very few ferals present in the neighborhood. The houses were empty. We saw almost none outside. It was the best situation we could have hoped for." Wyatt scratched his head as he thought. "You'll have to bear with me as there are a few possibilities we discussed. But once the boy attacked and was in a frenzy, ferals appeared out of nowhere."

"More talkers?" Randall asked.

"No. They were normal ferals," Liv supplied.

"But it wasn't just the few that we had seen around. It was like dozens of them just crawled out of the woodwork," Wyatt continued. "It was like they were lying in wait."

"That's bullshit," Randall said. "The ferals don't hide. They don't lie in wait. They just attack. They are mindless animals."

"Even animals can set traps." Max looked pointedly at the man. "That is what you're implying, right?" She waited for Liv and Wyatt to agree before continuing. "That is a large leap." She clasped her hands together on the table. "If they can set traps, rudimentary as they might be, then we must be very careful in the Dead Zone. Nothing can be taken at face value."

"That is our point entirely." Wyatt nodded in agreement. "The virus is mutating or has at least in one instance. The ferals seem to be adapting and learning."

"I don't think this mutation is an isolated incident," Liv interjected. "I think there are more instances of mutation out there. When Ramsey was killed, the feral moved extraordinarily fast. It leaped onto the top of the truck. I've been wondering if that was a mutation."

"Maybe he was just athletic," Kraus explained. "We have seen that those folks who were better runners before infection show better physical endurance when infected."

Liv nodded. "True, but this feral didn't have legs. I have a hard time believing it could have moved so quickly with that kind of disability. I think it was a mutation that enabled it to do that. And if that is the case, who knows what other kinds of mutations are happening out there."

Max nodded, her lips pursed in thought. "That makes sense. Viruses have a greater chance to mutate as they infect more people. This virus has infected how many? Millions? I think billions would not be an overestimation when you consider the impact across the globe. That makes the chance of some kinds of mutation very high. I guess, kind of like the flu, it changes all year long because it infects so many people."

"But what about the idea that the other normal ferals are changing?" Kraus asked. "That seems like a bit of a stretch. Can viruses mutate within the host?"

Liv shook her head. "No. There's a difference between adaptation and mutation. I think that would be more of an adaptation." Liv leaned back in her chair, blowing out a long breath. "Though, the truth is that we just don't know very much about the virus and what is left of the host's brain function."

"What, you mean like there might be something left of the person inside?" Kraus leaned forward.

"No, no." Liv shook her head. "I doubt that. To be honest, I don't even really want to think about that. But basic brain function. We know the brainstem is intact. Otherwise, they would stop breathing and their heart would stop beating. As far as we can tell, most of the frontal lobe is destroyed. The virus erases memories.

Perhaps some of that remains intact and gives them some slight capability for basic reasoning. Maybe we didn't see much reasoning during the outbreak because they have to relearn it much like a child learns to reason as they grow."

The tension in the air was so thick that Liv almost couldn't breathe. The implications that the ferals could learn and grow the longer they were infected was nightmarish in a world that was already fraught with nightmares.

"If that is the case," Max started slowly, "then there is a solid chance none of us will survive much longer."

"So, what do we do?" Randall asked, a sneer curling his lips.

"Well, we sure as hell don't give up. I don't know about you folks, but I've survived too damn long to roll over now." Max fixed her steely gaze on the others around the table. "People have been fighting wars with each other for as long as time. This ain't no different. We're fighting a war against an enemy that, for now at least, is stupider than us. If we're smart about our decisions, we'll last a hell of a lot longer."

"We should probably work on defense mechanisms. At the very least, we should work out an alert system, so we can get a heads-up when the ferals are approaching," Wyatt suggested. "Could Ralph rig up some kind of triggered alarm?"

"Probably." Matt shrugged. "I'll ask him."

"It wouldn't hurt to try and devise some tactics for breaking up hordes that approach the farm and how to tackle the ferals once they're here," Liv added.

"Sounds like a plan." Max nodded. "We'll start there."

"I hate to ask this, but what do we tell the others?" Liv asked. "Shouldn't we tell the rest of the survivors around the Slag?"

Max pressed her lips together into a thin line. "I suppose we should. I think the best way to handle that would be to have each of us talk with our respective people. Smaller groups mean we can answer any questions and help everyone move on. We don't want to start a panic."

"What about the Collier colony?" Liv asked. "If we are truly to be allies, we need to warn them."

Max waved off Liv. "Take your people and give folks at Collier a heads-up. Your people saw all this, so it's not news to them."

Everyone slumped down in their chairs. No one wanted to leave the meeting. No one wanted to go talk to the other survivors. No one wanted to deliver the news that things were potentially changing again. All around her, Liv saw blank faces as the others pondered what other changes the future might hold.

How could they survive if the ferals were becoming better hunters?

DAY 31

"Mutations can't occur that quickly." Jackson waved his hand dismissively. Liv was about ready to pull out her hair. She had spent the last thirty minutes trying to talk some sense into the man.

"Listen." Liv slammed her hands harder on the table than she had meant to. "Mutations can occur randomly at any time. It is as simple as an improperly copied gene. It's a goddamned dice roll. That's all. The ferals are mutating. Not all of them, but the mutations are out there. It has made some of them better hunters. We ran right to the goddamned kid, thinking he was someone who needed our help."

"He probably was," Jackson spat back. "The kid was beyond your help. End of story. He was just too far gone."

Liv ground her teeth together as she held back the fury she wanted to release upon the man. "Crazy isn't contagious. How do you explain what happened to my raider?"

"Are you sure about that?" Jackson asked, raising a skeptical eyebrow as he looked over Liv. "Just look around you. What makes you think the whole world hasn't gone mad?"

"Fine." Liv drew in a deep breath and stood up abruptly. "We came here to warn you, and we've done that. Whether or not you want to listen is entirely up to you. I just thought you cared about the wellbeing of your people and would want to know." The comment was a low blow, and she knew it.

Jackson's chair clattered to the floor as he shot out of it. "How dare you accuse me of not caring about these people!" he snarled. "Who the hell else would have taken care of them?"

"Then maybe you shouldn't be so dismissive of new threats." Liv leaned forward, planting her hands firmly on the table. "Ignoring new threats is the quickest way to get yourself and the rest of your colony killed. The ferals are changing. If we don't change too, we'll die."

Jackson looked like he was about to reach across the table and smack Liv, but she didn't flinch away as she stared him down. Wyatt moved a few steps closer to her, every muscle in his body tense.

"What harm could it do to take precautions and keep your eyes open?" Liv persisted.

Jackson closed his eyes, running a shaky hand through his hair. Finally, he scooped his chair back up and plopped back down in it. "I've seen a lot of shit in my time, but the world just keeps surprising me."

Liv returned to her own seat. "It does open up a whole new can of terrifying."

Jackson shook his head. "I...apologize for my behavior," he said slowly. "And thank you for bringing word to us. I'll make sure my men keep an eye out for anything odd."

"We did not mean to cause any trouble," Liv said, trying to extend an olive branch. "Since we are trying to be allies, we felt it was important to warn you."

Jackson massaged his temple and nodded. "There are so few people left." He suddenly sounded very weary. "It is important that we stick together. That's exactly why I stayed here." A wry chuckle escaped his lips. "I could see the writing on the wall. This wasn't something that was just going to blow over in a few days or even a few weeks. When people started showing up, I decided to stick around. If this really was the end of the world, I figured we had to band together to survive."

"This isn't the end of the world. It is the birth of a new world. It's foolish to think that the end of our species means the end of everything." Seti broke his usual stoicism. The entire room turned to look at him.

Jackson laughed outright this time. "Oh, yeah? Do you think this really is the death of our species, or do you think we'll have a place in this new world?"

"I think that depends on us," Seti said simply. "If we work to make a place for ourselves in this world, then there will be a place."

Jackson stared hard at Seti for a moment before turning back to Liv. "Y'all have thought about this way too much."

"What's left to do at the end of the world besides think?" Liv shrugged.

"Fair enough," Jackson conceded. He pushed himself up from the chair. "It's almost time for dinner. Let me thank you folks for coming. Why don't you join us?"

"We wouldn't want to intrude," Liv said. They knew the Collier's food stores were low. She couldn't imagine taking from it further.

"Please, I insist. I have to say, making this alliance work has been pretty one-sided so far. Let me make up some of the difference by giving you guys a meal." Jackson opened the office room door and motioned for the raiders to follow him. Reluctantly, Liv stood and followed Jackson down the hall.

They entered the large, open warehouse. Quiet murmuring drifted through the room. Compared to the last time they had been here, it sounded absolutely chaotic. The aroma of barbeque drifted through the air, and Liv's stomach somersaulted.

"It's not too fancy, but we managed to get a few cows that were grazing in a pasture not far from here." Jackson smiled. "Damn things have been roasting all day. Since we don't have any way to refrigerate leftovers, we need to make sure there aren't any."

"And you guys haven't had a problem with infection via the meat?" Liv asked tentatively.

Jackson chuckled. "No. Nothing like that." He frowned. "Have you guys not been eating meat?"

"No." Liv shook her head. "To be honest, after seeing what I saw during the Midnight Days, it pretty much lost all appeal." Liv grimaced. All the blood, brain matter, and body parts. The images of ferals digging into their still screaming victims rose unbidden from her memories of the first few days. She could still hear the sound of ligaments and muscles tearing as the ferals ripped chunks out of their victims. Liv gagged as she quashed the memory back down.

"You folks really are strange," Jackson muttered.

"Hey, eggs, beans, and salad aren't really a bad diet." Liv shrugged.

"I can't say I'd turn my nose up at something fresh," Jackson admitted.

"Nothing fresh." Liv shook her head. "Not anymore at least. Hopefully, in the next few months, we'll be drowning in fresh vegetables. For now, it's all canned and preserved."

Jackson chuckled. "One can dream, right?"

A long table had been set up to slice the meat. One man carefully sliced slabs off a leg, while another expertly separated ribs.

Jackson inhaled a deep breath. "I know you aren't a fan, but I have never smelled anything so glorious."

"Me either." Jay took in a deep breath, a smile spreading across his face.

"Well, don't stop on account of me." Liv found a spot to sit down and wait for the others to get their food. A small array of canned fruit and vegetables had been placed out, but Liv couldn't bring herself to eat something that could be saved.

Wyatt plopped down next to her, his plate piled with hunks of meat. Liv looked away, swallowing the bile that rose in her throat.

"What?" Wyatt asked. "I got some for the both of us."

"You can have it all."

"What? You don't want any?" Wyatt jiggled a piece of the cooked meat in front of her face. Liv tried to swat his hand away, but he quickly snatched it back, shoving the food into his mouth with a large satisfied grin.

"You are disgusting," Liv said dryly.

"Maybe." Wyatt shrugged. "But this is the best stuff I've had all month," Wyatt said through a mouth full of food.

"You have fun with that," Liv said flatly.

Wyatt swallowed. "Killjoy."

"Gross," Liv shot back as Wyatt shoveled more food into his mouth with a smile.

The large doors to the warehouse slammed open, the sound echoing through the room. Everyone went silent, turning toward the doors almost as one.

Three men stood in the doorway. "Jackson!" one of the men shouted.

"Here!" He stood up and hurried toward the men. The room remained silent as they spoke, though their voices still couldn't be heard. When Jackson turned to look around, his face was set in grim determination. The big man made a beeline straight for Liv and the other raiders.

When he reached the group, he knelt down. "If you wish to leave, you must do so now."

"What? Why?" Jay asked. "I just started." Jay gestured to his food.

Jackson ignored Jay's complaint. "There is a large horde moving up the highway. We're going to take care of them. But if we fail, this building will be squarely in their path. So, you must leave now or get trapped here until the horde passes."

"How many?" Liv asked.

"Thousands. My men don't have an accurate count, but the horde was the largest we've seen."

"What can we do to help?" Ry asked.

Jackson shot a skeptical glance at the woman before returning his gaze to Liv. Liv nodded in agreement. "How can we be of use?"

"I could not ask you to do anything like that on our behalf." Liv could see that the words pained him. He needed their help.

"You didn't. We are offering," Liv said.

Jackson lowered his voice further. "Listen, we have nothing to offer to repay you for such a thing. You guys could get killed. I couldn't ask you to do that for free."

Liv held up her hand to stop him. "We talked about it earlier. There are too few of us left. We couldn't leave you to defend yourselves. We need to stick together." Liv lowered her own voice, leaning in toward Jackson. "But if we help you, I want you to start trusting us, so we can start working together. No more of this tense bullcrap we've been dealing with."

Jackson's lips were set into a grim line as he sat back. "I think that sounds more than fair." Liv nodded. "All right, gather yourselves. We need to move out now. We only have a few hours to figure out what to do about the horde."

Liv threw all her weight against a sedan. Wyatt did the same on her left and Ry on her right. Slowly, the car began to tip until it suddenly rolled, the windows shattering as it hit the ground. With a few extra shoves, they pushed it into place in line with the other cars.

Her arms were sore. Swinging the sledgehammer had given Liv more upper body strength than she had ever had, but tipping over cars was an entirely different story. Jackson had mobilized dozens of people, forty-five of the strongest survivors at Collier. But they had so many cars to move.

"How many more?" Ry puffed as she leaned against the car.

"I don't know." Liv shook her head as the next car pulled up. The driver jumped out and ran off to retrieve another.

Ry groaned but moved toward the vehicle.

"We're cutting it close." Wyatt gritted his teeth as they all threw their weight against the car. For a moment, it didn't move, and Liv wondered if they were simply going to run out of energy. Slowly, the vehicle tipped before it crashed down like the last. Just like the previous sixty or so the trio had already tipped. Others were working frantically alongside them. Some scavenged what they could from the vehicles and siphoned the gas. Others pulled the cars into place. Many worked on tipping the cars and locking them together just right.

In all, they had six rows of vehicles. Each approximated fifty cars long. The wide arc of interlocking vehicles was impressive.

A loud whistle pierced the air. All the workers stopped, turning their attention to the spotter, who stood on the roof of a truck parked further down the highway.

"Horde! Retreat!" The cry bellowed across the highway.

Liv could see the horde on the horizon. The ferals looked like a mass of specks. Nothing significant yet, but through their sheer numbers, they kicked up a trail of dust that obscured everything behind them. How many ferals would it take to churn up that much dirt?

Liv snatched up her sledgehammer and dropped it into the loop on her belt, jogging back to their vehicle. Her arms and legs shook as she ran. She would pay for this tomorrow. She would probably pay for the exertion for a week.

Wyatt hopped into the driver's seat alongside her and started up the car. The convoy was already retreating down the highway. Liv grabbed her jacket off the floor of the car and pulled it on. The idea of adding more layers to her already hot and sticky skin was awful, but if the barrier didn't hold, she needed to be prepared.

After a few minutes, the vehicles once again pulled over. Jackson climbed out of his car and pulled himself onto the hood, watching down the highway with a set of binoculars. Liv pushed open her own door and walked over to join him.

"How's it looking?"

"They haven't reached the barrier yet, but I think we got away without sending them into a frenzy."

Liv nodded before realizing that he wouldn't see the gesture. "That's good. If they stay dormant, then hopefully, they just follow the curve of the barrier."

Liv hated not having her own binoculars. She needed to make a point of finding a pair for herself. She hadn't needed them until now, but it couldn't hurt to have a set.

A few others got out of their vehicles and gathered around Jackson as they waited for the horde.

"Approaching the barrier." Jackson's voice was clipped.

Liv could hardly breathe. If the ferals pushed through the barrier, they would either have to retreat to Collier and wait for the horde to pass or stand and fight. She didn't like the idea of being trapped in a building surrounded by thousands of ferals. The Collier survivors had shown amazing discipline when it came to noise, but that would be too risky.

Jackson's breath hitched as he stared intently through the binoculars. Liv tensed, waiting for the news that their plan had failed.

"The first few have hit the barrier...they're turning." Jackson's voice was barely a whisper.

Ry grabbed Liv's shoulders. "We did it!" she whispered excitedly.

No one made much noise, but a few of the survivors pumped their fists in the air triumphantly. Others hugged. A few whispered to each other, broad smiles plastered across their faces.

"The cars are shifting back under the weight of the horde." Jackson hadn't taken his eyes off the highway. Liv was positive he hadn't even blinked. Her heart fell. If the cars were pushed out of line, if a gap was created... "But the horde is still turning."

Wyatt took Liv's hand, squeezing it in excitement. She looked over to him. A broad smile covered his face. "It worked," he mouthed. She squeezed his hand back.

The horde was still coming. The end wasn't in sight yet. Though they were mere specks on the horizon, Liv could see the writhing mass they created.

She took a step closer to Wyatt. "How many do you think there are?"

Wyatt shook his head. "I don't know."

Thousands. Ten thousand. More?

"How did they amass such a large horde?" Liv didn't expect him to have the answers, but she couldn't keep herself from wondering.

Wyatt squeezed her hand but didn't say a word.

The questions buzzed around Liv's head. Were hordes like this forming elsewhere? Was this something that would become more common? Had they just directed the horde toward an innocent group of survivors? What would the Slag do if such a horde was headed in their direction?

DAY 33

Liv walked down an empty street. The road was cracking. Tiny bits of grass grew through the cracks, creating lace with the pavement. The buildings around her were succumbing to vegetation.

Once carefully manicured medians had grown out of control. The bushes had grown huge, spilling over the curbs and into the street. Vines crept up the sides of the buildings. Trees grew tall and leafy without pruning.

"Liv!" Liv spun around. Jen stood down a side street. A smile lit her face, and she waved. "Liv!"

The woman looked just as bubbly as she had ever been, her fiery red hair gleaming in the sunlight. Liv's feet pounded against the pavement as she rushed toward her. Liv couldn't bring herself to slow down as she neared. Instead, she slammed into her full force, wrapping her arms around Jen.

They staggered a few steps together before regaining their balance.

"Well, it's good to see you too," Jen giggled, squeezing Liv tight.

Liv gave Jen one final squeeze before pulling back. She had missed the woman. They hadn't known each other long, but in a few short days, Jen had become a best friend.

"I…I…I miss you," Liv stammered through her tears.

"I miss you too." Jen's voice hitched. "But it's ok. Don't cry. If you cry, I'll cry." It was too late. Jen was already crying as she pulled Liv into another hug.

Liv wasn't usually one who hugged a lot. She tried to keep a bubble between herself and others, but right now, she didn't mind. She had truly missed Jen's company at the Slag.

"Why don't we take a walk?" Jen motioned down the street.

"Is it safe?" Liv hesitated. The streets looked entirely deserted, but the idea of walking in the open made her anxious.

Jen shrugged. "As safe as can be. No one has been here in ages."

Liv jogged a few steps to catch up with Jen. She couldn't help but stare at the woman.

"This place is so beautiful. It'll be even better in a few centuries." Jen breathed, taking in the crumbling city around them.

"Are people gone?" Liv asked. Jen nodded. "Are the ferals gone?" Jen nodded again.

Jen held out her arm, stopping Liv in her tracks. Liv pulled her sledgehammer from her belt, ready to fight off whatever Jen had seen. Instead, Jen pressed her fingers to her lips. A wolf loped out of a shattered door. It paused, lifting its nose and scenting the air. After a moment, it broke into a run. Four more wolves burst from the door, following on the heels of the first.

"Beautiful," Jen breathed.

Liv watched the wolves race down the street. "Is this what will happen when everyone is gone?"

"Yes. The Earth will return to what it was before. The animals will rule the land, and the planet will be green again." Jen reached up, plucking a flower from a creeping vine that had started to consume a long-abandoned car.

"So, we are going to survive?" Liv's stomach clenched. "How much longer do we have?"

Jen's lips turned down. "I don't know. A week. A year. A century."

"*Will Elli survive?*" The words made Liv's throat feel like sandpaper. She wasn't sure she wanted to know the answer, but she couldn't stop herself from asking it.

"*Not everyone will survive, Liv. Most won't.*" Jen turned to face Liv. "*That's the world. That's the way it has always been.*"

"*Will Elli survive?*" Liv persisted, desperation clawing at her insides.

"*What if I said no? Would you give up right now?*" Jen asked.

"*I…*" Liv's mouth opened and closed as she tried to come up with an answer. "*Does that mean no?*" she croaked out.

"*I have to go.*"

The street was suddenly filled with people. Hundreds of them. Pressing in against Liv. She began to panic. It was like being in the center of a horde. She had to get out. She had to get out before they ripped her apart.

A face caught her eye. A soft smile. Gentle eyes behind thin-framed glasses nestled in a face framed by light brown hair. The same features Liv had known all her life.

"*Mom,*" Liv breathed, reaching for the woman.

As Liv tried to push through the crowd toward her mother, she began to recognize the other faces. A friend from college. A coworker. The neighbor boy who lived down the street. They were all smiling. They all looked relaxed as they stood in the street of a city that had been reclaimed by the apocalypse.

They were all dead.

Jen grabbed Liv's hand. "*You can't go,*" Jen said firmly, holding Liv in place.

"*But…*" Liv turned back toward her mother. "*But I just want to see my mom.*" She could feel tears sliding down her cheeks.

"*I know,*" Jen said quietly, "*but not now.*" Liv could feel her breath coming more quickly. She just wanted a hug, to say I love you, anything. "*Liv,*" Jen said firmly, "*the end is here. We'll see you soon enough but not now.*"

Liv's brain stopped. "Soon enough?"

Jen pulled Liv into another tight hug.

Liv sat up, gasping for air. Sweat covered her skin in the humid and stifling room. Jordan and Jay were asleep on the floor. Liv grabbed her shoes and tiptoed out of the room. Outside the door, she frantically jammed her feet into her boots.

"Where are you going?" Liv jumped at the voice. "Sorry, I didn't mean to startle you," Wyatt said quietly.

"I just…I need a walk." Liv didn't know what she needed. The dream was still swirling around in her brain, muddling her thoughts.

"Want some company?"

"No…yes…" Liv shook her head. "I don't know." She sighed, pulling her long hair back into a ponytail.

"How about I come, but we don't have to talk. We can just walk together," Wyatt offered.

Liv nodded, heading down the hall toward the front door. She didn't know where she was going. It didn't really matter. She just needed to walk. To do something.

She could still see the dream so vividly in her mind. The bright sunshine lighting up the city. The brilliant colors of the vegetation. The wolves running through the streets.

The face of her mother. Gentle and kind as she had always been. Her mother had been a constant source of support. She had talked Liv through many problems, offering advice.

But her mother was dead. She had been killed in the first few days of the outbreak, most likely by her father.

Jen and Corey had died for her. She had only known them a few days, but the laughably mismatched couple had protected her and Elli as they trekked through the infected streets. When they had been overwhelmed by the infected and the end had drawn near, both had sacrificed themselves for her and Elli and allowed them to escape. Their blood was on her hands. Liv hadn't wanted anyone to die for her. She wanted her parents back. She wanted Colin here. But the world wasn't fair. It didn't care what she wanted.

She could feel the tears rolling down her cheeks.

"Why did this happen?" Liv said quietly, not looking over at Wyatt.

Wyatt let out a heavy sigh. "I don't know." She hadn't expected him to know. She didn't think anyone knew. And knowing why wouldn't change that it had happened.

"I had a dream," she began slowly, "about what will happen in the years to come. Everything will keep moving forward without us. To be honest, it wasn't really bad. Everything was doing just fine." Liv nibbled on her lip as she thought more about the dream. "My friends were there. People I haven't heard from since before the outbreak. My parents..." Liv scraped her boots against the ground. "I met a couple during the first days. They saved Elli and me when we had no way out. They were wonderful people. Jen was so bubbly and happy. Corey was blunt and vulgar, but...they helped us when they had no reason to do so."

"They sound like wonderful people," Wyatt commented, encouraging Liv to continue.

"They're dead or feral at least." Liv swallowed the lump in her throat. "We got caught by a horde while crossing Highway Seventy. Corey tried to draw them away, but he...didn't make it. When Jen and I got cornered, Jen sacrificed herself to allow Elli and me to escape."

The tears were flowing again. The image had been burned into Liv's brain. She was sure it would be there until the day she died. Corey pressed his bloody face to the tiny shattered window in the school's side door, Jen embracing him. The look of pure happiness on her face for just a brief moment before he ripped out her throat.

"That was very noble of them."

"I didn't want them to," Liv snapped. "I didn't want them to die for me. I didn't want that hanging over my head. I didn't want my parents to die or my friends." Liv shut her mouth. Millions of people had died in the last month. Most of them during the first few days. The Midnight Days. That didn't make the people she loved any different. They were all the same.

Only the survivors were different.

"Why was I different? Why did I survive?" Liv spun on Wyatt. "There isn't anything special about me. I'm not particularly strong. I don't have any survival skills. I'm not a genius. I'm not important. So why me? Out of all the people that died, why did I survive?" she demanded.

Wyatt pressed his lips together. "Sometimes, it's nothing more than dumb luck." Liv growled and jumped up to pace. "During the first days, many good officers died. A lot of them were more experienced than me. Some were better shots. Some were stronger…it was just luck that I survived.."

"Do you think this is lucky? Being here? Outliving our friends and family? Not knowing if we'll have food tomorrow or even if we'll be alive?"

"Would you rather be dead?"

No. Liv couldn't respond. She didn't want to be dead, but that didn't make the reality of their situation any easier.

Wyatt let out a long sigh. "I spent many nights…and days, if I'm being really honest, wondering how things would have been different if I had gotten home sooner. At first, I thought this was better. They weren't suffering through this, but that's not the way Sarah would have looked at it. If the roles were reversed and Sarah was here instead of me, she would try to live better. To live for the both of us. I can't say that I'm doing that, but I know she would want me to go on and make the best of things."

Liv nibbled on her lip. "But doesn't that pressure feel...crushing? How do..." Liv suddenly deflated, all her energy draining away. "How do you live knowing that you are living for others without getting overwhelmed?"

"Pft!" Wyatt chuckled. "I can't possibly seem that collected. There are days that it is an awful burden." He fell silent for a moment, staring at some imaginary point in the darkness. "But most of the time, it just means I'm able to get up in the morning. For now, I think that's enough. Maybe later it will mean more. Maybe it never will..."

Liv fell silent thinking about what Wyatt had said. She took in a deep breath, sucking in the smell of grass and decaying foliage.

Finally, Liv let out a long sigh. "I wouldn't rather be dead." She plopped down in the grass, tilting her head back to the stars. The grass was dry and prickly against her skin. "But sometimes, it's just all too much."

Wyatt sat down next to her. "Maybe you need to stop looking so far ahead for a little bit. A month ago, things took a very drastic turn. Things changed and everything we thought lay ahead of us ceased to be. That doesn't mean that things are all bad. We're alive...and doing relatively well, even if everyone who should be here isn't."

"One day at a time." Liv tested out the words and chuckled to herself. "You're talking to someone who has an obsessive love of lists and planning." Liv paused, watching a satellite drift passed the stars. How long would it be until the last one decayed from orbit and plummeted back to Earth? "But it doesn't sound like a bad idea. I could give it a try." She laid back in the grass. "I've always liked looking at the stars. It's just amazing how small they appear but how large they really are. It kind of helps put things in perspective."

A comfortable silence fell between them. Liv's eyes danced back and forth across the stars as she looked from one to the next.

Wyatt sat up. Before Liv could react, he leaned in toward her. His lips were soft as they brushed against hers. Tentatively, she rose up to meet him. She wrapped her arm around his neck. Suddenly, his lips were crushing against her. Liv could feel a desperate need welling up inside her. She needed to be close to someone. She needed someone to comfort her. She needed Wyatt.

Suddenly, Liv pulled away. She and Wyatt locked eyes. Hurt and confusion stared back at her.

"I...uh...didn't plan that," Wyatt mumbled, giving Liv a goofy grin.

"I can't do this." Panic bubbled up in her chest. "I'm sorry, but I can't. Colin is alive." Colin might not have made it here yet, but she knew that, if he was alive, he would make his way to the Slag.

If...

What if he wasn't alive anymore? Would she ever know?

"It's all right." Wyatt's gentle voice interrupted her swirling thoughts. "I shouldn't have done that. I know you're married. I know he's out there." He sat back. "Why don't we just forget this happened?"

Liv smiled, forcing the panic back down. "All right." She stifled a yawn. "We should probably both get some rest. The morning will be here before we know it."

DAY 35

They were almost done.

Liv looked down at the list in her hands. Most of the items had been checked off but not all of them. They had to go out more and more often. It had only been two days since their last run, but they were burning through supplies. The population at the Slag had swelled to seventy-eight. Until the crops were ready to harvest, it was up to them to supply the Slag with food.

The survivors hadn't been pouring in, but they had seen a steady trickle. Mostly, people came in pairs or small groups. They hadn't seen a big group of survivors in a while.

Liv looked up from her list, watching the buildings glide by. A large motorcycle shop caught her eye.

"Oh! Pull over here!" The list fell from her hand as she gestured out of the window.

Wyatt mashed the brake and made a sharp turn into the parking lot. "What do we need here?" he asked.

"I have an idea. Let's go take a look."

Liv scanned the parking lot quickly. A few ferals were already dashing toward the car. Liv waited until one was almost at the car before throwing her door open, knocking the grimy man to the ground. He snarled up at her as she swung her sledgehammer up and brought it back down again on his head. Another was only a few steps behind him. Liv let go of the sledgehammer, pulled out her knife. She grabbed the woman by the throat, plunging the knife into the feral's eye socket. After a brief moment, she felt the crack of the socket giving way, and the woman went limp.

Liv looked around at the others. A few more ferals were scattered on the ground around the cars. Liv straightened her jacket, wiping the blood from her gloved hand on one of the feral's shirts.

"Anyone up for a new change of clothes?" she asked, waggling her eyebrows.

"I wouldn't mind some riding gear." Jay shrugged. "I'd look like a total badass." A big grin spread across his face, making him look like a kid in a candy store.

Liv rolled her eyes. "Ok, but that's hardly the most important thing."

"Pft! If I'm going to be tromping around in the Dead Zone every day, at least I can look like I belong here."

"Well," Liv continued, "biker jackets are made of leather, right?"

"Sure." Jay nodded.

"I thought we could snatch up a few and see how well they can protect us. I figure, if they are supposed to protect bikers from road rash, then maybe it'll help protect us from the ferals. My jacket has done pretty well so far, but something that fits properly would be even better." Liv pulled at the jacket that was at least two sizes too big.

The building was clear. The outbreak had occurred on a Saturday evening. The employees had probably locked up and gone home, not knowing anything was wrong. The raiders spread out in the empty store, perusing through the aisles for gear. Liv pawed through a rack of women's jackets. The bright green leather was buttery soft. Without thinking, she balked as she read one of the price tags. Before the outbreak, she would have walked away from the rack. Now, whatever was here came at the affordable price of free.

The neon colors on the first rack hurt her eyes. They might be great for helping riders stay visible to other motorists, but she wasn't too keen on getting noticed by the ferals. Instead, she turned to a rack full of black and grey jackets. She discarded the jacket she was wearing and pulled one off the rack.

Liv had never been a big shopper. She hated trying on clothes. She hated having to paw through the racks to find just the right top or dress. The apocalypse had cleared up most of her clothing qualms. They wore what they could get their hands on, but she had to admit it was nice to pick out something that she liked for once. It was strange the things that she missed.

Liv ran her fingers along the black leather of the jacket. A single red racing stripe ran down each arm. She had always liked red.

"Looks good!" Liv turned to see Wyatt pulling on a jacket of his own.

"Thanks." Liv smiled. She zipped up the jacket and smoothed the front. She didn't want it to be too loose. Loose clothing could provide a handhold for a feral.

Wyatt inspected his own jacket with a frown before pulling it off and hanging it back up on the rack. It was hard to abandon old habits. No one would be around to care if they threw the jackets on the floor, but it seemed wrong to just discard perfectly good clothing.

"We should probably take as many of these back as we can. Winter will be here before we know it, and people will need jackets." Liv turned back to Wyatt.

"Good call." Wyatt nodded, inspecting a pair of riding pants.

"What about helmets?" Rows and rows of helmets displayed on the back wall caught Liv's eye.

"What about them?" Wyatt frowned.

"They would be a good idea for when we're clearing houses or facing a horde. It'll restrict our vision, but if a feral gets in close enough to bear hug us, it'll be harder for them to find someplace to bite."

Wyatt shrugged. "I don't see why it would hurt."

Wyatt and Liv both moved toward the wall. The helmets had several different shapes. Some had visors. Thinking back to the feral that had vomited on Henry, Liv wanted one with a visor. A black helmet with red spikes down the center caught Liv's eye. She plucked it off the wall, turning it over in her hands. Finally, she pulled it on over her head and turned toward Wyatt.

A smile spread across Wyatt's face. "You look like a Trojan warrior."

"Pft! Hardly, but it's cool, right?" Liv tilted her head from side to side. The helmet was heavy and felt odd, but she could get used to it.

"It goes with the jacket." Wyatt nodded as he picked up a blue helmet and pulled it on.

"Hey, guys," Ry called. Both Liv and Wyatt spun around. Ry stared at them for a moment in their helmets. "Cool!" she said, her eyes briefly wandering over the wall before returning to Liv and Wyatt. "I had an idea. I was thinking we could add some armor plating to the gear." Ry gestured to the jacket she was holding, pulling at the sleeves. "I was thinking we could reinforce key points, like the shoulders, arms, legs, and sides."

"Is that something you could do?" Liv pulled off the helmet.

"Oh, yeah." Ry nodded enthusiastically. When Liv gave her a skeptical look, she continued, "Hey, Cosplay is expensive. You either have to shell out hundreds or thousands for someone to make the costumes for you, or you learn to make them on your own. I liked a lot of heavily armored characters, so I learned some metal work. We'd just need to get the metal curved right and sewn in with some padding. No big deal."

Liv laughed. "That's awesome. Yeah, let's give it a try. I'm all for something that's easier in the long run." The magazines did their job, but even with the padding, they still chaffed, and it was hot as hell.

"Don't get me wrong. It'll make everything heavier, and it might still chaff, but it should definitely be easier to get ready when we head out on supply runs or need to move quickly."

"Man, we're really turning into post-apocalyptic survivors." Jay was grinning ear to ear.

"I guess we do have to dress the part if we want to keep surviving." Wyatt nodded.

"I'm not dying any time soon." Liv's mouth set in a grim line as she pulled a pair of pants off a rack. "I'd rather be all decked out than try to look normal."

Liv eyed herself in a mirror. Her hair fell in a long braid down her back. Her face was leaner than it had been before the outbreak. She was leaner. The jacket and helmet gave her a bit of an edgy look.

So much had changed. So much was still changing.

DAY 36

Wyatt shifted from foot to foot as he waited for Liv. Ry stood next to him, fidgeting impatiently with a bag in her hands.

"Are we there yet?" Liv's slightly annoyed voice trickled to them on the breeze. "This is getting pretty old."

Liv rounded the corner. Jay had his hands over her eyes as Seti led her by the hand.

"We're here, ya party pooper." Jay and Liv stopped just inside the barn. "I'm going to take my hands away, but you have to keep your eyes closed."

Liv sighed. "Ya know, surprises became a lot less fun after the Midnight Days, right?"

"Only another minute." Liv's eyebrows shot up at the sound of Wyatt's voice. Wyatt helped Ry pull the garments out of the bag. He held up the pair of leather riding pants while Ry held the jacket.

"Ok." Ry shook out the jacket and held it in front of Liv. "Open your eyes."

Liv opened one eye cautiously before opening the other. "It's done!" Liv exclaimed, her whole face lighting up.

"Here, put it on." Ry shoved the jacket toward Liv with

anticipation. Liv slipped her arms in. It was heavier than it had been but still lighter than she had expected.

"How much did you add?" She ran her fingers over the leather, trying to find the changes.

"I put sheets of aluminum in both the forearms." Ry moved her finger from Liv's wrist almost to her elbow. "I put a collar in them that should protect our necks when we aren't wearing the helmets and a sheet on either side along the ribs. I tried to cover the easy access areas that the ferals tend to go for. There are, of course, weak points that aren't covered, but the leather should give you a second to react and take care of them." Ry stepped back, beaming. She turned to Wyatt. "The pants have plates across the thighs and calves." She drew her finger along the plates. A frown flitted across her face, momentarily erasing the smile. "I wanted to add something around the ankles, but I was afraid it would chaff too much."

"I'm sure it will be great as it is. It already feels better than the mess we've been wearing." Liv ran her fingers along the tall collar. It was rigid and sat just below her chin. The metal had been covered with more leather to make it more comfortable.

"Oh!" Ry exclaimed. "I almost forgot! Take it off again!" Liv pulled off the jacket as Ry bounced around excitedly. "Turn it over." Liv flipped over the jacket. On the back, four letters had been scrawled across the shoulders.

Thor.

"What do you think?" Ry asked excitedly. "I figured we could put nicknames on everyone's jackets. Something cool and strong. Thor seemed perfect for you since you always carry around that sledgehammer."

"I love it." Liv beamed, slipping the jacket back on and admiring it. "I can't wait to put it to use."

"It looks great on you." Jay slapped her on the back. "Now don't you feel like an ass for whining the entire way over here?"

"Well, you didn't have to cover my eyes the entire way…" A flush spread across Liv's cheeks.

Jay waved off her comment. "So, when do we get ours?" He turned to Ry. "I can't wait to try one on, myself."

"It really wasn't that hard." Her eyes danced back and forth as she thought. "Probably one or two days per set."

"I call dibs on the next one!" Jay said quickly.

"Psht! I get the next one if I'm making all of these." Ry gave him a light shove. "And you'll get it when I decide to make yours."

"Aw, come on." Jay followed her out of the barn.

Wyatt hung back, waiting for the others to leave. He scooped up the helmet off a bale of hay and passed it to Liv. "Want to try the complete look?"

Liv pulled her hair ties out, shaking out the tight bun she usually wore. She took the helmet from him and pulled it over her head. "What do you think?" Her voice was muffled by the helmet's visor. She picked up her sledgehammer, propping it against her shoulder.

"You look like you just stepped out of a post-apocalyptic movie."

She snapped up the visor. "Sounds like things look about right then." She pulled off the headgear. "I've got to admit, this feels a hell of a lot more comfortable than all the tape and magazines and towels."

"We'll have to give it a test run here soon," Wyatt said as they began the slow walk back to the house.

DAY 37

"Here." Ry snipped the final thread and threw the jacket at Wyatt. She had worked feverishly all night to get his gear finished before they went out again this morning. Wyatt didn't think she had slept all night.

"You're amazing." Wyatt snatched the jacket out of the air.

A large yawn overtook her face. "You bet I am." She gave him a half-hearted smile as she pushed her chair out from the table she had commandeered for her work. "Just bring me back something nice."

"Got it! One big bottle of the finest wine I can pilfer." Wyatt quickly pulled on the jacket. He was already late. She had worked so hard that it felt wrong to leave when she was so close to finishing.

Ry chuckled. "That actually doesn't sound half bad."

The alarm shrieked from the walkie on Wyatt's hip. He froze. Ry stopped her shuffle midway to her bed.

"Attention raiders! Attention raiders!" The call cleared the airwaves so that the raiders could communicate in an emergency without interruptions. "Ferals approaching from the east side of the farm trailing survivors.

Approximately fifty-five to sixty ferals and five or six survivors. They are approximately two miles from the clear zone. All hands ready and await Thor's orders."

Ry swore, mirroring Wyatt's own thoughts. The fence hadn't been erected on the east side yet. That was good for the survivors, but it meant the ferals would pour in too.

"I'll get ready." Ry pulled her own raider outfit out of a trunk at the end of her bed.

"Thor here." The radio crackled again. "Riders, split the herd. On-duty and standby, form up on me at the house. Weapons ready in sixty seconds."

"We'll be fine. You're exhausted. You need rest." Wyatt's mind buzzed, but he didn't want Ry getting hurt because she was too exhausted to fight properly. "I've got to go." Wyatt was already out the door.

"Be careful!" Ry hollered at him.

Wyatt shoved open the front doors just as the riders took off, their mounts thundering across the field. The horde had already broken into the clear zone around the farm. The raiders took off, following behind the much faster riders. Wyatt sprinted to catch up, slipping on his helmet as he ran.

As the riders approached the horde, Wyatt's heart fell. The horde was too close together. The horses couldn't get between them and the survivors. Kraus wheeled his mount around and changed tactics. The horse sidled up to the edges of the horde, careful to stay out of reach of the monster's fingers. A few infected peeled away in favor of closer prey.

The horde was closing in on the survivors. The survivors were dirty. It was hard to distinguish who amongst the group was human and who was feral. They would have to delve into the horde and hope the survivors were strong enough to fend off a few of the ferals on their own.

They closed the distance between themselves and the survivors quickly. Wyatt passed the first few people in the group, and suddenly, the world around him was plunged into chaos. Liv was already swinging her sledgehammer.

A feral lunged for Wyatt with a snarl. He swung his baseball bat, striking the creature in the temple. Another creature grabbed ahold of his forearm. Before the creature could bite, Wyatt jerked his elbow back, smashing it into the feral's face. The feral's grip loosened, and Wyatt spun around, smashing the reinforced bat into the creature's side. As the monster fell to the ground, Wyatt raised the bat and brought it back down on the monster's head.

Out of the corner of his eye, Wyatt saw Liv go down, a feral on top of her. Wyatt swung the bat with all his might, trying to clear away the ferals around him, but with each swing, others filled in the gap. A feral launched itself at him, and Wyatt threw his arm up. The feral latched on and bit down on the metal plate that Ry had sewn into the sleeve. A smile spread across Wyatt's face as he dropped his bat and snatched up the knife he kept at his hip. In one quick motion, he drew the knife and plunged it into the feral's eye.

As Wyatt stepped back and looked for the next threat, he realized there were none. Others were looking around for any remaining ferals. The survivors eyed the raiders skeptically.

Wyatt glanced around for Liv. She shoved the feral off of her and jumped to her feet. Assured she was all right, Wyatt turned away and did a quick headcount. When he counted all the raiders that were still standing, he breathed a sigh of relief. Among the still standing were seven new survivors. Wyatt wasn't sure if everyone in their group had made it.

Liv darted past him, and Wyatt's head whipped up, preparing for another onslaught. Liv peered at the edge of the tree line before suddenly sprinting forward. Wyatt had to stare hard before he saw the movement. A feral man was shuffling into the field as Liv raced toward him.

"Oh god!" One of the survivors let out a choked sob, covering his face with his hands.

Wyatt turned back to Liv. As she approached the man, she slowed. She stumbled, forcing herself to stay on her feet as she drew a knife. A few feet from the feral, she stopped entirely. The feral lunged, and she caught him by the neck.

Wyatt took a few hesitant steps forward as Liv struggled with the feral. In a flash, she brought the knife up, stabbing the man through the temple. As the feral collapsed to the ground, she collapsed with him.

A long, keening wail ripped into Wyatt's very soul.

Colin.

Wyatt swallowed hard around the lump in his throat. *She was right.* The man had been alive, at least until a very short time ago.

The raiders and survivors watched on in stunned silence.

"Get these people into the farmhouse." Wyatt grabbed Jay. "I'll take care of Liv. You take care of them. Don't send anyone back out until I bring her in." Jay nodded solemnly.

Wyatt jogged the few hundred yards toward where Liv sat crumpled in the grass. Liv had pulled Colin into her lap, holding his broken body close. The man had been ripped to shreds. Bite marks covered his arms and legs. Chunks of flesh had been ripped away. His entrails dangled out of a jagged hole in his stomach. Wyatt swallowed back the bile that rose in his throat.

Tears streamed down Liv's cheek as she held Colin close. She sat like a statue, staring into the trees. Not the trees. The void. A void had opened up before her, and she could not look away.

He wanted to comfort her. He wanted to say something that would take away the pain, but those words didn't exist. Instead, he stood back, watching over her as she mourned.

"You need to go inside." Wyatt's voice was gentle as he knelt down next to Liv. It had been hours. The sun burned bright in the sky, and if she sat out here any longer, she would end up with a heat stroke.

Liv didn't answer. She didn't even acknowledge that he had spoken. Wyatt gently took her arm and began to help her up.

"No!" She screeched, grabbing ahold of Colin's body.

"Liv, I won't let anything happen to him." Wyatt tried to catch her gaze. "You know I won't. Let me get you inside, and then I'll come back in and we'll bury him with the others."

Liv's chin quivered as she thought for a moment. Finally, she nodded, allowing Wyatt to help her up. She grabbed ahold of his arm as they walked, clinging to it as though her life depended on it.

Wyatt walked her over to the buckets on the porch. When they stopped and pulled the curtain, Liv turned to him with a quizzical look.

"Your hands."

Liv looked down at her red stained fingers with a dawning horror. "Oh god!" she shrieked, wiping at her hands in a panic.

"Here, let me help you." Wyatt unzipped her bloody jacket and gently tugged it off. Liv dunked her hands in the bucket of fresh bleach water, her panic subsiding into sobs as she scrubbed at them. With her hands clean, she leaned back against the side of the house, letting the water drip from her fingers.

"He was alive." Her voice was raspy. "He was alive earlier today." She turned to Wyatt. "He was so close. Why couldn't he have made it just a little bit further?" Her eyes begged him for an answer. She had asked him many questions that he couldn't answer, but this time, she needed an answer, and he didn't have it.

Wyatt pulled Liv into a tight hug. "I don't know. Liv, I am so sorry." He could feel the tears welling up in his own eyes as she began to cry again. He knew her pain well, and he would not wish it on anyone.

DAY 40

"You don't have to go," Wyatt told Liv as he leaned against the door to her room.

"Yes. Yes, I do." Liv pulled on her jacket and zipped it. "I can't just sit around anymore. It's killing me. I need to get up and get out. I need something to keep myself busy. I'm tired of doing nothing."

Wyatt nodded. "If you need something, let me know. I've been there," he said earnestly.

"Thank you." Liv gave him a weak smile. "I think right now I just need to be busy. I just...don't want to think about it." She sighed. "There'll be plenty of time for my stress-addled brain to work through it at night, I'm sure."

"Sometimes dwelling on it doesn't help." Wyatt shook his head. "I was ready to give up..." His eyes grew unfocused as he was sucked back into the memory for a moment. Then he shook his head and continued, "It was only once I got moving that things started to feel...better."

Liv placed her sledgehammer in the passenger side of the vehicle. "I think, right now, it's just better to take things one day at a time. It may not be the healthiest approach to ignore it, but I'd rather deal with the ferals than be thinking about…Colin." It felt like a betrayal to say the words, but they were true.

"It still hurts to think about Sarah and Ben…maybe that won't be true one day."

"Maybe one day." Liv jumped into the truck. "But today is not that day."

Liv wiped her brow. The work wasn't hard today, but it was hot, and they didn't have any relief from the sun's brutal rays. She finished hooking up the trailer hitch and walked up to the driver's side of the truck. Jay sat inside the cab. She rapped her knuckles on the window and gave Jay a thumbs-up.

As he pulled away, Liv mentally tallied how many trailers they had sent back to the Slag. Twelve so far. She let out a long breath. They had to hurry. They needed as many of the trailers as they could get. At least thirty to accommodate the survivors they already had, but they wanted a surplus, so they could continue taking in survivors.

"Ready for more?" Wyatt called to her.

"I'm ready for a nice cold margarita."

Wyatt groaned. "Don't you dare talk about anything cold."

Liv flashed him a wicked grin. "Sure would be nice, though." She fell silent as Wyatt pounded his fist against the front door of the trailer. They both listened intently, waiting for the sounds of a feral inside. But nothing stirred.

They hadn't found any ferals inside the trailers yet, and at this point, Liv doubted that they would. However, it still didn't hurt to be cautious.

Liv pulled open the door. Wyatt lunged through the opening. After a moment, he relaxed, beckoning Liv.

"Empty. I know I shouldn't be disappointed, but I could use a change of pace," he muttered.

The interior was just as pristine as all the rest. The trailer hadn't been touched during the Midnight Days. Liv walked the length of the trailer, peering into the bathroom to ensure it was empty.

Liv ran her fingers along the dusty countertop in the kitchen. The Slag wouldn't have the hookups required to make the trailers fully functional, but the survivors at the Slag would have their own separate spaces. Their own little home. After the cramped confines of the farmhouse, it would be a godsend.

With the interior cleared, Liv stepped outside, unrolling a long strip of painter's tape, and placed it across the door.

"Hey!" Seti's voice boomed. "Come look at this."

Wyatt firmly closed the door behind them, and they moved toward the other raiders. On the far end of the lot, Ry and Seti stood next to a section of downed fencing.

"What is it?"

Seti shook his head. "I have no idea, but you should check it out." He scratched his chin as he stared hard at the fence. Liv frowned as she strode over to them. Ry stood next to the sales building near the fence. They had seen the fallen fence when they had scouted the area. On top of the fence sat an overturned car, a decaying corpse still strapped into the driver's seat.

"Something about this doesn't seem right." Ry's words were slow. "It's bothering me." She walked around the car, inspecting it again. Liv walked with her, looking for something out of place. They had seen plenty of wrecked cars on the roads, panicked people who had tried to escape the ferals and had lost control of their vehicles. It was an all too common sight.

"There's too much damage," Seti said finally.

"What makes you say that?" Liv nibbled on her lip as she looked over the car again. It was a crumpled mess. The front end was smashed in. The passenger side was crushed. The windows had shattered, spraying glass in all directions. A tire was missing, and the front axle was broken.

"Well, the crash seems to have started over there." Seti carefully climbed over the downed fence and into the road. A line of long heavy tire tracks marred the road. Glass lay scattered around the end of the tracks, glittering maliciously in the sunlight.

"It looks like something was in the road," Ry continued.

"A horde maybe?" Liv crouched down next to the car, peering in.

Seti's jaw worked from side to side as he thought about it. "That makes sense for the tracks and the glass. They ran into a horde and got caught. Once they were surrounded, the horde broke the windows and got in. Except, that doesn't explain how the car got overturned on the fence."

"Maybe they tried to plow through the horde and overturned that way," Wyatt suggested. "There are a million different ways this could have happened. Without witnesses or more evidence, we really have no way of knowing."

"My point is," Seti pushed the point further, "we have seen some very odd things happening with the ferals. We may not know what happened, but it looks odd, and we should keep our eyes open."

"I agree." Liv stood up slowly. "If the ferals are changing, we really have no idea what will happen next. Stay sharp." Liv couldn't shake the feeling that something wasn't right. The hairs on her arms rose. "Now, we have a lot of work to do. I would prefer to not be out here all day *and* all night. Let's get back to work. But keep an eye on your surroundings for anything else that seems strange."

As Liv spun around to return to the trailers, she stopped in her tracks. The others beside her didn't move or make a sound either. Her eyes roved over the back of the small sales building, looking for an answer. Two large indentations. They sat almost level with her head. The brick had cracked and chipped, leaving a spiral of large spider web cracks in the side of the building.

"What do you think could have made that?" Jay's words were quiet, almost awestruck.

"I don't know." Liv reached out, gently running her finger along one of the cracks. "Let's just finish what we're doing and get out of here. I'd rather not find out."

DAY 58

The car bumped along as Liv looked at her map. The Slag was dangerously low on medication. They had gotten lucky so far that no one had been seriously hurt or became ill, but their luck wouldn't hold out forever. The map had a few locations Liv wanted to check out.

Mercy hospital was just across Highway 61. They would have everything the Slag could possibly need, but the place was crawling with ferals. Perhaps, if their plan with Walmart worked, the Raiders and Collier could try the same thing there. There were some schools nearby. The nurse's office would have a few things, but likely it would be more basic first aid supplies.

All of the pharmacies in Troy were too close to Walmart. If they made too much noise, they would draw the horde straight to them. While the horde around Walmart had dwindled dramatically in size, it was still too large for them to want to tackle.

That left the veterinary clinics. Most antibiotics that were given to animals were the same antibiotics used by humans. Liv had circled several places on her map. Hopefully, they would be entirely untouched.

Wyatt circled past the clinic. A dozen ferals milled around in the parking lot and street in front of the clinic. They snarled and dashed for the car.

"Just make a loop around the building." Liv twisted in her seat to watch the building. "There aren't many. It's not worth our time to try and draw them off."

"Gotcha." Wyatt swung the SUV into the parking lot, circling behind the building. The windows were intact. The glass front door was closed and unbroken. The building looked mostly untouched. Liv could feel her heart lifting a bit. Maybe they could catch a break for once.

Liv unbuckled her seatbelt and heard Eric and Ry in the back followed suit. "On three. One…two…three!" The SUV halted abruptly, and Liv threw her door open, jumping out and pulling on her helmet. Her feet pounded against the pavement as she sprinted for the first feral in the pack. The creature was missing her arm at the elbow. The head of the humerus pushed through her skin like a balloon surrounded by knots of shiny scar tissue.

With a growl, Liv pulled back the sledgehammer and swung, aiming for the woman's head. The weapon connected with the woman's ear. Her head snapped around with a sickening crunch, and she tumbled to the ground like a rag doll.

The next feral was right behind the first. Liv wouldn't have time to bring up her sledgehammer. Instead, she kept it low, smashing into the feral's knees. The creature's legs buckled and collapsed. As Liv raised her weapon to finish him off, he snarled at her, unaware of his imminent fate. Liv slammed the hammer down on his forehead.

Liv looked around. Wyatt finished off one feral. Ry was wiping the blade of her sword on a cloth. Eric stood by the car. His eyes were wide, and his bow was still in hand.

"How are you doing?" Liv said quietly as she stepped over to the tall man.

"Good." He seemed unsure about his words.

"Are you sure?" Liv persisted. She understood why he might be shaken. Eric had only just arrived at the Slag and safety and had gone back out into the Dead Zone again. He had to be tough to still be alive, but she needed to be sure he could handle being outside the safe zone again.

"Yeah." Eric took a breath and steadied himself. "These last few days have been hard. I guess I just hadn't realized how hard."

Liv swallowed. "I know." Her voice softened.

Eric's eyes grew wide. "Damn. I can be such an idiot." A deep flush came to his cheeks.

Liv put up a hand to silence him. "He was your friend, too. You have every right to be upset."

Eric nodded. "I'm so sorry, Liv. I really am. I just wish he could have at least made it to say goodbye."

"Me, too." Liv took a breath and steadied herself against the wave of emotions that swelled up and threatened to overwhelm her. "Are you going to be all right?"

Eric nodded fervently. "Yeah, I'll be fine."

Liv squeezed his shoulder before turning back to the others. "All right. We're going to split into two groups. Ry and Eric,"—she nodded to the pair—"you guys check the front facing rooms. Wyatt and I will check the back facing. Sound good?"

"Sounds good." Ry and Eric nodded in unison.

"Then let's go." Liv marched toward the door. She laid her hand on the door handle, checking to make sure the others were ready. As they assembled behind her, she took a breath and pulled on the door. It opened. Liv let out a sigh of relief. She hadn't wanted to go smashing windows and drawing attention to themselves if the door had been locked.

The interior was dark, but light trickled through the blinds. The clinic looked normal. It wasn't strewn with garbage like some of the houses that had been occupied since the Midnight Days. It simply looked like it was closed for business and would open again the next morning.

Maybe they had finally caught a break.

The two groups split. Ry pushed open the door that led behind the desk. She and Eric disappeared around the corner and into the building's dark interior. Wyatt laid his hand on the door to the first room, looking to Liv for confirmation that she was ready. Liv nodded, moving to stand just behind him. Wyatt silently turned the knob and pushed open the door.

The room was empty with only a few chairs and a small exam table taking up space. Liv moved to the next door, laying her hand on the knob. She and Wyatt locked eyes, and they nodded at the same time.

Liv pushed the door open, jumping inside. Again, the room was dark and empty.

Without warning, a heavy weight fell right on top of Liv. She let out a muffled yelp as arms wrapped around her, teeth gnashing in the small opening of her helmet. Liv pushed hard against the creature, trying to hold it back. The chairs clattered across the ground as they struggled together. A tacky substance slung to Liv's clothes as they came in contact with the creature. With a hard kick, she sent the feral sprawling across the ground.

The creature picked itself up, a low growl emanating from its throat. The man was completely naked, except for a thick green gel that covered his entire body from head to toe. As the man placed a hand on the wall, Liv pulled out her knife and lunged forward. The knife sunk into the man's eye, pushing through the socket and into his brain. The man's feet collapsed, and he slowly slid to the floor, his hand still stuck to the wall.

"Jesus!" Liv ripped off her helmet. "Where the hell did he come from?" She whirled around to Wyatt.

The door on the other side of the exam room burst open. The first thing Liv saw was the shotgun pointed straight at her. The gun was being held by a woman almost a full head taller than Liv. The woman looked cleaner than most of the survivors that came from the Dead Zone. She wore a pair of lavender colored scrubs that almost looked new.

At her feet stood three dogs, a three-legged German Shepherd, a Shar Pei, and a Border Collie. They all watched the raiders, all three entirely focused and simply waiting for the word from their master.

"Whoa! Whoa!" Liv said, clutching her sledgehammer.

"We aren't here to hurt you," Wyatt said from behind Liv. "We didn't know anyone was here."

"Were you bitten?" The woman's eyes were wide and wild. The Shar Pei took a step forward, his lips pulled back in a vicious snarl.

"No." Liv shook her head vehemently.

"Put your gun down." Eric's powerful voice echoed down the back hallway.

The woman glanced back. The dogs wavered, trying to split their attention in two directions. "I won't put it down, but I won't point it at you folks anymore. Fair enough?" Her brow was creased. The gun didn't mean much. With the pack of dogs at her feet, she probably didn't even need it.

"Fair enough." Liv made her voice loud enough, so Eric would be able to hear. The woman glanced down the hall and relaxed a bit.

"Quiet." The dogs instantly stopped growling, though they remained at attention. "Sorry, about," the woman gestured to the infected man, "I wasn't really expecting visitors."

"Flashlight please." Liv crouched down to the feral. Wyatt handed her his flashlight, and she clicked it on. In the bright halogen illumination, the man was even more disgusting than he had felt. A thick yellow mucus covered his skin. It clung to every inch of his body like sap.

"What the hell is this?" Liv breathed.

"I don't know." The woman crouched down next to Liv. "He managed to creep inside a few days ago when I was bringing in supplies. I assume he was clinging to the overhang of the roof. I trapped him in here, but I hadn't worked up the nerve to try to kill him off yet."

"Wait, backtrack." Wyatt's voice was full of disbelief. "He was hanging from the overhang? Like hanging upside down?"

The woman nodded. "I assume so 'cause he was hanging from the ceiling when I came back in. He almost got the drop on me. Luckily, the dogs warned me." She scratched the golden's ear. "They're a good bunch." Liv followed the man's outstretched arm. It still stuck to the wall, holding him partially upright. The beam moved upward still. Mucus dotted the ceiling. Handprints stood out in spots, testifying to the woman's words.

"What the hell?" Eric breathed, his eyes glued to the ceiling.

"The monsters are changing," the woman said matter-of-factly.

"We've seen a few but nothing this...bizarre," Liv said, her voice filled with equal parts amazement and horror.

"I actually would like to study this guy a bit." The woman stuck out her hand. "My name is Doctor Lauren Edwards."

"Liv." As Liv took Lauren's hand, the dogs relaxed. A few even laid down on the floor, their tongues lolling out of their mouths.

"Liv, really?" Lauren chuckled.

Liv shrugged. "Seems true so far." She turned to the rest of the raiders. "This is Wyatt, Ry, and Eric."

"Well, would you folks mind helping me get him into a surgical room?"

"How about you bring him back to the Slag? Our home," Liv asked when Lauren gave her a puzzled look. "We have other survivors there, and admittedly, we could sure use a doctor."

"Oh, I'm not a people doctor," Lauren admitted. "But I could certainly help a few people. How many survivors do you have?"

"The last count I heard was eighty-four."

Lauren's eyes grew big. "I had no idea there were that many people left in the world. Sure, I've seen a few survivors here and there, but they have been so few. Mostly, it's just been the infected. There are so many of them." Lauren's eyes grew sad. "But I couldn't leave. All of my medical equipment is here."

"We could help you move it," Wyatt jumped in before she continued that thought too much further. "We could take anything you need back to the Slag. We even have mobile homes set up as housing on the farm. I'm sure no one would object to you commandeering one for your research and medical needs."

Liv nodded earnestly. "We have many good people at the farm, who are just trying to survive. We could really use your help." Liv gestured to herself. "The raiders and I go out for supplies. If you joined us, you'd have no need to risk your life getting things for yourself. You could just study the ferals and treat people."

Lauren regarded Liv skeptically. "Keep in mind I am not a virologist. I'm not an expert on the infected. I've just been dissecting them when the opportunity arises and trying to figure out what I can to pass the time. Nor am I a human doctor. My medical knowledge gives me a leg up on the average Joe, but that doesn't mean I can do everything."

"We understand." Liv nodded respectfully.

"And I cannot move all my equipment. Some of the lab machinery is just too big and too delicate to move. We may have to come back at a moment's notice if I need to run tests."

Liv nodded again. "We would be more than happy to bring you back. A little more knowledge could really help us all."

Lauren eyed Liv skeptically for another moment. "All right. I'll go with you." A look of relief crossed Lauren's face, and she relaxed with her decision made. "Just let me gather my things, and then we can head out."

DAY 59

Liv sat down at the long dining room table. She wasn't the first one there. Kraus lounged in a chair opposite her. They still needed Max, Randall, and Lauren. The woman had opted to speak with them about what she knew already. Liv was both excited and afraid. What new horrors would greater knowledge bring?

"So what do you think this woman is going to tell us?" Kraus leaned forward on the table.

"I have no idea." Liv blew out a long breath. "Hopefully, that there can be a cure or a vaccine."

He nodded. "I don't know if I think a cure is possible, but a vaccine would be something. Imagine not being afraid to be bitten." His eyes glazed over as he relished in the idea.

"It would really make a difference. You could still get ripped to shreds by a horde, but if you didn't have to fear one..." Liv shook her head, wiping away the beautiful, fear-free future that blossomed before her. "I don't know if we should get our hopes up just yet."

Max strode in, followed closely by Randall, and plopped down in her customary seat at the head of the

182

table. Randall sat directly to her right. Lauren was only a few steps behind, a bag slung over her shoulder. Her pack of pups followed her into the room, sticking close to her side. Liv perked up, curious what the bag might contain. Liv gestured for Lauren to sit down next to her with a nod.

"Good day," she said without looking up as she dug through the bag. The poor woman looked flustered as she pulled a stack of papers out of her bag and shuffled through them. "I don't believe I've met all of you. My name is Lauren Edwards. I am…was a veterinarian. I have been studying the infected since the outbreak, though that does not make me an expert." She finally sighed, looking up from her work. "So where do you want to start?" Her eyes fell on each person sitting at the table in turn.

"Why don't with start with what is causing the infection?" Liv offered. "Is it a virus? Bacteria?"

"Parasite. The infection and the symptoms that cause people to appear feral, as you call them, is caused by a parasite similar to Giardia, which causes food poisoning. Now, when I say similar, that is not entirely accurate. It's the closest comparison I have, but it's like comparing apples and oranges. They're both fruit, and that's about where the similarity ends."

"What does that mean as far as treatment?" Kraus asked.

"Nothing. Some parasites, like worms, are very easy to treat. Others…not so much. This is not affected by normal treatments. As far as I can tell, the treatments that kill the parasite are ineffective. At best, the treatment kills the host, but more often than not, it does nothing." Lauren shuffled through her notes.

"If it is a parasite, how is it transferred through saliva?" Randall asked. "Aren't parasites usually larger as far as disease goes?"

"Yes. They are." Lauren nodded enthusiastically. "It seems that the microscopic eggs settle in the saliva and bloodstream, while the mature parasite settles elsewhere in the body, predominantly in the brain, but in some cases, it will form colonies elsewhere."

"What does that mean?" Max asked, leaning forward intently.

"It means a lot of different things. It really just depends on where the parasite settles. In the case of the man that was locked in my office, the parasite had settled in his sebaceous glands. These glands are responsible for producing oil around the hair follicles. When the virus entered there, these glands changed, and what they secreted changed, resulting in the sticky goo that covered the man."

"What you are saying is that the parasite is altering the host's bodily functions?" Liv asked.

Lauren nodded. "Yes, but this isn't something rare to those instances where the parasite settles outside of the brain." She frowned, searching through the papers again. "I don't quite understand it yet...but the parasite invades every aspect of the host and remakes it to suit the parasite's own needs. Take healing, for instance. The infected have a greatly increased healing capability. The problem for the hosts is that, once that healing is initiated, it doesn't stop. This results in lumpy knots of scar tissue that we have started to see on the infected."

"With the parasite's strong capability to preserve itself and the host, is there any better way to kill the ferals without having to go for the head?" Liv thought she already knew the answer, but it didn't hurt to ask.

"No," Lauren shook her head dismissively. "Unless you can get a direct shot to the heart, the parasite will start to repair and restructure the body in less than a minute to preserve the host. Since the parasite has already destroyed pain sensors throughout the body, the host often doesn't know anything is wrong. The parasite repairs the damage, and the host goes on."

Liv held her breath. She had one more question to ask, but she wasn't sure she wanted to know the answer for sure. Not after killing so many ferals. "Are they alive or dead?"

"Alive," Lauren said without hesitation. Liv's shoulders slumped. She had known the answer. Dead things didn't bleed. Lauren reached into her bag and pulled out a jar. Inside the jar, suspended in liquid, was a brain. "However, they are only alive in the sense that their body is alive." Lauren pushed the jar to the center of the table, so everyone at the table could see it. "The frontal lobe is completely destroyed, along with many of the areas that control higher functions. That kind of damage can't be repaired. The parasite has altered these people beyond anything we can correct."

Liv leaned in to take a look at the jar. Sure enough, the brain inside was riddled with holes. The delicate folds of the brain had turned to mush in parts. However, the stem that controlled vital functions, like breathing and heartbeat, was entirely untouched.

"Is there any hope of a vaccine?" Kraus asked.

Lauren blew out a long breath. "I honestly don't know. This parasite is unlike anything I have ever seen. Since it is repurposing the body for its own needs, the immune system doesn't even really react to it." She fidgeted with her papers. "And I don't have the proper lab equipment to create such a thing." She stopped, considering her words carefully. "I would like to say it is possible, but I don't know how. Perhaps if I could run some tests on someone who is immune I could figure out more."

"No one is immune," Randall stated.

"Someone is always immune," Lauren shot back. "Just because we haven't seen it doesn't mean they don't exist. No disease has a one hundred percent mortality rate. Even if it is low, there is always a percentage of people who are immune."

Liv leaned back in her chair, thinking over what the veterinarian had just said.

"So we need to find someone who has been bitten but didn't go feral?" Max's jaw worked as she thought.

"Exactly."

"That's like finding a needle in a haystack," Liv stated in exasperation. "How could we even go about finding someone like that? It's not exactly like people run around announcing their presence nowadays."

"I don't know." Lauren shook her head dismissively. "I didn't say we had high chances of creating a vaccine. Even if we did manage to find someone that is immune, we'd have to find the proper lab, hopefully, one with a generator and preferably a virologist…"

"In other words, we'd need to hit the lottery," Kraus summed up.

"We'll keep our eyes out for survivors in the Dead Zone. We always do." Liv pushed away the dissected brain. "The rest of your information was very helpful." Lauren grimaced as if she disagreed. "If we find anything of interest while we're out, we'll bring it back to you."

Lauren nodded, shuffling her papers back into a pile and putting them back into her bag. "Thank you."

DAY 67

Liv heaved up a long twelve-foot post and dropped it into the hole. Max fussed with a level, pushing the post until it was straight with the supports. Another person hurried over, pouring concrete into the hole around the post.

Liv hated building fences. She and Colin had rebuilt a small section of fence at their home. Digging the post holes had been the worst part, and Liv was happier than she cared to admit that she had not been tasked with the job.

Carefully, Liv released the post and stepped back, so Max could check one more time. Level. They were so close to being done. Other folks were already securing the large sheets of aluminum.

"Damn. It's hot as hell out here," Max grumbled, glaring at the sky. "I can't wait for the winter to get here."

"I'm not looking forward to the winter," Liv groaned, wiping the sweat from her own forehead. "That will have its own challenges."

"Don't go spoiling my fun, woman," Max scolded, ambling off to the next post hole ten feet away.

Liv snatched up her water bottle and gulled down the liquid. It was warm, almost hot, as it hit her throat. The warm liquid wasn't nearly as thirst-quenching as she had hoped. Liv would have given almost anything for ice.

The radio squawked, the high-pitched beep making everyone turn toward Liv. "Attention raiders! Attention raiders!" Liv's heart leaped at the call, and she turned up the volume. "Ferals approaching from the south down the main road. Survivors unknown but probable. Approximately twenty-five ferals a half a mile from the gate. All hands ready and await Thor's orders."

Wyatt, Jay, and Seti were instantly at her side. None of them had worn their gear. It was too hot, and Liv was sure one of them would have passed out in all the gear. Ry and Eric were on duty, but they would need some backup.

"Thor here," Liv spoke into the radio. "On duty, meet me at the house. T-minus two minutes."

Liv scooped up her sledgehammer and turned to the others. "We don't have time to get our gear from the house, but they'll need back up." She cursed herself. She should have brought her gear out here with her. "Be careful everyone. We don't have our gear, and that means we're vulnerable."

"We all survived the Midnight Days without it. We can do it again," Seti said reassuringly.

Liv nodded. "Just make sure to watch your partner's back. It'll be all the more crucial."

As they approached the house, Ry and Eric were already waiting outside.

"Where's your gear?" Ry asked in confusion as she fell in line with the rest of the raiders.

"Inside," Liv stated. Ry opened her mouth as if to protest but closed it again.

The road up to the Slag from the main road was long, but the gate reared up quickly. One of the guards was waiting and swung open the gate. Jay pulled the truck to a quick stop just outside, and the raiders piled out. The raiders quickly formed up shoulder to shoulder.

"Eric, stand back and pick off the ferals with your bow," Liv ordered. The guards watched over the fence with rifles, but she would feel much better with Eric at their backs. The horde could already be seen further down the road, their screams echoing off the trees.

As they jogged toward the mass, Liv's eyes flitted over the faces, looking for any indication that one of the ferals might be mutated. It was hard to distinguish between all the different dirty and snarling faces.

Except two. A mother and son ran hand-in-hand at the head of the horde. They weren't infected. Liv broke into a run. The pair didn't have a large lead on the ferals. She could see the fear etched into their faces, tinged ever so slightly with relief.

A feral suddenly pushed its way to the front of the horde. In a few powerful strides, it closed the gap between itself and the woman. It reached out with dirt crusted fingers and grabbed a fistful of the woman's short choppy hair. The woman screamed, shoving her son forward and out of the feral's grasp.

Liv pushed her feet to move faster. They were out of time.

An arrow zipped by, slamming into the man's eye socket. The feral crumpled to the ground. Unbalanced by the feral's hold on her, the woman stumbled. The few precious seconds were all the horde needed to catch up to the woman.

Liv raised her sledgehammer over her head and brought it crashing down on a head that clung to the woman's arm. The woman reached for a knife with her free arm and stabbed at another.

The horde crashed in around Liv. The sledgehammer had become like a natural extension of her own body.

Liv side-stepped as another feral lunged for her, kicking it to the ground. With a swing, she caved in the creature's skull. Another reached for her with clawed fingers. Liv back-pedaled as she tried to put some distance between herself and the creature. Suddenly, the feral toppled, an arrow sprouting from its head. Sporadic pops punctuated the ferals' howls.

Without any time to think, Liv swung again. This time, her sledgehammer connected with a woman's temple. Most of her scalp had been peeled off her head, white scar tissue covering the bone.

Another scream pierced the air, and Liv whirled around. A feral had sunk its teeth deep into the woman's shoulder, blood bubbling up around its lips. The woman collapsed under the creature's weight, disappearing from view as the last few monsters dove in for a meal.

Ry was the first to reach the woman. With one swing of her sword, she separated the feral's head from its body. She stabbed another through the back of the head. Liv pulled out her knife and jammed it into the last feral's temple.

The woman was a mess. In the few short seconds the creatures had, they had ripped a hole in her stomach, spilling her insides onto the dirt road. As a cough racked through her, blood splattered across her lips.

"Mom?" Liv's head snapped around to the boy. Silent tears streamed down his face.

"Ry, take him back to the house and fetch Lauren!"

"No!" the boy screamed and thrashed as Ry scooped him into her arms. "Mom!" Eric rushed over to help her, keeping her from being pummeled.

Liv sank down next to the woman, taking her hand. "Don't worry," she told the mother through the lump in her throat. "Your son is safe. We'll take care of him. We're better off here than most." She gently squeezed the woman's hand.

"Do you promise?" The woman grimaced, squeezing Liv's fingers tightly as she bore through the pain.

"Yes." Liv nodded earnestly. "I have a daughter of my own. She lives here happily. We'll take care of him like he is our own."

A smile flitted across the woman's face before quickly washing away under another wave of pain. "Kill me," she managed. "Please kill me before I change." The woman's injuries were so grave. Even if she was immune, could she even be saved? "I don't want to forget him." Tears shone bright in her eyes. "Please."

Liv gave the woman's hand a reassuring squeeze. "What is your name?"

"Rebecca." Wyatt breathed. Liv's eyes darted back and forth between Wyatt and the woman.

The woman relaxed a bit. "Wyatt...I am so sorry...about Sarah and Ben."

Wyatt knelt down and took Rebecca's hand in his. "Don't worry about Dylan. I'll take care of him. I'll take care of him as if he was..." Wyatt couldn't bear to say the last few words.

"Thank you." A tear slid down her cheek.

Without another thought, Wyatt drew his weapon, brought it to Rebecca's forehead, and fired. Her body jolted as the shot ran through it before relaxing in death. He sucked in a deep breath, carefully placing the woman's hand across her chest.

Wyatt pushed himself to his feet and Liv leapt up to follow him. On the other side of the gate, they could still hear the boy shrieking.

"We were neighbors…before the Midnight Days," Wyatt muttered. "Dylan and Ben used to play together. We lived next door to Dylan's father, Robert. Robert and Rebecca divorced last year…it was hard on Dylan."

"I'll go with you," Liv said solemnly. "He should know we are all here for him."

His feet felt like lead as he stepped back through the gate. He didn't want to do this. He didn't want to tell a child that his world was gone. Wyatt walked back to the house, trying to think of what he would say. He pushed open the front door, his feet scraping against the wood.

"Mom?" a quiet voice called from the kitchen. That single word crushed him, and each step was more difficult than the last.

As Wyatt rounded the corner, he was met by the boy's hopeful smile as he shoveled a large steaming spoonful of oatmeal into his mouth. As his eyes fell on Wyatt, the smile faded from his face. He chewed the bite slowly and swallowed.

"Mister Ward? Where's my mom?" Dylan asked, his eyes locked on Wyatt.

"Dylan, your mom…she…" the words caught in Wyatt's throat as he saw tears welling up in the boy's eyes. All the things he had thought about saying fled, and he was left speechless as he watched the boy crumble. "She didn't make it."

"You're lying!" the boy screamed, taking Wyatt by surprise. He jumped off the stool, tipping it over and sending it clattering to the ground. "You're lying! Where is she?!" Dylan threw himself at Wyatt, his fists flailing through the air.

Wyatt caught Dylan by the wrist and pulled him into a bear hug. The boy broke down into sobs as he clung to Wyatt.

"What will I do?" Dylan looked to Wyatt with tear-stained cheeks.

"Where is your dad?" Wyatt immediately wished he could take back those words. Dylan's face crumpled as more tears burst forth.

"He's a monster." The boy wailed, burying his face in Wyatt's shoulder.

Liv knelt down next to him. "You can stay here with us. I know it's scary." She couldn't imagine how terrifying this all was to the child. He had suddenly found himself alone in a world that was already brimming with horror. "You'll be safe here, and we'll make sure you're taken care of."

"But...but..." Dylan's chin quivered. He leaned back against Wyatt, sobbing, and Wyatt squeezed him tightly.

Liv didn't know where to begin. They had all lost someone. They had all experienced the horrors of the Dead Zone. But she could never imagine how this child must feel being among strangers in such a terrifying new world.

"Come on," Liv said quietly, motioning for Wyatt to follow her. Wyatt scooped Dylan up in his arms and stood. Together, they moved into the living room and sat down on the couch. Dylan had fallen silent. The boy just stared off into space. Into the void.

"Mama!" Elli's head poked around the corner, and her face lit up as she darted across the room. Liv cringed. She had far too little time with Elli these days, but she was afraid cuddling with her own precious child would send Dylan over the edge. Elli threw her arms around Liv's neck as Liv scooped her up.

Nana Eve hobbled into the room. "So sorry, Liv." She stopped short as she saw the little boy cradled in Wyatt's arms. "Well, who is this handsome young man?" Her voice was warm and gentle, but Dylan didn't respond.

"His name is Dylan. He'll be staying with us now," Wyatt said, not wanting to go into more detail about his arrival.

"I see." Nana Eve nodded, the smile fading from her face as she understood the meaning. "Well, Dylan, it is a pleasure to meet you. Derek will be glad to have another boy like you to play with when you are ready."

"Derek?" Dylan asked listlessly.

"Yes," a small smile returned to Nana Eve's face. "He's a youngster about your age."

"I don't want to play." Dylan's mood immediately soured.

"That's all right, dear." Nana Eve hobbled forward a few more steps. "We aren't going anywhere. You take all the time you need."

It took hours for Dylan to fall asleep. Elli had only taken moments to doze off in Liv's arms. Though Dylan didn't move, if Wyatt tried to shift, the boy would clutch for him and start crying anew.

Dylan sobbed even in his sleep. Wyatt's face twitched as he held the boy, his arms wrapped around Dylan like a vice. His gaze was far off, his mind somewhere else. As Dylan began to relax, slowly drifting to sleep, so did Wyatt. He smoothed the boy's hair, his fingers gentle and loving.

"We need to think about teaching the children how to survive." Wyatt's voice was low when he spoke. "They need to know what to do if...if we aren't around to protect them."

Liv swallowed hard around the lump in her throat. "Do you really think they would be able to fight in the face of a feral?"

Wyatt's shoulders lifted in a slight shrug. "Perhaps the older ones, but I don't think it could hurt. If it saves just one child, I think it would be worth it."

"It would be." Liv nodded in agreement. "I'll talk to Max and find someone to do—"

"I'll do it." Wyatt cut Liv off. "I want to do it. I want to help these kids stay safe." He insisted, his jaw set. "I can teach the little ones like Elli to hide, where they should hide, and that they need to be quiet and wait for an adult to find them. I can teach the older ones how to find a safe place, some survival skills like finding food, and maybe firing a gun."

Liv's eyebrows shot up. "Are you sure that's wise?"

Wyatt frowned as he thought. "For some of them, I think it would be a good idea. I'll get a feel for the kids and who can be responsible enough to handle it."

Liv let out a sigh, her shoulders slumping. "All right. I wish we didn't have to. I wish they could stay kids for a just a little longer, but I do think it's a good idea."

"If we teach them to survive, then maybe they'll be able to become adults." Wyatt's grip tightened around Dylan. Liv scooted closer to Wyatt, pressing her shoulder against his.

DAY 72

The Slag buzzed excitedly. The survivors from Collier would be here soon, and everything was almost ready for their arrival. Max had decided to throw a large party before they went to clear out Walmart. They would have more than enough supplies upon their return and could afford one lavish night.

A few had come from Collier that morning with three deer to roast, along with some other supplies to help prepare the feast. The smell of the sizzling meat wafted across the farm and made Liv's mouth water despite herself. While she hadn't eaten any meat since the outbreak, she was sure that streak would end tonight.

Everyone had been hard at work to prepare for the party. The large dining room table had been moved outside and set up as a buffet. Dozens had been working since the early morning to make food for the large group.

"Attention!" The call came over the radio, and Liv's heart sank. They needed just one peaceful moment. "Caravan approaching from the main road…" The words trailed off for a moment. "There are ten cars and a bus."

"Is it Collier?" Liv asked into her radio.

There was another pause at the other end of the radio. "The lead vehicle just started waving their flag. It's them!"

A wave of relief washed over Liv.

The vehicles pulled in just on the other side of the trailers and parked in the large swath of cleared ground. Jackson stepped out of the lead vehicle, a smile plastered across his face. He looked around, and when he spotted Liv he strode over to meet her.

"It's nice to see your home finally." He took in the large farmhouse and the trailers, the barn, and the green fields. His lips pressed into a thin line. "You have a fine place here."

"Well, make yourself comfortable and eat. The cooks have been working all day. I wouldn't want all their hard work to go to waste."

Jackson took a deep breath of the fragrant air. "Oh, that won't be a problem." Liv looked the man over. In the daylight, she could see more details that she hadn't noticed in the dark cavern of the Collier building. His face was gaunt, and he was skinnier than she remembered. Liv looked around as the other survivors from Collier exited the vehicles. Their clothes hung loosely from their bodies.

With a jolt, Liv realized they had been in a far worse situation than she had thought. They had been starving. Liv swallowed around the lump in her throat as she watched the procession of malnourished people head toward the house.

"I want to thank you for trusting us." Her lips set into a grim line as she turned back to Jackson.

A smile spread across Jackson's face. "We got off to a rocky start," the man admitted. "Hopefully, this is the dawn of a prosperous future for both of our people. Thank you for helping us. I know you and your people worked double time to help us." He stuck out his hand to Liv, and she shook it. Liv noted how bony his fingers felt.

"Please make sure your people eat their fill," she said firmly. "There's more than enough for everyone."

"It smells wonderful! You folks have certainly outdone yourselves."

Liv nodded. "We all need our strength for tomorrow, so we figured we would make a party of it. There's been far too little to celebrate recently."

Jackson nodded solemnly. "I'll take it. Oh!" Jackson's eyes lit up, and he yanked open the back door of his car. "We found something the other day that we thought was perfect for the occasion." Liv raised her eyebrow questioningly as he spun back toward the vehicle and dug through boxes in the back seat. After a moment, he turned back to Liv, producing a bottle of whiskey. "We came across a liquor store that had hardly been touched and figured that a few drinks might be a nice addition to the feast." He beamed with pride.

"That sounds wonderful." It really did. A few drinks with the celebration sounded like heaven, even if they wouldn't be cold. "You didn't find any tequila, did you?" Liv asked hopefully.

Jackson's eyebrows shot up in surprise. "I wouldn't have pegged you for a tequila drinker."

Liv shrugged. "I won't turn down a nice margarita."

Jackson chuckled and turned, digging through the backseat again. After a moment, he produced a golden bottle of Jose Cuervo. "All yours. I don't have any margarita mix, but I have this." In his other hand, he held a jug of pineapple juice.

"Ah, well that'll work just fine." Liv accepted the bottles. "I'm sure everyone will be especially excited for your contribution. Just make sure you can function tomorrow."

"Killjoy," Jackson said with a smile.

"Now, let's go eat." Liv slapped him on the shoulder, and they ambled toward the tables where Max had just placed the first large tray of meat from the spit. Liv piled her plate high with a fresh salad, glazed carrots, mashed potatoes, and added a few chunks of the juicy beef to her plate. She made her way over to where a group of raiders had gathered on a blanket and plopped down next to Wyatt.

"What is that?" Wyatt pointed a finger at the meat. "It looks disgusting," he teased.

"Join us! Join us! Join us!" Jay chanted. After a moment, Seti and Ry joined the chant. As Wyatt and Ava added their voices, the chant carried across the field, causing others to turn and stare.

"Well, it smells delicious." Liv popped a piece into her mouth before she could think about it too much and change her mind. It was more delicious than she remembered. Jay whooped and clapped.

Wyatt chuckled, picking up his own plate that had been piled high with meat and vegetables. He shoved a bite into his mouth.

"Man, I can't remember the last time we ate this well," Ry said around a mouthful of food. "To be honest, it was probably well before the outbreak. I am not a cook. I probably would have ended up poisoning myself if I hadn't found the Slag."

"The only thing that would make this better is a nice cold beer," Jay added between bites.

Wyatt groaned. "We aren't going to talk about anything cold."

Liv's eyes lit up, and she reached into her bag. "It may not be cold, but I do have a surprise, courtesy of Jackson and the Collier survivors." All eyes turned toward her as she pulled the bottle out of her bag.

"Dude! What took you so long?" Jay exclaimed.

"Jackson brought it. Collier found it on one of their raids and saved it for today." Jay tossed his cup of water into the grass and stuck it out for Liv to fill. Several others followed his example. When the others had full cups, Liv filled her own, swirling the amber liquid with her finger before taking a drink. She winced as the sour tang of alcohol washed over her tongue. She had poured a little heavy, and the drink was oddly warm. As the initial surprise faded, Liv found herself enjoying the drink.

"I can't wait to be able to relax a bit after tomorrow." Jay took a long swig of his own drink. "Enjoy some of the finer things again like toilet paper." While the Slag hadn't run out of toilet paper, keeping it in stock had become a constant struggle.

"You know what I'm grabbing tomorrow?" Ry said after a sip of her own drink. "A book."

A smile spread across Liv's face. She had loved reading before the Midnight Days, but she had so little free time and even less of it now. "I always thought the apocalypse would have more free time than this. No job. No bills. No obligations. More time, ya know?"

"Hey, I'm not saying I'll get to read a lot. If I only read one page a day, I'll be a happy woman."

"It would be nice to pick up some things to do just for fun. I think it would be good for everyone to do something more than just survive," Ava agreed between mouthfuls of food.

Liv nodded and took a sip of her drink. "We should have the run of the place. I don't see why we can't bring back some extras."

Liv pushed away her empty plate. "You know what I want? Coffee." Liv's mouth watered just thinking about it. She wouldn't have access to an electric coffee maker, but she could steep the grounds like tea. It had been almost three months since her last sip of the sweet elixir, and at this point, anything would do.

Ry groaned in agreement. "We're going to be living the high life."

"Mommy!" Elli toddled over from where she had been playing in the grass. The child threw her arms around Liv as she plopped down in Liv's lap.

"Are you having fun, baby?" Liv wrapped her arms around Elli and kissed the top of her head.

"Yeah." A broad grin spread across Elli's lips.

"That's good." Liv gave Elli a squeeze.

"Elli!" Dylan dashed over, Lauren's large German Shepherd close behind him. A broad smile lit up the boy's face as he reached out to scratch the dog's ear. "Come on! Come play!" It warmed Liv's heart to see the boy smile. Nana Eve and the other children had really helped him with the transition. Nana Eve put everyone at ease, and the boy was no exception. But what had helped Dylan most was the dog. The instant he had laid eyes on the dog, he had become attached, and the dog seemed smitten as well. The pair went everywhere together.

Elli scrambled out of Liv's lap. "Come on, Mama!" Liv heaved herself up, waving to the other raiders as she trailed behind Elli and Dylan.

The children were playing tag. Their shrieks and giggles rang through the air as a girl of nine chased the other children. As the girl reached for Elli, Dylan snagged Elli's hand, pulling the toddler aside just in time. Together, they darted off, laughing.

The children were fast. They easily darted around, their little legs switching directions in an instant as they wove and dove around each other. Liv ran until she thought her sides would split. Despite her ragged breathing, the children continued to play, and she marveled at their endless energy.

Liv made her way toward a table where Jordan and Jay sat with Max and Randall.

"There she is!" Max shouted happily.

A broad smile spread across Liv's face. "I wasn't aware I was missing."

Max waved away Liv's snarky comment. "Sit! Sit!" A crooked smile was plastered across her face as she motioned Liv to a plastic lawn chair. "I don't think you've had nearly enough to drink." She poured a drink into an empty cup and passed it to Liv.

"Well, I do have work to do tomorrow—"

"Pft! You need to live a little. Lord knows, we all have a lot less time here than we thought." Max's face twisted as she thought for a moment. "You know, I don't say this often enough, but I'm proud of what we've accomplished here. Damn proud." Her chair wobbled precariously as she leaned back. "I have to admit I was skeptical when all of you raggedy survivors started showin' up on my doorstep. I wasn't sure I could turn any of you into proper farmers." Max looked around at the nearly two hundred people gathered in the clear zone. "But we've done more than that. We've created a community out of strangers. It's really something." The old crone held up her cup. "Cheers to all the hard work we've accomplished."

The others held up their cups and clanked the flimsy plastic together. Liv took a long swallow from her own.

"Thank you, Max, for taking us all in during our hour of need." Liv raised her cup again.

"To the generosity of one old bag. Without her, we would certainly be dead." Jay raised his cup as well. Jordan punched him lightly on the shoulder.

"You watch your mouth." Max's eyes narrowed as she raised her cup. "I will throw you right back out into the Dead Zone with all the ferals."

A goofy grin spread across Jay's face, and they touched their cups together again. "You wouldn't do that. You love me too much." Liv suppressed a giggle. She had no doubt that Max would throw out anyone if she had half a mind to do so, but she wouldn't throw out Jay.

Max rolled her eyes and downed the rest of her drink. "You're lucky you're funny…"

Liv turned, feeling eyes on her. Wyatt watched them from where he stood with some of the Collier survivors. Her heart fluttered for a moment.

"If you'll excuse me…" Liv pushed herself up from the table.

Max turned in her seat and spotted Wyatt. He gave the woman a quick wave. A large cat-like grin spread across Max's face. "I see." She nodded.

"What does that mean?" Liv asked, her brow furrowing.

Max heaved a heavy sigh and shrugged. "Well, go on." Max waved Liv away. "Don't keep him waiting." A deep blush rose on Liv's cheek as she polished off the rest of her drink before striding over to Wyatt.

"Having a good time?" Wyatt separated from the group he had been chatting with.

"Yeah, it's nice having everyone together for once." Liv looked around. Many people had settled into groups as they sat around chatting and eating. Laughter drifted across the field. The buffet table had been thoroughly demolished. Some scraps remained, but the group had eaten its way through much of the food. "I think this is the most socializing I've done in…" —Liv shook her head— "as long as I can remember really. Before the outbreak, I preferred to hang out in smaller groups. Just close friends, ya know? This is different, though. It's nice to know there are so many of us left."

Wyatt nodded knowingly. "Want to take a walk? I was thinking about stepping out for a minute and getting some peace and quiet."

"Sure." As they walked side by side, their shoulders brushed together, making Liv's skin tingle.

They strolled leisurely across the clear zone, heading toward the tree line. Cicadas serenaded them from the surrounding oak trees as they approached. The sounds of the party fell behind them, turning into a quiet murmur in the background. The sun had set, but the last few rays still poked above the horizon. The first few stars twinkled in the darkening sky.

"Are you ready for tomorrow?" Wyatt asked, breaking the silence. Tomorrow would be dangerous. One of them could be killed. Both of them could be killed.

Liv let out a small nervous laugh. "Yes and no. I'm ready to have the supplies, but I'm not really a fan of running headlong into a horde."

"We'll be fine. We'll take it slow and steady. If we can keep our heads about us, we should be able to come out on top," he reassured her.

"I know." Liv nodded. "There are going to be a lot of us there, between us and Collier. We've been planning for this for so long now. I just can't help but stress about the details. That's how I've always been."

"That's what makes you a good leader."

Liv stopped, glad the darkness hid her flush. Instead, she turned to gaze up at the sliver of moon that hung in the sky. They were such a small speck in the universe. No one cared if they lived or die. No one would care if the entire Earth burned. The universe would keep existing without them.

Instead of depressing Liv, it made her feel more alive. Their problems were small and temporary. If they persisted, they could get through them.

Liv ripped her gaze away from the stars and studied Wyatt. They had been through so much together over the last few months, coming closer and closer together. He had seen her at her worst and helped raise her back up. She swallowed hard as he met her stare.

Emotions swam in his misty gray eyes.

She fought the urge to look away. For so long she'd been denying her feelings for Wyatt. But right here, in this moment, she couldn't remember why. He was strong, loyal, and set her blood on fire. *Ah, to hell with it.*

Before she could rethink her actions, Liv forward, pressing herself against his. Her lips met his, tentative at first.

After a split second, he let out a groan and wrapped his arm around her.

Liv's skin tingled as desire rose within her. She wrapped her arms around Wyatt's neck, her fingers running through his short, soft hair.

He deepened the kiss, turning it into something wild and desperate.

Liv pulled back, gasping for air.

"Are you sure you want to do this?" Wyatt's breath was ragged as he whispered in her ear.

Liv rubbed her cheek against his, luxuriating in the feel of his skin on her own. The contact set her skin on fire.

"Yes." She could barely get her brain to form the singular word. "Do you?"

Wyatt's crushing kiss was all the encouragement she needed. She pulled herself back just enough to tear off her t-shirt. Wyatt's hand roved over her bare skin, stealing her breath and making her shudder against him.

As they collapsed into the grass in a tangle of arms and legs and crushing need, they kicked off the last of their clothes.

Liv wrapped her arms around Wyatt as he moved on top of her, feeling the strong muscles that shifted as he moved. His lips traced the curve of her neck, and a shiver raced across her skin. She arched against him, her fingers digging into his back as waves of pleasure rippled through her. Shutting out the rest of the world, she gave herself over to him.

Much later, as they lay panting in the grass, Liv's gaze once again fell to the stars, their twinkling beauty falling on her. The world outside their intertwined bodies seemed far away like a bad nightmare.

Wyatt pushed himself up onto his elbows. "I love you," his voice was barely a whisper.

Liv pulled him back down to her, kissing him deeply. "I love you too," she repeated, breathlessly. Her chest tightened as she clung to him. For once, everything in the world seemed right again.

DAY 73

Liv chewed on her lip as she stared out of the window at Walmart. Abandoned cars filled the parking lot, sitting about haphazardly wherever they had been left. Dozens of ferals milled aimlessly among them.

"Don't get antsy." Liv's voice was level as she spoke into the radio, portraying a calm she didn't feel. "Wait for them to come to you."

The vehicle sat patiently as the ferals raced across the parking lot. Figures darted out of the shattered glass doors on both ends. Fewer emerged from inside than they had hoped for. Perhaps there weren't as many inside as they had expected.

The first feral slammed into the truck, not even slowing down. A second followed closely behind the first, the horde closer behind them.

"Go?" The woman sounded shaken.

"A few more seconds." The ferals in the parking lot were converging on the vehicle, but only a few had actually reached the truck.

As they stepped into the street, Liv brought the radio back up to her lips. "Go. Keep it slow," Liv reminded. "Let them keep up with you. Keep them interested, just keep them off the vehicle."

The truck jumped, and a few of the ferals were thrown off. Some clung to the sides, desperate for a meal. The truck started its slow roll down the street, pacing just faster than the ferals could run.

Liv turned her attention back to the parking lot. She couldn't see any heads above the cars, but that didn't mean they weren't there. They waited patiently as the truck made its way down the main street and turned down a side road. The truck would continue its slow progress until the ferals had been led far enough away and before rejoining the rest of the group to gather supplies.

"Ready?" Liv turned around in her seat to look at Jay, Seti, Ry, and Ava.

"Hell yeah!" Jay exclaimed exuberantly. Ry and Seti gave Liv a solemn nod.

"Let's do this," Wyatt said resolutely, patting Liv's thigh.

"All right. All squads move in. It's that time," Liv said into the radio.

"Roger that."

"Got it," the teams responded. A group of Collier survivors would head in through the main entrance with Liv. Jackson would head in the second front entrance with his own crew and the remainder of the raiders. A third group, comprised of Collier survivors, would head in the back. All the groups would slowly converge toward the center of the store.

Wyatt pulled the car forward to the edge of the parking lot. They wouldn't be able to bring it right up to the door. The parking lot was a sea of smashed vehicles, and they couldn't find a way wide enough to the front.

As Wyatt pulled the car to an easy stop, Liv grabbed her sledgehammer and hopped out.

"Remember," she shouted at her group, "stay in your pairs. Your buddy watches your back, and you watch theirs. Stay radio silent if possible. We don't want to wake up the whole damn store if we can avoid it. And stick to your department. Keep checking and rechecking your department for any ferals that might have wandered in."

She looked over at her group of survivors. Eleven stared back at her. Each team was comprised of twelve survivors who were capable of fighting their way through a fully infested store.

"Be quick. Be quiet. Be safe," Liv told them. Wyatt looked to her with a smile as she parroted the words he had said to her in one of her darkest moments.

He pulled her in close, planting a soft kiss on her lips. "Don't get killed."

"Pft!" Liv shoved him away. "You just keep them off my back." She slid her helmet on and turned toward the parking lot.

Nothing moved between the cars. She picked her way between the vehicles, squeezing between bumpers and climbing over hoods. Her eyes constantly roved over the ground as she looked for ferals caught underneath the cars or with mangled legs that couldn't stand.

As they approached the door, Liv holstered her sledgehammer and pulled out a long hunting knife. They needed stealth if they could. The sledgehammer would not make quiet kills.

Darting from the last car, she sprinted to the doorway. Glass crunched under her boots as she slid up against the wall. With a flick of her wrist, she flipped up the visor on her helmet and peered inside.

Empty.

Liv motioned the others forward and darted just inside the door. The interior was dark, the only light coming from the shattered doors and a few small, high up windows.

The helmet would be impossible to use in the dark interior, so Liv pulled it off. As her eyes adjusted to the darkness, the shapes began to materialize around her.

The smell hit her before she could fully see what was in front of her. Rot rolled over her like a tidal wave, and Liv gagged into her sleeve. She quickly pulled out a small container of vapor rub and dabbed some under her nose. It didn't help. The pungent odor permeated every inch of the building. Now, it was just mixed with menthol.

As her eyes cleared, she looked around once again. Overturned stands littered the ground. Garbage covered the floor. Rotted fruit and vegetables had long been ground to mush that was smeared across the floor. And the ferals. Hundreds of them stood still in the darkness of the store.

Liv swung her hand up, calling the others to a halt.

There were just as many as they had imagined. The monsters clustered together in the aisles, but none of them moved. Instead, they stood still, swaying ever so slightly as they slept.

Each step was agonizingly slow as Liv crept forward. She approached a feral near a large display of soda. The man's eyes were closed. He shifted back and forth, keeping himself balanced as he slept on his feet. A large knot protruded through his torn and blood-stained shirt, scar tissue stretching and pushing at the fabric on his shoulder.

Liv stood upright before the feral, but he still didn't move. In one swift motion, she drew her knife and jabbed it into the man's eye. Before the man could hit the floor, Liv caught him, slowly easing him down.

She looked back to the others and motioned for them

to do the same. One after another, they speared the ferals. Their progress was slow as they moved down the large main aisle, clearing the way through the rest of the store. Countless bodies were strewn across the floor like dropped dolls.

A loud bang resonated through the store. Around them, the ferals jerked. Liv's breath caught in her chest as she took a few steps back. A feral shriek cut through the silence, echoing through the large building. It was quickly joined by others until they became a deafening roar.

Liv pulled out her sledgehammer and swung at a feral that stood to her left before the woman could even come fully awake, the blow crushing the feral's skull. Without hesitation, she swung again, this time sending a man to the ground. Wyatt leaped forward, slamming his baseball bat into the man's forehead.

Her sledgehammer sailed through the air. Blood and gore trailed in its wake. The floor became littered with bodies as they pushed their way deeper into the store. Liv turned down the first aisle of clothing. Ferals streamed down the narrow aisle toward them.

She swung her sledgehammer, catching a feral in the shoulder and sending it to the ground. Wyatt struck like lightning, jamming a knife through the feral's temple.

As they reached the middle of the aisle, Liv stopped. The ferals surged in toward them, but the shelves forced them down to only a few at a time.

Liv swung her sledgehammer again. It slammed into one feral's temple and knocked another down as it followed through. She quickly swung the weapon over her head, bringing it down hard on the second feral's head.

The ferals pushed in. Each of them scrambled to get closer as they pushed down the aisle. Liv dropped the sledgehammer into its loop and pulled out her knife again.

A flash of movement caught her eye. A naked woman crouched on top of one of the tall shelves, her body covered head to toe in thick mucus.

"Climber!" Liv shouted over the screams of the ferals. Wyatt was a better shot than she was. In a flash, he drew the Glock at his side and fired. The woman's head snapped back, and she toppled over, her limbs sticking to the shelf as she slowly slid down.

The ferals in the aisles used the momentary distraction to push in closer. Wyatt fired six more shots behind Liv before he spun and fired five more shots at the ferals in front of Liv. As they fell, the others surged forward.

A feral man surged through the horde, shoving and clawing his way to the front. His shoulders were lumpy and disfigured. Knots of scar tissue had grown up to cover them, making his neck seem almost comically short.

He lunged at Liv, his fingers hooked like claws as he reached for her. Liv threw her forearm up, and the man grabbed ahold of it, slamming her into the shelf as he did. His fingers dug into her arm painfully. With a snarl, he clamped down on the plate sewn into her jacket. As he gnashed against the leather, Liv plunged the knife deep into his temple. The feral crumpled, ripping the knife from her hand as he fell.

The lines were thinning out as Liv grabbed for her screwdriver. The ferals weren't packed as closely together. Sporadic pops of gunfire echoed through the store.

They were winning.

Relief coursed through Liv's veins. They were winning. They just had to keep going. She spared a quick glance over at Wyatt. His face was contorted into a vicious snarl as he grabbed a feral by the tattered remains of its shirt and plunged his knife into the thing's skull.

She couldn't help but wonder how the others had fared. Was everyone still alive? Liv shook the thoughts from her head. They would know soon enough.

The aisle was empty. A single feral rounded the corner, dragging a mangled leg behind him. Liv leaped forward, quickly dispatching the creature, and spun back toward Wyatt.

"Is that all?" Her breathing was ragged as she looked around. Bodies lay like a carpet across the tiled floor. Blood splattered the shelves. Wyatt was covered in bits of gore, and Liv imagined she looked the same.

A maniacal cackle escaped Wyatt's lip. "That wasn't enough?"

Liv blinked in disbelief. "I guess..." Shrieks and snarls still echoed through the store, though there were considerably fewer. Liv had to fight the urge not to run off and help the others.

"Come on. We need to keep the clothing department clear. Maybe you'll get some more action."

Liv made a face at Wyatt as she passed him. Together, they carefully picked their way through the bodies. Liv found the feral with her knife still embedded in its skull. She ripped the weapon free and crept down to the end of the aisle. Cautiously, Liv leaned out and looked down the main aisle.

Empty.

One by one, they cleared the other aisles. Few ferals had remained behind as the others had been drawn into the sounds of the embattled survivors.

A feral that was missing the lower half of its body slowly pulled itself across the linoleum. A knotted mass of flesh extended from its abdomen like a gigantic wad of bubblegum. It raised its head and snarled at her. Liv jammed her screwdriver into the creature's head and moved on.

A scream cut through the store. Not the cry of a feral, but the pure scream of someone in pain. Liv and Wyatt froze. Her hand hovered over the radio. Could they really let others die without doing anything?

Liv locked eyes with Wyatt as they listened for other sounds. The shrieks of the ferals had died down. The store had fallen into silence.

A lone gunshot split the silence, and Liv's shoulders sagged. Wyatt squeezed Liv's hands as he passed her and took the lead.

Many of the racks had been overturned. The contents spilled across the floor and created an uneven mess. A pile of clothing shifted. Wyatt hefted his baseball bat and carefully pushed the clothing aside. A hand shot out of the pile, grabbing hold of the bat. Wyatt wrenched the bat free as the feral thrashed underneath. With a mighty swing, he brought the bat down again and again, until blood soaked through the clothing pile and the creature stopped moving.

They stepped into the large aisle that ran through the center of the store. Jay and Seti stepped out from the crafts department a few moments later. The smile was gone from Jay's face. His eagerness drained away. Ry stepped out alone.

"Harvey?" Liv knew the answer, but she had to hear it.

"Dead," Ry said quietly. "A leaper got him." Liv swallowed around the lump in her throat. Harvey hadn't been more than a shadow of himself since his twin had died.

Others slowly trickled into the wide aisle. Liv's group was missing two more of the Collier survivors. Jackson's group lost four after someone had tripped over some debris. The group that had come through the back had only lost one.

Eight dead.

"All right." Jackson's voice was even louder in the silence. Dejected faces turned toward him as they processed the losses the victory had cost them. "It's been a long day already, but we have a hell of a lot more ahead of us. This place is going to smell even worse by the time the sun sets. We need to get everything we need out before then because I sure as hell don't want to waste time carrying out all these bodies." The survivors groaned as they stood.

"Take the bodies of our dead to the vehicles," Liv called out. "You," she pointed at two people from the Collier colony, "find some tarps and wrap the bodies. Take them back to Collier and the Slag for burial. Tell them we'll be returning with everything we set out for." The men nodded, trudging away slowly.

Liv heaved a large box of cereal into the back of the U-Haul. For a moment, she leaned against the edge of the truck and huffed. The late afternoon sun beat down on them mercilessly. The sunburn on her cheeks made her skin prickle. The two trucks that were going back to the Slag were nearly full. The extra-large U-Hauls contained everything they would need to get through the winter, everything they needed to get their colony off to a good start and keep it there.

Wyatt gave Liv a weak smile as he set a box down on the edge of the truck. Ry pushed it toward the back, finding a place for it to fit and make the most out of the space. Though Ry didn't have to carry the boxes from the stores, Liv didn't envy her. The girl had sat in the sweltering truck all day. The inside had been hot in the morning and had quickly turned into a furnace as the sun got higher in the sky.

"Quit slackin'," Wyatt chided with a devious smile.

Liv's brows furrowed at him. She pushed herself away from the truck and followed him back toward the store.

"You should take your own advice," she snarled back as he fell in step with her.

"Oh, right," Wyatt said sarcastically.

They were back at the cereal aisle. Hundreds of boxes still sat on the shelves. It would keep for months, and even after it was stale, it would still be safe to eat, so they were taking back every box.

"Hey." Jay slid to a stop at the end of the aisle. "What do we still need most, clothing or beds? Ry wanted me to ask you because we won't have enough room for both." His shoulders were slumped, and there were dark circles around his eyes. They were all exhausted, but after this, they would get to rest, at least for a little bit.

Liv straightened up from her box, stretching her back as she thought. "Grab the mattresses. The stores are full of summer clothes. What we really need is winter clothes." Jay nodded and trudged away.

"We're all going to have real beds soon," Wyatt said, revelry in his voice. "I never thought that would be such a luxury." Wyatt had been sleeping in a sleeping bag on the floor with several other men since he arrived. Priority for beds and rooms were given to families, who could fit multiple people into one bed and would use the entire room.

"It's amazing the little things that we took for granted." Liv closed her box of cereal. "I never thought I'd be so happy to have so much toothpaste."

Wyatt nodded. "Truly, we'll live like kings now."

Liv giggled and hefted her box. The cereal was light, but the box's large size made it awkward to carry.

Tires screeched and doors slammed, stopping Liv in her tracks. A cacophony of shouts rose outside. Liv dropped her box and sprinted to the front door. At the last second, Wyatt grabbed her arm and yanked her back from view.

"Just wait." He motioned for her to be silent and listen.

Liv peered around the door. Three vehicles had pulled up to the loading docks. A dozen strangers stood around the trucks, guns in hand.

"Well, look what we have here. You folks are so kind to have packed up all our food for us." Anger made Liv's blood boil, and she gripped Wyatt's arm tightly to keep herself in place. "Now, why don't you folks just back away nice and slow."

"Hey, man." Jay's voice rang loud and clear. "We've worked our asses off for this stuff. We aren't just going to give it to you. If—"

"Back the hell up!" the stranger shouted. Footsteps scuffled across the ground, quickly followed by a loud thud.

Liv bolted up and strode through the large bay doors. Jay lay on the ground, with another man kneeling on his back.

"Excuse me!" she belted out, her voice ringing across the concrete. A man whipped around to face her. Suddenly, a dozen guns were all trained on her. Liv didn't allow herself to falter as she strode toward the stranger standing over Jay. "But I'm sure there must have been a misunderstanding."

"Well, I do believe so." A broad cat-like grin spread across the man's face. The man was tall with a shaved head that had become so common as bathing became less common. The man had the same lean look that came with surviving on the bare minimum in the apocalypse. "Do you know these folks?" The man gestured to the survivors around the trucks.

"I do. They are my people." Liv crossed her arms in front of her.

"Well, they seem to have some of our stuff. If they return it, we can all be on our way."

Liv made a show of peering at the trucks. "I don't see any of your stuff. All I see are the supplies my people died for." There was an icy tone in her voice. "You can't have them." Liv laid her hand on the Glock at her hip. Footsteps sounded behind Liv, and Wyatt stepped up next to her right side.

"That's a real shame." The man nodded slowly.

"You heard the lady." Jackson stepped up, flanking Liv on the left. "Now, why don't you just move along?"

"Your people died for these, you say?" Liv didn't answer the man. Every muscle in her body tensed. "It'd be a shame if more of them had to die for these things and we still had to take them from you." The man's gun snapped up in a heartbeat, and the loud report rang out.

Jackson gasped, his hands flying up to his chest. Blood seeped through his fingers. Liv grabbed him as he sank to his knees.

As the raiders made to move forward, the strangers whirled, pointing their guns at as many people as they could. The strangers were outnumbered, but they had better firepower.

Liv quickly motioned over one of the Collier survivors to help her keep pressure on Jackson's wound. The woman slowly complied, waiting to see if the strangers would allow her to do so. They only stared at her impassively as she took a few steps forward.

"Don't worry," Liv whispered in Jackson's ear. "Just hang on. We'll get you fixed up." She wasn't so sure. His breaths were wet and ragged. He coughed, blood splattering across his lips. Frothy blood bubbled up from the wound with each desperate attempt to pull in a breath.

Jackson reached for Liv, and she took his hand. "Don't let them take a fucking thing." It pained him to say each raspy word. Liv pressed her lips into a thin line and nodded. She took the woman's hands, placing them across the wound and forcing her to press hard, though she knew the efforts were all in vain.

Liv turned her attention back to the strangers as she stood. "We could have shared. There was more than plenty for everyone." She shook her head. "Now, you will get nothing." Her limps shook as adrenaline coursed through her veins.

The man chuckled. "You must have a death wish." He strolled forward a few steps. "Or don't you get it yet?" He pointed his gun directly at Liv's head. "We will take it whether you want us to or not. This is the apocalypse, sweetheart. Only the strong survive, and we are the strong."

A deep thud reverberated through the air and shook the ground. Everyone stopped and looked around as the ground shook again, tremors traveling through the soles of their boots.

As the stranger turned away, Liv saw her opportunity. She struck out, her fist landing across the stranger's jaw. His head snapped around, and he folded to the ground. As his gun clattered to the ground, Liv darted in, snatching it up before he had a chance to reach for it. She nested it against her shoulder, pointing the rifle directly at the man. The same man who had shot Jackson. All the other men turned directly toward her, dozens of guns aiming toward her.

The man let out a harsh laugh as he held his cheek. "Did that make you feel better? Because you are sure as shit—"

A thud sounded again, and a creature walked around the side of a long wall that separated the loading docks from the rest of the store. At almost twelve feet tall, the creature towered over the SUVs clustered there. It walked on two legs. Long, thick arms dangled down at its sides. Muscles bubbled up in lumps underneath its skin, turning the creature into only a vaguely human mass. Its head sat nestled in a knotted mound of shoulder muscle, its neck entirely buried and immobile. Chains dangled from the creature, folds of flesh enveloping them and making them part of the beast.

No one moved as the creature scented the air. The creature turned to face the survivors, its beady eyes buried in the twisted flesh that surrounded its head. Liv flinched as it let out a thunderous roar. It brought up a fist and slammed it down on the hood of an SUV, denting the metal.

"Fire!" The strangers let loose a volley of gunfire as the creature fell onto all fours, galloping toward them like a gorilla. It moved with a terrifying speed that didn't seem possible with such a distorted body. Bullets sprayed across the creature's body, marked by red spots and oozing blood, but the creature didn't even seem to notice them.

Liv drew her weapon, firing directly at the creature's head. A bright red spot blossomed just center of the monster's forehead, but the creature didn't stop.

"Run!" screamed Liv. She spun, running down the dock and diving behind a stack of pallets. The pallets behind her wouldn't protect her from the monster, but hopefully, she could gather herself for a moment and figure out what to do.

A split second later, Wyatt slid in behind the pallets and was quickly followed by Ry.

"What the fuck is that thing?" Ry huffed.

Liv carefully peered around the pallets. The monster bared down on a cluster of the strangers. The fire didn't ease up as they held their ground. Its skin was coated in blood, its own blood painting the beast red.

The creature reached out, grabbing a man around his midsection. It effortlessly lifted the man in the air and slammed him back down on the ground, leaving a bloody splatter on the asphalt. The man's scream was cut short, and his body went limp as the creature tossed him away.

The strangers scattered, but one man was too slow. The monster snatched him up too. With another thunderous roar, the creature shook the man violently before ripping him in half.

"Jesus." Liv ducked back behind the pallets.

"What is that thing?" Ry repeated.

"A variant?" Liv shook her head. "That's the only thing I can guess."

"That thing doesn't even look human." Ry's eyes were wide. The creature bellowed again, and the three of them ducked down even further, trying to make themselves invisible.

"We have to get out of here. Now," Wyatt said firmly.

Liv peered up over the pallets again. Though one car was smashed, the others were intact. With their losses so far, that should be enough vehicles to get them all home. "Do we know where everyone is?"

"No." Wyatt shook his head dismally. "Everyone just kind of scattered."

Liv blew out a long breath. "We can't leave them behind. We have to gather as many people as we can before we leave." She crouched back down, turning to Ry and Wyatt. A plan was forming in her brain, but it was more suicidal than anything. "We have to kill that thing."

"How? You saw what happened when the Strong tried to take it out. Even headshots didn't do anything." Wyatt shook his head.

"That thing's head is covered in like…muscle armor." Ry blanched at her own words. "What are we going to do?"

"I think we need to spread out. We each run a separate direction. Find as many people as we can and then get the hell out." Wyatt and Ry nodded. Liv peered up. The monster was chasing some of the Collier survivors toward the vehicles. The beast was too fast; they would never make it.

"Go!" Liv scrambled over the pallet and darted across the dock. Ry raced down the other side, and Wyatt moved more cautiously across the open ground to the far side.

As Liv passed the first truck, she found a group of Collier survivors huddled inside. Her feet slid as she skidded to a halt.

"Can one of you drive this thing?" A man nodded quickly. "Good. Get in the cab. Get ready to go. The rest of you look out for other survivors. I'll be sending some of them your way. Get ready to get them and the supplies out of here." This trip could be all for nothing. They had lost too many people to go back home empty-handed.

Eric's head poked out from the back of the other truck pulled up to the loading dock. "Liv?"

A tired smile flitted across Liv's face, and she jogged to the second truck. Jay sat slumped against the inside of the truck. "Thank God you guys are all right."

"Where's everyone else?" Jay asked through clenched teeth.

Liv shook her head. "We're trying to find out. Can one of you drive this thing?"

Eric nodded quickly. "I can probably figure it out."

"Good. Get in the cab and get ready. We're leaving now." Liv didn't wait for him to respond before she left them behind.

The beast snatched up a woman and threw her. Her body hit the wall with a sickening thud, and she crumpled to the ground. Ava spun and fired. The beast screamed in rage as the bullets peppered its face and chest. It snatched up Ava, bringing her to its lips and ripping off her arm.

Ava's scream was cut short as the beast tossed her aside, and she rolled across the ground in a heap. Liv winced as her limp body hit the ground.

As the others turned to fire at the monster bearing down on them, the creature raised its fists. It batted one man away like a rag doll. The creature flailed in a fury, smashing into several cars, breaking windshields and smashing hoods and roofs.

Liv pulled up short. The beast was tearing through their cars. They had to do something, or they would never be able to get away.

"Hey!" she screamed. In one swift move, she pulled her sledgehammer from her belt and slammed it against the large steel pillar that held up the overhang above the dock. The clang of metal on metal was loud as she smashed her sledgehammer against it over and over.

The beast spun. As its small, beady eyes fell on her, all of Liv's muscles tensed. The monster barreled toward her, closing the distance quickly. Liv turned and ran further down the dock as she tried to lead the creature away from the trucks.

The beast slammed into the metal support, the thick beam bending ever so slightly under the creature's force. The beast pushed itself away, roaring in frustration. It turned as it searched for her.

"Hey!" another voice called out as a burst of gunfire cut through the air. Wyatt advanced on the beast, firing quick bursts at the monster's head.

The beast bellowed as Wyatt turned and ran. The creature dropped down onto all fours, quickly closing the distance between itself and Wyatt.

Liv ran back to the truck. Ry was shepherding a handful of the Collier survivors toward the trucks. Liv immediately changed course, running for the woman in full armor.

"Give me your sword," she demanded, shoving her sledgehammer at Ry in exchange. Ry offered her the sword, hilt first. Liv nodded a quick thanks and raced back to the truck.

"Boost me up!" she screamed at Eric and Jay as she snatched her helmet out of the back of the truck.

Without question, the two men locked their arms together, lifting Liv high enough that she could reach the top of the truck. The metal scorched her fingers as she pulled herself up through the narrow gap between the top of the truck and the overhang.

"Get to the trucks!" Liv screamed as she raced across the top, desperately trying to ignore how high up she was. The truck rumbled to life underneath her.

The loud report of a gun echoed off the building, and a bullet whizzed by Liv. On top of the truck, she would be a sitting duck for the Strong, but she couldn't turn back.

Another shriek caught her attention. Liv spun in time to see a pack of ferals descend on a few of the Strong. The ferals were being drawn in by the sounds of the beast. The horde flowed around the building, the trickle quickly becoming a stream of bodies. They would be overrun in no time. They had to leave now.

As he neared the front, Wyatt darted around the corner of a massive stack of pallets. The beast hit the stack, sending pallets flying through the air.

"Get to the trucks!" Liv shouted with all her might. Hopefully, Wyatt and any other survivors would hear her over all the noise.

Wyatt hesitated a moment before barreling toward the trucks. The beast was right behind him. For a horrifying moment, Liv thought he might not make it as the monster ate up the distance between them. It reached out with one long arm, its fingers almost grazing Wyatt's back.

Liv surged forward, running the last few steps across the top of the truck. She leaped over the gap and landed on the cab, sliding down the small incline. Her stomach jumped into her throat as she wobbled precariously. Her feet hit solid metal again, and she ran a few more steps before leaping down to the hood.

Two more steps.

She locked eyes with Wyatt. His eyes grew wide as he realized what she was about to do. He suddenly dodged to the right, forcing the beast to turn and follow him. The creature turned its back to the trucks as it grabbed for him again.

Jump.

Liv was flying through the air. Her arms pinwheeled as she fought down the sudden panic that welled up inside of her. She smashed into the beast's shoulder and latched onto the chain that dangled around the creature's neck. The chains dug into her palms as her entire weight fell on them. The beast pulled up short, bellowing as it tried to reach for Liv. The monster's massive arms couldn't bend enough to reach her as it flailed.

The chains snapped violently around Liv's hands, threatening to break every one of her fingers as the beast thrashed about in a rage.

With all her might, Liv hauled herself up the chain. It only took a few pulls, but her arms shook with each movement and threatened to give out. As she reached the creature's misshapen head, the chains disappeared underneath the beast's skin as the muscles had grown over them.

A long bulky finger grazed Liv's helmet as the creature continued to flail.

Liv pulled Ry's sword from her belt. Holding onto the chain with one hand, she reared back and stabbed the blade as hard as she could into the beast's skull. It cut through the muscle and hit the skull. The beast screamed at the assault, spinning in circles that threatened to throw Liv off.

But the beast did not fall.

Gritting her teeth, Liv yanked the sword out and stabbed over and over at the creature. Blood poured over her hands and clothes as it spilled from the split flesh. She would penetrate the skull or carve it straight out of the mass of muscle. She didn't have any other choice.

She felt more than heard the wet crunch as she finally cut through the monster's spinal cord. The beast let out a gurgling high-pitched scream. Its legs tangled as they suddenly became useless. The beast pitched forward, and the ground rose up too quickly.

Liv tightened her grip on the chain and sword, but it did no good. As the beast collided with the ground, Liv was thrown forward, tumbling through the air for a horrific moment. When she hit the ground, it felt like every bone in her body might snap in half. The world around her wavered.

"Liv! Come on. Wake up!" Wyatt's voice sounded far away. Her helmet was carefully tugged off her head, and suddenly, the light was blinding. She screwed her eyes shut against it as the throbbing in her head threatened to drown her. "Oh, thank God." She could hear the relief in Wyatt's voice.

Liv cautiously opened one eye and then the other. The sun was still blinding, and her head throbbed, but it was bearable. Every inch of her body ached.

"Get her up!" Jay barked. "We have to go now!" The sounds came rushing back. Ferals screamed all around them. Gunfire steadily punctuated the air. Footsteps pounded against the ground.

"Come on." Wyatt didn't wait for a response. Instead, he scooped Liv up in his arms and spun around, making the world sway unsteadily around her.

The beast lay on the ground in a mass of unmoving muscle. Ferals were swarming into the docking area now.

Ry ran at Wyatt's side, cutting down ferals that got too close. Jay ran ahead of them, clearing a path. One of the trucks was gone.

A bullet pinged off the asphalt, and Wyatt pushed them faster. Liv's head whipped around as she tried to figure out where the bullets were coming from. Behind the wrecked cars. The Strong were pinned down by the horde flooding into the area. Most of them were focused on fighting the ferals, but one man had his weapon aimed at them. Another shot hit a feral in the shoulder as it came between them and the gunman.

"Collier?" Liv asked, her voice weak.

"Gone as soon as the beast was down," Wyatt puffed.

The second truck lurched forward. The back end swung around, bringing it closer to them. Jay vaulted in, quickly followed by Ry. Together, they reached down for Liv as Wyatt lifted her up.

Wyatt pulled himself in. "Go! Go! Go!" He screamed into the radio. The ferals were already climbing into the back of the truck, their fingers reaching for the survivors.

The truck lurched again, throwing off some of the ferals. Liv pulled out her knife, stabbing at the stubborn ferals that still clung to the back.

The truck rocked dangerously as it rounded a corner too quickly. The contents in the back shifted. They hadn't been able to finish packing. The load was unstable. Jay jumped up, throwing his shoulder against the boxes to keep them from toppling.

Liv looked up, watching the horde wash over the ruined vehicles and the Strong just before they rounded the corner out of the docking area. She stabbed down at the last few ferals angrily before leaning back. Ferals trailed in the wake of the truck, their legs pumping furiously as they tried to keep up with the vehicle.

She stuck her hand out for the radio. "Take us home the long way."

"Will do." Eric's voice was grim. "Glad you made it, Liv."

"Me too." She clipped the radio to her belt as they slid in the back of the truck as it turned a corner more gently this time.

Liv finally looked around. A few of the volunteers from the Slag, some of the Collier survivors, and all of her raiders, except Harvey and Ava, huddled in the back. Twelve people in total. Liv wondered how many they had actually lost.

She hung her head. Were the supplies worth it? Were they worth every life lost? They had made a victory and suffered defeat all in the same day.

"Are you all right?" Wyatt put his arm around her and gently pulled her close as Ry pulled down the large rolling back door.

"I don't feel great, but I'll live." Liv smiled weakly.

"That was absolutely epic." Jay held his hand up for a high-five.

Liv stared blankly back at Jay. She hadn't brought down the beast to look cool. She had done it to put an end to its rampage. To prevent it from following them back to the Slag. To keep it from creating more like it.

As the smile faltered on Jay's face, she returned his high-five. "I'd rather not do anything like that again."

"What even was that thing?" one of the men from Collier asked.

Liv shook her head. "A variant. We've never seen anything like it either. The variants we've seen have looked more...normal."

"If that thing was a mutation of the virus...then what are we going to do?" Ry asked quietly.

"What we've been doing," Liv stated simply. "Keep surviving until we can't. What else can we do?"

The truck fell into silence as it continued to bump along the road. Eric slowed as the ferals fell behind. They followed a long and winding back road. Eventually, they would have to angle back toward the Slag. They were all tired. They all wanted to rest. Most of them had been up for well over twenty-four hours at this point.

Suddenly, tires squealed, and the vehicle rocked dangerously as Eric stomped on the breaks. They were thrown against the supplies as they slid across the floor of the truck.

"Strangers in the road." The radio crackled quietly.

"The Strong?"

"Don't know." Eric's reply was barely audible.

"Get out of your vehicle!" The muffled shout reached Liv's ears and instantly set her heart racing.

"Get ready, everyone." She made sure to keep her voice low as she pulled out the AR-18 she had taken from the Strong. She was desperately low on ammunition.

In the back of the truck, they had nowhere to hide. The best they could hope for was to surprise the strangers when they opened the back.

Feet scuffled outside of the truck, quickly followed by the cab door slamming closed.

"Who are you?" an unfamiliar voice demanded.

"Nobody." Eric's voice was quieter. "Just trying to survive."

"What do you have in the back?"

"Nothing, nothing. I use it as a mobile safe place." Eric lied. Liv's stomach clenched. Would their lie work? What would happen if it didn't?

Footsteps marched in their direction. Dozens of them. Liv flicked off the safety, aiming straight at the door. As the door slid open, she was blinded by the sunlight. They had been in the back of the truck for long enough that her eyes struggled with the quick change in light.

"Put your weapon down!" the voice screamed at them. Dozens of people stood at the back of the truck. Half of them had guns. Some just held various blunt weapons, ready to fight.

Liv's breath caught in her throat. If they opened fire, they wouldn't survive. They might be able to take some of the strangers with them, but they would be cut down like fish in a barrel.

"We don't want a fight," Liv said. "We just want to go home. Let us pass, and we'll leave you in peace."

A woman who looked at Liv down the barrel of a shotgun chuckled. "I don't think so." Liv's grip tightened on her rifle. "I'll only ask you kindly one more time. Put your weapons down. All of them." She emphasized each word dangerously.

Liv and Wyatt locked eyes, and he shook his head imperceptivity.

Liv gritted her teeth. "Live to fight another day," she said to the others in the truck as she slowly lowered her weapon to the floor. "Put your weapons down."

A broad smile spread across the woman's face. "Atta girl." Liv growled. She wanted nothing more than to punch the woman in the throat.

Soft clanks sounded around her as the others set their weapons down. Liv pulled out her sledgehammer and set it down, along with the screwdriver. A small knife was tucked into her boot, but she left it.

"Now, get out. Slowly. One by one. Any sudden movements or if anyone tries anything, we'll kill all of you," the woman instructed.

Liv moved first. Slowly, she climbed out of the truck. She wasn't sure she could have moved quickly if she had wanted to. Sitting had given her sore muscles time to tighten up.

"Now kneel," the woman demanded. Liv's heart hammered as she knelt down in the middle of the road. "Put your hands on your head."

"I'm not sure I could if I wanted to. This has not been our day," Liv said with a sigh. She leaned forward, splaying her hands out in front of her.

"Clearly." The woman glared down at Liv for a moment before she turned back to the truck. "Next! Move it!"

Wyatt walked up slowly and kneeled a few feet from Liv. One by one, the others climbed out and kneeled in the road. If they were going to die, Liv wished they would just get it over with. The strangers went by, patting down each of them. As they approached Liv, she tried to steady her breathing.

A man's hands roved over her quickly as he felt for weapons. He paused and removed the knife from her boot, showing it to the woman. Without a word, the woman pulled her leg back. Liv tried to curl in around herself, but it didn't do any good. The woman's boot connected squarely with her ribs and left Liv gasping for air.

"I told you to put everything down. Anyone else want to admit that they kept something?" the woman asked the line of prostate captives. "The next one to hide something gets a bullet." Reluctantly, Ry pulled a screwdriver from her sleeve. A man from Collier removed a small pistol from his pants. "Good." The woman nodded enthusiastically.

"What's in the truck?" the woman asked again.

"Supplies," Liv answered with the truth. It didn't make sense to lie anymore. The strangers would more than likely search through the boxes anyway. "Just ordinary supplies we need to get by."

"So you lied to me?" The woman spun on Eric.

"Stop!" Liv cried out as she pulled her leg back again. "Leave him alone. He was protecting us. Wouldn't you do that for your people?" The woman stalked over to Liv, hauled her foot back and kicked her hard in the ribs again. Liv collapsed onto the ground, coughing and heaving. Wyatt moved to stand, but Liv's hand shot out, grabbing ahold of his and pulling him back down.

"Don't," she choked out the word.

The woman looked Liv over. "Fine," the woman sneered. "You want to be your people's hero? Any punishment that would be doled out to them now goes to you."

"Danika!" a female voice barked. The woman's head snapped up. For a moment, her eyes grew wide. Danika dropped to one knee, bowing her head. Liv looked around. All the other strangers had done the same thing.

The steady *click click click* of footsteps was the only sound around them. Shiny leather pumps stopped directly in front of Liv. The toes that peaked out were painted a deep scarlet red.

"Strangers?" the voice asked.

"Yes, my queen." Danika did not look up.

"The same ones?" The voice had a hard edge that made Liv tense.

"No, my queen, but I fear they are from the same group."

"I see." The bright pink shoes turned back toward Liv. "Stand," she commanded, nudging Liv with her toes.

Liv pushed herself up slowly. Her ribs protested every breath she took. The woman that stood before Liv was dressed head to toe in pink. She wore a bright pink sleeveless A-line dress that matched her shoes. Her wrists were adorned with thin silver bangles that jangled as she flicked her perfectly curled blonde locks away from her face. Her makeup would make any beauty guru jealous.

The woman looked Liv up and down, noting every bruise and smudge of dirt or blood.

A condescending smile crossed the woman's face. "Take them alive. We'll need to find out more about their colony." As soon as the words left her lips, the others leaped into action. Liv was tackled to the ground. The air rushed out of her lungs, and she struggled to breathe as someone wrestled her wrists back and zip-tied them together.

The woman bent over, taking Liv's face in her hands. "You shouldn't have come here, sweetheart."

With all the force Liv could muster, she spit in the woman's face. "Bite me," Liv challenged.

The woman stood back slowly and wiped the spit from her cheek. "How charming," she said flatly, wiping her hand on Liv's shirt.

A feral shriek rang in the silence. As the other strangers closed ranks around the woman, she motioned for them to stand down. A man handed her a small ax.

The feral broke through the tree line, sprinting for the fresh meat. The woman broke into a sprint despite the tall heels she wore, making it look effortless. As they neared one another, neither stopped. The woman ran full force into the feral, sending it sprawling on its back. Before the thing could recover, she planted her foot in the middle of its chest, raised the ax, and brought it down in a powerful swing. She swung again and again, before bending down and picking up the head.

The queen leisurely strolled back to Liv. "I am not afraid of you or your people, sweetheart." She shoved the snapping head into Liv's face. Teeth snapped inches from Liv's face, and Liv recoiled from the disembodied feral.

"Take them alive," the queen ordered. "Let's go home."

DAY 74

Charlie sat in the tree line, staring at the cars. Fourteen of them huddled in a group. His group. But he didn't want to go back. He couldn't. He was a failure. Charlie's shoulders sagged as he turned away from the camp.

"Where do you think you're going?" Charlie nearly jumped out of his skin. His leader stood before him, arms crossed. He hadn't even heard him walk up.

"Nowhere." Charlie tried to stand tall.

The man nodded. "Where's the rest of your squad?"

"Dead."

"Dead?" His eyebrows shot up. "What happened?"

"We were ambushed." Charlie realized his mistake as the words left his lips. His leader's lips contorted in fury.

"You were ambushed?"

"By a monster," Charlie rushed to explain. "Like nothing I've ever seen. It was one of the freaks, but-but mutated. Out of control. Bigger than anything I've ever seen."

"By a monster?" The leader rocked back on his heels. "You don't say."

"I swear it's true." Even Charlie could hear the pleading in his voice now, and he tried to fight it down. "Go back to Walmart. It's on the loading dock." He grasped at straws. He wouldn't believe him either if he hadn't seen it with his own eyes. The thought of the monster sent a chill down his spine. "I killed it!" he blurted out. "That's why I'm the only one who survived."

The frown deepened across his leader's face. "Charlie," the man's voice was soft, and Charlie feared that more than his raging anger, "do you actually think I'm stupid enough to believe that?" He cuffed Charlie, sending him sprawling into the dirt. "Look at you. You're a blubbering mess. You failed, and you still dared to come back to me empty-handed. What do I always say?"

"The strong take what they want. Only the strong...only the strong will survive. We are the strong." Charlie sniffled, picking himself up from the dirt.

"Are you strong?" The man knelt in front of him.

Charlie couldn't answer him. No answer he gave would be acceptable. He would be a liar, or he would be weak.

The man stood, dusting himself off. "That's what I thought." He turned to walk away.

"Wait!" Charlie shouted. "Wait. Wait. Wait. Weren't you looking for someone? Cameron? Connor?"

"Colin?" The man whipped back around toward Charlie.

"Yes! Yes." Charlie nodded enthusiastically.

"Did you find Colin?" The man's finger traced the long scar on his face that ran from his cheek to his hairline.

"No, Samuel." Samuel sneered in disgust as Charlie hurried to continue. "But-but-but I found his wife. Didn't he call her Liv?"

"He did. Did you find her?"

"I did. I did." Charlie nodded. Maybe he would survive after all.

"Where is she?" Samuel said coldly.

Charlie deflated. "I-I-I don't know. B-b-but she's close."

Samuel stepped back. "Kill him. We'll find them on our own."

One of the other men stepped forward, pulling a pistol from his waistband.

"No. No. No. No—" Charlie's words were cut off as his brains exploded out of the back of his head. Charlie's body sagged to the ground, blood pouring out of the hole in his head.

Samuel strode through the trees toward the cars. If Liv was close, then Colin couldn't be far. Samuel's fingers danced across the ugly scar on his face. A growl escaped his throat.

He would find them.

He would make them suffer.

He was strong.

Continue the series with...

Downfall
Book Five of the Death & Decay Series

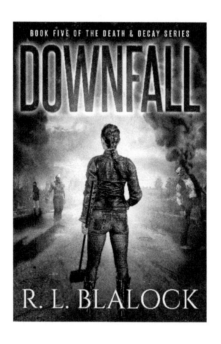

Coming Winter 2018!

MORE BOOKS BY R. L. BLALOCK

The Death & Decay Series
The Darkest Days: Book 1

Devour: Book 2

Divided: Book 3

Distortion: Book 4

Downfall: Book 5 (Coming Fall 2018!)

Undead Worlds

Includes the short story

Defenseless: A Story of Death & Decay

Undead Worlds 2 (Coming October 2018!)

Includes the short story

Dominion: A Story of Death & Decay

R. L. BLALOCK'S FAN NEWSLETTER

There's a lot of books in the pipelines right now. More Death & Decay, a brand new sci-fi universe, and a secret project that I think you're going to love. There's going to be a lot of news to share. If you want to get the latest updates on new releases, sign up for my newsletter.

As a thank you for signing up, you'll get a copy of Defenseless: A Story of Death & Decay straight to your inbox.

ABOUT THE AUTHOR

R. L. Blalock's love of reading started young. As a child, her father would read stories to her before bed every night. In middle school, she and her best friend bonded over books and writing. Her love of zombies, though, started later in life. In 2008, when R. L. Blalock first watched the remake of Dawn of the Dead, she instantly fell in love with the genre.

Born and raised in Sacramento, California, R. L. Blalock now lives in St. Louis, Missouri with her loving husband and precocious three-year-old daughter. Their family also includes three pets: Memphis, a Pitbull/German shepherd mix who prefers to spend his days cuddling; Dixie, a Pit bull/Akita mix who greets everyone with excited squeals and enough kisses to last a lifetime: and Pazuzu, the Green-Cheeked Conure who thinks she's a dog.

During what precious little free time she has, R. L. Blalock likes to read whatever dark and twisted book she can get her hands on or scare herself silly with the same nightmarish kinds of video games.

You can connect more with R. L. Blalock through her newsletter, website, Facebook, Instagram, Twitter, or Goodreads.